I0654429

Stacked

Case

Andy Gruse
STACKED CASE

Stacked

Case

A novel by

Andrew Thomas Gruse

The first printing of this book was in 2016.

Re-edited and re-released in 2018.

ISBN: 0692059997

ISBN-13: 9780692059999

To Benjamin and Matthew:
You two continue to inspire me.
Don't ever stop.

To Heidi: "Someday"
Has finally arrived.
At least one has.

To the Non-Believers:
Up yours

-Andrew Thomas Gruse

Andy Gruse
STACKED CASE

Chapter 1

Zachary Stack secured a Sig P229 into the shoulder holster and concealed the weapon under his tan spring jacket. He squinted at the bright sun and looked down the street. "Would you live out here?"

New houses, all too big with mortgages even larger but with yards too small. Nice lawns in the front with a freshly planted tree too close to the house. Two separate lawn care trucks drove past, having completed their assault with liquid fertilizer. Artificial green, Zack thought. Here today, gone tomorrow. Nothing like keeping up with the Jones's.

"Me? Can't afford it. Plus, I'd have to put my kids in a different school. You?"

Zack eyed a two-story brick house, large white pillars standing majestic beside wide concrete steps leading to the front door. "Would be nice, but I'll never afford to live out here." A 'for-sale' sign stood in front of it. "What do you think that one goes for? A million?"

"At least," he smiled at Zack. "That sounds like the edge of commitment. I'm impressed." The lieutenant pointed at the gun. "You think you're going to need that thing?" Lieutenant Ted Barnes, Baltimore

PD, stared at the private detective. The two had become close friends; close enough to allow the lieutenant to let Zack enter the house alone of a man involved in industrial espionage.

"Haven't used it yet and I don't plan to today. Just give me five minutes with the guy."

Barnes looked at his wristwatch. "I'll give you three. One of these days you're going to cost me my job."

Zack smiled. "And force you to seek work in an honest field? I shudder to think."

"Screw you. Three minutes and don't get stupid."

"The guy's wife has been missing for three days. Don't count on me behaving." He felt a vibration in his front pocket, grabbed his cell phone and looked at the text. He stared at it, exhaled and slid the cell phone into his front pocket.

Lieutenant Barnes scratched his ear with his pinky finger. "What is it?"

Zack rubbed his forehead. "Just a text letting me know the electric company is about to shut off the power if we don't pay our bill."

Barnes nodded. "Liar. Get going. I have back-up on the way."

Back to work. Zack walked down the street, up the narrow cobblestone brick sidewalk, hopped the three stairs neatly dressed to look like the same brick-red cobblestone pattern of the walk and was about to knock on the door when he saw it cracked open.

Zack pushed open the heavy steel door with the faux wood finish and looked into the foyer. Four suitcases sat on the marble floor. He stepped inside and saw two airline tickets atop the suitcases.

A creak in a floorboard sneaked through the silence. Zack dodged to a wall; his thoughts betrayed him. The text weighed on his mind. Force it out. Concentrate. Be patient. Adrenaline surged; he stepped around the corner.

A fist slammed his jaw. Zack hit the floor, winced and saw the menacing stare of Doug Granders. Hate filled his eyes, his fists clenched. "You made a mistake, hotshot. You came to the wrong house."

Doug tried to kick Zack; Zack swept his leg around and knocked Doug off his feet. Zack got to his feet and rubbed his jaw. "No, I'm at the right house. And you're not going anywhere. Where's your wife?"

"Hopefully rotting in hell." The man got to his feet and charged Zack. Zack grabbed his arm, twisted it and ran Doug's head into a wall, busting a nice cloned Rembrandt and threw him to the floor.

"Where is she?"

"Go to hell!"

Granders started to get up, but Zack kicked him in the stomach. "Don't move." Zack walked past and slammed his heel into Granders' head. He grabbed a high-backed wooden chair from the nearby dining room and placed it over Granders. Zack sat on the chair, his arms crossed on the back, his chin rested on his forearms.

"Hard way or the easy way. Tell me where she is, and I promise not to leave you incapable of reproducing."

Granders' lips curled. His face turned red with rage. He struggled to move the chair but could not dislodge it. "I told you to go to hell. I'm not telling you nothing."

"You're not telling me nothing?" Zack leaned forward on the chair. The leg brace pressed against Granders' neck. "That's not proper

9

English. How did an idiot like you get a white-collar job? Now, where is she, Dougie?"

Veins bulged from his forehead; sweat beads covered his beet-red face as he fought for each breath. "What's it to you?"

"She's been missing for three days, you're about to leave the country, and since she's paying me to follow you, I'd like to find her." He pressed forward further. "Where is she, Doug?"

Doug gagged. "I... I don't know!"

"Where's the broad you're cheating with? I'd like to ask her."

Doug's bloodshot eyes bulged. His knuckles turned white on the chair legs.

"Listen, moron. I'm told I'm a bad liar. So, take it from me: you're a horrible liar. Last chance before I use my knife. I'm not very good with it, either. You may wish to talk quickly." Zack waited as Granders went limp. A trickle of bloody saliva crawled down the side of his face, but he still would not answer. "Have it your way."

Zack reached into his pocket and heard footsteps behind him.

He saw the broad swing the pot. It smashed the side of his head, knocked him off the chair. She swung the pot again while he crashed into the wall and Granders jumped from the floor. The pot slammed into Zack's elbow, and he felt another blow on the cheek. He thought he heard voices and shuffling feet, hoped it was the cops, but his world went black.

* * * * * * * *

Sometime later, he found himself sitting on the rear bumper of an ambulance, the acrid scent of smelling salts in his nose and the burn

10

of rubbing alcohol on his forehead and his cheek. His vision cleared, the sun shaded a nameless paramedic. He looked away from the paramedic, and Lieutenant Barnes leaned against the side of the ambulance, his arms folded across his chest with a smug look on his face.

"One of these days Zack, you might not be lucky enough to have me bail you out."

Zack touched the side of his face and grimaced. "When that day comes, I guess you'll get to say I told you so."

"Dude, when that day comes, I won't want to." Barnes checked his wristwatch. "How is he?"

"May have a slight concussion," the paramedic said. "Nasty contusion on his cheek, though. We'll need to take him in for X-Rays."

Barnes nodded. "Ok. Did you find anything out about the missing Mrs. Granders?"

Zack shook his head. "Doesn't sound like Doug knew where she was, but I don't believe him. Couldn't get anything else out of him before frying pan lady whacked me."

"Well, things just got interesting. As you know, the last time she was seen was four days ago. Detective Sybach has pretty much determined you were the last one to see her. We better find her." He looked up. "I have to go. Keep in touch."

Andy Gruse
STACKED CASE

CHAPTER **2**

The X-Rays were negative, and he was told to wait for the doctor to release him when the curtain was pulled back and in walked Julie Fletcher. He was always happy to see her, his girlfriend of three years, but this time it didn't feel like it would be a good visit.

She sat on the edge of the bed, her sandy blonde hair pulled back into a ponytail the way he liked it, and she smiled her infectious smile at him. "How's your head, babe?"

"No kiss hello?" She leaned forward and kissed him. "It's fine. Still in one piece. What are you doing here?"

"I'm a reporter, and you promised me a story."

He leaned back and shut his eyes. "Is that all I am to you? A story?"

She met him when she was doing a freelance article on veterans returning from the Middle East. He was lying on the floor in the airport terminal, and she tripped over him. After a ten-minute apology from her, he asked her to have a drink with her, and they had been together ever since. "You know exactly what you are to me." Another kiss made him feel better, but his mind swirled with more than the fuzz from being knocked out. Granders' missing wife was atop the list, but a close second was the text he received.

"I know. But how did you know I was here?"

"Ted told me. He said you got a text that gave you as he said: pause." She ran her hand through his short hair. "Talk to me."

He loved her ability to cut to the chase. One of the many things he loved about her. Her persistence to get to the bottom of things was one of those double-edged swords, though, and this was one of those times.

"Your silence suggests that you're trying to hide something from me."

He didn't look at her. Looking at her would ruin it. He'd been lying most of his adult life, but when he looked at her, he struggled to do it successfully. Thus, he had stopped trying early in their relationship. Avoidance was a lot easier. "It's family stuff, that's all."

"Really? Do I finally get to meet your family?"

"They don't live around here." He finally looked at her. "I think it's best if I go alone."

She sidled closer to him. "Oh, nonsense! Take me with you. I've been dying to meet your family since our first date. That was years ago. Remember?"

"How can I forget?" He felt her shoulder nudge his. She expected more. "Look," only he couldn't formulate a sentence after that. *Don't look into her eyes.* The voice of reason added its two cents: *She's going to find out sooner or later. Get it over with.* "Just let me take care of this. When it's over, we'll talk about it."

"Talk about it? When it's over? For Christ's sake, Zack! You're hiding something from me. You know how I know that? You won't look at me!"

14

No doubt about it. Finally, he looked at her. Her eyes conveyed more than just pleading. He had stopped trying to describe the blue in her eyes after someone showed him the color cerulean. He never heard anyone use cerulean to describe the color of eyes, but it fit Julie's eyes. He loved those eyes. And she tried to control him again with those damn eyes. "It's more like refusing to share rather than hiding."

"You're pathetic. I can find out you know. I mean, that's my job! I'm an investigative reporter, remember?"

"I don't know where to start. I don't know anything yet."

"About what?"

He tried to think of how to phrase it without telling her what he knew and what he couldn't but what he knew he should have from day one. "Shit," he mumbled.

"What is it, honey? Talk to me?"

"I will, I promise," he told her and saw the look of disappointment on her face. "I just need a couple of days to figure out what the hell is going on and then I'll tell you everything."

She stared at him with a look that would have burnt a hole in most men. He wasn't sure if he was used to it and immune or just dumb. Without another word, she left the hospital bed and hospital without him.

Zack laid back and thought. The missing wife of Doug Granders, Kate Granders, faded away as he thought of the text. One simple headline from a newspaper in a small city in Northwest Indiana that said: "Darnell Whittaker released on parole; screams frame. Names likely murderer!"

He took a deep breath. *Well, Darnell, what the hell are you up to now?*

Andy Gruse
STACKED CASE

CHAPTER 3

Michelle Borman disliked being in the office after dark. It was a fear she had since Zack and Andre were honorably discharged from the Marine Corps and the two started their detective agency. Michelle did the administrative duties that the two guys had no intention of doing. She had known Zack since he was seventeen going on eighteen and the two had been close from day one. They dated at first, but the time apart did them no favors and then discovered they were better as friends. When he asked her to help him and Andre run the business, she gladly accepted.

But she still hated being in the office after dark. Michelle's fears started when working alone one night finishing filing and billing and sorting mail when strange noises came from Zack's office. It was dark, the wind was blowing, rain pelted the windows and the unmistakable sound of a chair scraping against the floor scared the daylights out of her. Instead of running, like Zack always encouraged, she investigated. She peeked inside the door, stepped inside, and Zack, dressed in a Batman costume leaped from behind the door howling and grabbed her around the waist. The humor of his practical joke, which caused her to nearly lose control of her bodily functions, had escaped her then…and now. She had been officially freaked out after dark ever since.

So, this evening, after the clouds blocked the setting sun and her two private investigators failed to call in and let her know where they were, her freaked-out meter peaked.

She sat at her desk and did her duties as best she could. Mrs. Baumgartner and her once-missing-but-now-retrieved Bichon Frise would command a nice paycheck. But there was something about that light coming from Zack's office. It wasn't turned on earlier, was it?

She rose from her chair slowly. Michelle looked at her watch, a gift from Zack from after he entered the Corps many years ago. Eight pm. The door handle was cold; it always was, but this time it was eerie. She turned the handle and heard a noise inside his office. Her breath stopped, but she forced herself to continue.

Suddenly, a light flickered, she pushed open the door, and a man shoved away from Zack's desk. She jumped in fright.

"Hey, 'Chelle. What are you still doing here so late?"

She let out a deep breath and leaned against the door as she shut it behind her. "Zachariah, how the hell did you get in here? You're supposed to be at your apartment resting!"

Zack rubbed the side of his head. "Yeah, I know."

Michelle looked around the room for a secret entrance but didn't see one. How did he get inside?

"Umm, what's going on, Zack?"

He was reading from the computer monitor. "You sent me a text while I was working, and I felt compelled to come back here and get up to speed."

Michelle walked to his desk and sat on the edge beside him.

"This is three days old."

18

She wanted to say she knew it was three days old but instead stared at him.

"A lot has happened in three days."

She felt her heart drop to her stomach. "Zack, I thought you'd want to know but wasn't sure if you should know."

"Darnell Whittaker was released, and his lawyer immediately proclaimed his innocence and wrongful imprisonment." He looked at Michelle. "Blamed it on race."

Michelle didn't try to hide her frown. "Are you going to tell me how you got into your office without me seeing you?"

Zack's face was red, but the right-side was showing bruising already. She didn't like the puffiness or the redness in his eyes. He rubbed his forehead.

"His lawyer seemed determined to find out who really killed Frank Staechel," he said. "In fact, he swore it was his dying mission in this article."

"I thought you'd find that interesting," Michelle shifted on his desk. She folded her arms across her chest.

"Why didn't you tell me?" He eyed her as only he knew how. Even with the puffy and red face and the bloodshot eyes, his gaze was penetrating.

She didn't know what to say.

"His dying mission happened within forty-eight hours, while fishing. He drowned, the article says," Zack again rubbed his forehead. "What are the odds?"

"My first thought was astronomical," Michelle offered. "That's why I didn't say anything."

He leaned back in his chair and inhaled deeply through his nose. "Was this before or after you understood that he implicated David Staechel in the murder? And why did you choose to inform me right before I entered Granders' house today? Are you trying to mess with my mind or just that obtuse?"

She bit her tongue. She was one of only two people who understood the depth of this matter. "Call it a no-win situation for me. On the one hand, I don't want to piss off the boss but on the other hand when he starts doing things that put himself in danger, in my shoes, what would you've done?"

Zack shook his head. "Darnell was arrested for possession, and his lawyer drowned in a fishing accident." He clicked off the computer monitor. "They swear he's innocent and named Frank's oldest son as the most logical suspect in the murder and you wait three days until you tell me?"

She understood his incredulity but knew he wasn't seeing her side. "David Staechel has been missing for over sixteen years. For all we know, they presumed he's dead. Either way, if they think he's the murderer, so what? David is long gone. Let them search all they want. Darnell violated his parole and is going back to prison. His lawyer doesn't know how to swim yet was dumb enough to go fishing out on Lake Michigan?" She stretched her arms and cocked her head. "I'm not the obtuse one here."

Zack rose from his desk and grabbed a backpack from near the wall. He unzipped it and opened a desk drawer. He shoved in a box of forty caliber shells along with his Sig P229.

"I can't let this go, 'Chelle, you know that."

20

She stood straight, her arms re-crossed. She knew him well enough to know what would happen next. She had only one card to play. "What about Julie? Have you told her? Can you let her go?"

He zipped the backpack shut and snapped to attention. "Don't go there. You know what this is about. It doesn't include her."

"It will though if you disappear. Is that what you're thinking? You'll go back to Indiana and save the day? Keep Darnell from going back to prison and what else, Zack? What else do you think you'll accomplish?"

She watched him clench his fists. He wasn't a threat to her, but she understood his anger. She had dealt with it so many years earlier when she first met him. She just didn't understand why he wanted to risk everything he had worked so hard for since then. He was a different person, a different man. A new man.

"Perhaps my conscience finally got the best of me."

She stepped close to him; close enough that she could feel the heat of his breath on her face. "And in the meantime, what happens to those of us that care for you so much right now, Zack?" He stood still. "If you go back, you'd be opening up doors the defense never even thought of. For more than just the murder of Frank Staechel. Are you ready for that?" She moved closer. "Darnell's lawyer is dead. Are you ready for that? And I know how you feel about Julie. You aren't thinking!"

Zack rubbed his forehead again. Michelle suspected the blow from the frying pan, information courtesy of Lieutenant Barnes, was more than just a bump on the head. He turned to the desk and grabbed the backpack.

"Don't tell me you're going there, Zack. Please tell me you're smarter than that."

Zack walked past her, ignored her as she reached to stop him and hesitated at the doorway. "We both knew this day would come. Julie will ask questions. Answer them." He frowned and stepped through the doorway. "I don't expect to see her again anyway."

Zack left the office, went outside and unlocked his motorcycle on the street. He sat on it, took a deep breath and grabbed his cell phone to call Lieutenant Barnes.

He answered on the third ring.

"What do you want?"

Zack smiled, but the smile left quickly. "Ted, I need to leave town."

Ted Barnes was silent.

"I really can't explain right now, but it's something I have to do."

"Right now, you are one of two or three suspects in the disappearance of Kate Granders. I asked you not to leave town."

"And you know damn well I'm innocent. Hell, she owes me money, why would I make her go missing? Look, Ted, I have my cell phone with, so you can always find out where I am and I'm not running from anything. I just need a couple of days."

Barnes exhaled. "Doug Granders so you know, and his mistress will likely make bail by the end of the day tomorrow." Zack was silent, so Ted continued. "Even if the DA presses charges he'll still make bail. Hell, we aren't even sure the industrial espionage charges will stick. Where are you going and why?"

Zack thought about it. The ramifications Michelle alluded to lined up one by one and formed a deep line in his head. "Indiana. A place called Michigan City."

"I asked why?"

Zack nodded. "To investigate a murder. That's all I can say. I'll keep in touch."

Andy Gruse
STACKED CASE

CHAPTER 4

Eighteen hours on a motorcycle cramped and contorted Zack's body. Stretching his back at the first red light in his hometown felt good. He flicked open the visor of his helmet. Sixteen plus years and it seemed like only the gas prices changed. He flicked the visor shut, popped the clutch and rolled through the intersection.

Late May in Northwest Indiana. The air was different than anywhere else. Even going thirty on the bike he could smell the water of Lake Michigan. The plumes of steam from the power plant filled the sky to the northwest and the steady feel of moisture, humidity from the lake, crept inside the helmet and reminded him of the ever-present threat of popcorn showers and thunderstorms.

The main strip heading north-south in town was littered with gas stations and fast-food joints; the scent of deep-fried oil tickled his nose and reminded him of how hungry he was. He hated fast food, especially after living near the Inner Harbor in Baltimore where seafood was always fresh, but that aroma, the pungent, salty, fatty food delight emanating from the burger joints always smelled appetizing.

He passed empty lots where used car dealers tried and failed, emptier buildings where grocery stores and nurseries moved in and out biannually, it seemed, and larger and newer grocery stores fighting for survival with the Wal-Marts of the world built closer to the people than the superstores on the edge of town. Old town becomes new town becomes old town.

He stopped his BMW motorcycle at the next light, watched the multitude of mini-vans cross through the intersection and realized that this was Anytown, USA. Except this was his hometown, and he hadn't seen it in over sixteen years.

Two miles further into town his stomach got the best of him. He stopped the bike at the familiar pizza place he enjoyed throughout high school. It hadn't changed.

Flat roof, worn white panels instead of windows and slightly angular, the building looked out of place amongst the fancy window-laden high rises and neon flashing restaurants of modern times. But this place was established because of its unique charm and personality and the awesome pie they served inside. The aromas from this place made the burger joints' smell nauseating. He smelled the enticing, what is it? A fragrance! Not a scent or an aroma; this was a fragrance. Oregano, basil, the blend of cheeses and that tomato sauce was absolutely unforgettable.

He walked inside, recognized no one and sat alone at a booth. The only seating in the place was booths. Deep, dark, heavy wooden tables anchored to the walls lined the outside of the rectangular eating area. Each bench was covered with initials and words carved in by patrons over the years announcing their visit. The evidence was lacquered into eternity each year. He couldn't remember which table he'd left his mark upon. He rubbed his forehead again; his head hurt. He looked about the restaurant. With no light from outside, the ambiance was somber. This was a quiet place. Only a few amber bulbs gave enough light to see what you were eating and the people at your booth.

A waitress, middle-aged, thin with dyed light blonde hair handed him a menu which hadn't changed either. He ordered a large pepperoni and sausage pizza and after she left realized that not only could he not eat that much but couldn't transport it very well on the back of his motorcycle either.

As he waited for dinner, he checked his phone. The memory was full of text messages, emails and voicemails but there were too many calls to look at. He put it on the table in front of him and rested his head in the palms of his hands.

Pizza arrived. Steaming, the cheese still gooey and if he grabbed it too soon, it would all...damnit...be left behind on the cardboard it was served on. The plastic fork took care of that problem, but the even distribution of the cheese, pepperoni, sauce, and spices was ruined. Best to cram this one in as fast as possible and not make the same mistake on the second. Even the crust inspired the taste buds to accept nothing less.

Truth be told, the pizza was the only thing he missed about this town. He watched people enter the restaurant. Families of four sat at the booths. Couples holding hands smiling from ear to ear sat in a booth. Kids ran to the jukebox, put in the quarters and some music started.

Zack grabbed a second steaming piece of the pie, the cheese stayed properly in place, and he waved it front of his nose to savor the aroma one more time. Screeching female voices filled the air from the jukebox. He cringed. The music had changed, too. Back in his day, Duran Duran was the wildest the music got or the theme from the Pink Panther. Elvis, Sinatra, Dean Martin and Burt Bacharach used to highlight the jukebox and not surprisingly, it fit so well. This wasn't even music.

Zack returned to his phone as he finished his third and fourth pieces. The only person that didn't leave a message, that he wanted to talk to the most, was Julie. He swallowed the guilt along with the fifth slice of heaven; at least he hoped heaven had pizza this good.

He had the rest boxed, finished his water, paid the bill and stepped outside. Still light, plenty light, at half past six and it was warm yet too. A city police cruiser drove past, following a group of teenagers on the four-lane strip. Hoping to harass, ticket or just plain scare, Zack guessed.

He dialed a number as he sat on his bike and watched traffic flow past. Midway through the first ring, a harrowed voice filled his ear.

"You're alive, that's nice to know," she answered. "Do you know what I've been dealing with since you split last night?"

"Relax, Michelle." Zack put the key in the ignition. "I need you to get some information for me. I need to know where they're keeping Darnell Whittaker and whether he can have visitors. If he can't, arrange for me to meet him under the guise of his new defense counsel or something. Do that right away."

"It's almost eight o'clock here. It's too late tonight."

"Don't tell me what you can't do, just tell me you'll do it, all right? Has Julie called?"

"Why would she?"

Zack looked at the phone. That sounded like venom. Where did that come from? She had never sounded like that about Julie before even with him and Michelle's past relationship.

Zack slid the boxed pizza into his bag and strapped it to the seat behind him. "If she does," he didn't know what to tell her. "Look,

28

'Chelle, just work with me, all right? Darnell sat in prison because of me. He's not going to go back. I need some info so do your thing and get back to me as soon as you can." He waited for her response.

"He ended up in prison because the state-appointed attorney didn't care about another black kid getting thrown behind bars. If I recall, you had no choice but to leave town."

Yeah, he'd had a choice. He started the bike. The engine purred, and idling was barely audible. "Barnes found out anything with Kate Granders?"

"No, and 'Dre isn't too happy about you dishing your cases to him while you do whatever the hell it is you're doing."

He rolled his eyes. Fatigue swept through him. "Jesus, you're insufferable sometimes. Just get that information to me as soon as possible."

He heard a loud sigh. It sounded like discontent. "Zack, you were warned never to go back. Remember? The story you told me was that a gun was pressed against your head while you were told that. Am I missing something?"

A fleabag motel sign with half the letters unlit flashed ahead. He stared at it as his heartbeats counted off the seconds. "No, that's what happened." His voice sounded rusty in his ears. "That was a long time ago. Maybe things have changed."

"You're right." The sarcasm dripped. "The dirty pig probably turned over a new leaf and upon seeing you will apologize and welcome you back into town."

"That would undoubtedly save me a lot of trouble."

"Zachariah, I'm serious. You haven't thought this out like I have, and this is not a good idea!"

"Yeah, well, times change, 'Chelle."

"People don't, Zack."

"Then I have the advantage because the same guy who put the gun to my head is also the same sonofabitch that married my mom." He disconnected and looked at the setting sun. The horizon filled with purples, reds, and oranges. "And now, Warren," he said aloud to no one, "the step-son that hates your guts has been implicated in the murder case that made your career. We've come full circle."

CHAPTER 5

Julie Fletcher stopped outside the doorway of the Dre-Zack Detective Agency and took a deep breath. She stared at her hands, shook her head at what she learned the previous day and moved a single-diamond ring from her right hand to her left ring finger. She sighed, opened the door and bounded up the stairs to the office.

Before she opened the door atop the stairwell, she put a smile on her face and walked to Michelle's desk, but instead of sitting at a chair or standing and waiting for Michelle to acknowledge her, she sat on the edge. Michelle finally looked away from the computer.

"Good morning." Michelle raised one eyebrow. "If you're wondering where he is it's not here."

"I know that." Julie winked. "And I know he won't tell me where he is, and I doubt you'll tell where he went." She pulled an apple from the bag carried under her arm.

"So, what's left?"

Julie took a bite of the red apple. "Well, you tell me. I don't mind figuring it out on my own. But you could make my day a little easier."

Michelle leaned back in her chair. Julie watched Michelle's eyes. They traveled from her watch to Julie's left hand and then to the right

31

hand. She saw Michelle's glance hesitate at her left hand and a faint flush on her cheeks. "All I know is that he went back to where he grew up."

Julie swallowed another bite of the apple. "He told me the same thing." Her teeth snapped off another chunk of the fruit. "Honesty." She wiped her mouth. "Interesting."

"I have a lot to do here so if you could hurry this up." Michelle punched a key on the computer keyboard in front of her and checked her now-empty coffee mug.

"I can see how busy you are." Julie stole a look at the computer screen. "Look, he told me he went to high school here in Baltimore. I checked. He didn't. In fact, I spent my entire day yesterday checking every high school in the greater Baltimore area. There is no record of a Zachariah Stack anywhere. Besides the records he gave to the Marine Corps that they somehow verified, there is no record of him pre-sixteen years ago." Julie smiled and took another bite. "These are delicious; you want one? It's a Honey-crisp. Hard to get."

"No thanks. I had a muffin. What are you getting at?"

"You created a false identity for him when he met you all those years ago, didn't you?"

Michelle let out a deep sigh, leaned forward and crossed her arms on the desk. "What do you really want to know?"

"He told me he had a family thing he had to take care of. What did he mean?"

"I'm guessing that it means he had a family thing to take care of." Michelle leaned back in the chair again, her arms folded across her chest. Julie stared at her, awaiting more. Michelle shook her head. "I've never met his family, so I wouldn't know."

"The only records of a Zack Stack in Maryland, Virginia, Delaware, and D.C. aren't him if the pictures are accurate. So, who is he?"

Julie watched Michelle think about this question. She never felt like she was competing for Zack with Michelle, but she was aware of their past relationship. She trusted Zack but could see that Michelle cared for him. She was looking out for him. Protecting him. Julie wondered if it was as his ex-lover or as his friend?

"He's who you think he is, Julie." Michelle leaned forward again. "I'm not sure I should tell you where he is. It could get dangerous."

Julie watched Michelle steal another peek at the diamond on her ring finger.

"Oh please. You told me about his going to Doug Granders house, and that was dangerous. Were you hoping we'd both end up unconscious?"

"This is different." Michelle rose from her chair and walked to a coffee pot. Julie sneaked another look at the computer screen and saw the home screen for the La Porte County, Indiana Sheriff's Office.

The pungent smell stimulated Julie's desire for a strong cup of caffeine. Zack hated the smell and wouldn't let Julie drink it when he was around. Always said it would stunt her growth.

"Would you like a cup?" Michelle seemingly read her mind. "Don't worry. Zack isn't going to walk in and see you with it."

"I'd like one then, thank you." She tossed the apple core into the garbage and took the strong, black, hot coffee and sipped it. The instant kick reminded her why she liked coffee. "Now, back to Zack. He didn't grow up around here and has lied to me about the first seventeen years of his life. You don't want to tell me where he is, fine. Did he tell you to not tell me where he is?"

Michelle stared at the bag under Julie's shoulder with the laptop tucked inside. Julie understood the silence. The next one to talk loses. Michelle tapped her fingernails on the desk and shook her head. "He's investigating a murder." Michelle lost. "The murder of Frank Staechel. You should be able to find it online."

* * * * * * *

At ten that morning, Zack entered the county jailhouse building to see a prisoner. The wait for Michelle to send him information irritated him. Since he had arrived in town, he noticed his hands wouldn't stop shaking, and his stomach was in knots. Nerves. Not a good time for that.

He was searched, deposited his belongings which consisted of his watch, sunglasses, motorcycle helmet, wallet, cell phone and the key to the bike in a tray, signed his name, walked through a metal detector and was lead down a long hallway. The faded, rusty orange paint of the hallway walls peeled in the corners and showed water stains on the ceiling. A fluorescent light flickered.

He looked at the officer. The officer smiled. "Budget cuts. May or may not get that fixed this year."

Zack nodded and smiled. The officer opened a metal door with a narrow window on it, and Zack stepped inside the visitation room. "Cubicle six," the officer told him. Right in the middle of the row of chairs, separated by a small partition that was meant for privacy but offered none. There were no other people there to visit.

He sat on the metal chair and stared through the glass that separated the visitor from the convict. Then he heard a gated metal door creak open and a black man walk through, wearing a bright orange jumpsuit, followed by two guards. They pointed him to the chair and stayed behind.

The years didn't change Darnell Whittaker that much. But his face was harder. The edges were not round anymore. They were square, chiseled, angry. His hair was shaved to less than a quarter inch, and he had a one-inch scar on the left side of his face. Zack looked for tattoos but only saw a cross on his left forearm.

Darnell sat down and stared at the man across from him. Zack picked up the phone and waited. The recognition in Darnell's eyes was evident as was the anger and hatred. Or was Zack just thinking that because of his own guilt?

Darnell picked up the phone and moved it to his ear slow.

"My name is Zack. I'm your new defense attorney." Darnell was silent. "I'm here to help you."

"Go to hell, white man." Darnell started to hang up.

"Wait, wait, wait!" Zack urged. "Just hear me out."

"Why should I listen to you?" Each word dripped with resentment.

"Because I know you didn't kill Frank Staechel."

Darnell stared at him long and hard. "And how do you to propose to help me?"

"If I get you out of here, I need you to trust me and work with me. Can you do that?"

"I've spent the last sixteen years of my life in a jail cell because of a white man, and now you want me to trust one? Screw you, man. That's all I got to say."

"And you were released and ended up back in jail in three days. Is that my fault?" Darnell had risen from his chair but stopped. He looked at Zack.

"It was a bogus drug charge. I didn't do nothing, man. Those cops don't want me out 'cuz they know I know the truth, and my lawyer is gonna prove it. You can talk to him if you want to talk to me, man."

"Your lawyer is dead." They eyed each other. Darnell smiled and shook his head.

"He's dead, Darnell. That isn't a joke."

Darnell's smile disappeared. Zack saw a moment of hopelessness in those eyes. "You may not trust me, but right now I'm the only one you got." He didn't blink. "Man."

Darnell moved the phone back to his ear. "You ain't lying?"

"No. Killed in a boating accident on Lake Michigan a couple of days ago."

Darnell stared at him. He didn't blink. "So little Davey has come back home. How nice."

"I don't know who you're talking about. My name is Zachary Stack, and if you want help, you're looking at your best hope." The silence was deafening, and Zack knew this was a battle. He who speaks first loses, he thought. Darnell smiled and shook his head.

"How are you going to help me?"

"Tell me why the hell you were stupid enough to be caught carrying a bag of crack three days after you were released from prison?"

"I ain't never done a drug in my life. Even in the joint, never took as much as a damn aspirin. I didn't do no wrong to get in there; I sure wasn't gonna do wrong inside. Whitey cop finds me at my uncle's church late one night, throws me against the wall and when he searches me, he drops a bag from his own pocket. The whitey cop he's with says it's mine. What am I gonna do? I say it ain't mine and the man tries to break my jaw. I ain't resisting arrest, too. So here I am." He leaned back in the chair. "Now what's little Davey doing back here?"

"I told you, I don't know who that is." The moment Zack entered the building, he was aware of the cameras and inside this room was no different. He never looked up. "You call me Zack, or I walk out that door, and you rot in prison."

Darnell smiled. "You know I didn't do it, huh?"

"I'll have you out by the end of the day, but I need your word you'll work with me. You can't slip up again."

"Rumor is that Mr. Staechel was offed by his own kid. What do you think about that?"

Zack stared into the brown eyes of Darnell Whittaker. "Let's find out together."

Andy Gruse
STACKED CASE

CHAPTER 6

The fist hit Zack hard. Almost the same place Doug Sanders hit him. His cheek split, and he wiped the blood from his face. Zack recognized the look on Darnell Whittaker's face: hatred, contempt, anger. Zack shook his head and lifted himself from the ground.

Darnell came at him again; this time a kick to the abdomen sent Zack rolling. Zack coughed and held his stomach. "What the hell are you doing?"

"It's called sixteen years of payback!"

"I just got you out of jail." Zack sat on his rear and coughed. "Ungrateful SOB."

Darnell scoffed. His fists relaxed. He shook his head and walked away.

"Where the hell do you think you're going?"

"Away from you."

Zack got to his feet and walked after him. "And where do you think you're going to go? Huh?"

Darnell stopped and faced Zack. "I never killed anyone, but every time I think about how I spent the last sixteen years and realized it was because of you, I'm tempted to make an exception."

"Yeah well, good for you. But you aren't going anywhere."

"You can't stop me."

"How far do you think you'll get before the cops find you and bust you for something else?"

"Don't even try to be my friend, man!" Darnell turned away.

"I'm trying to save your life, you idiot!"

Darnell's fist came at Zack again. This time Zack blocked it and landed a quick blow to Darnell's stomach. Darnell drove his shoulder into Zack and pushed him backward. They slammed into a tree.

Darnell grabbed Zack's shirt and lifted him higher. "I ain't doing no more time for you, man! We go our separate ways here and now."

"No, we don't." Zack slammed his forehead into the bridge of Darnell's nose. Darnell stumbled backward. He straightened and charged, but Zack knocked him down with a right cross. Zack touched his face as Darnell stood. "I placed my business's future on us solving this."

"That's your problem, whitey."

"You don't have anywhere else to go."

"Well, I ain't going anywhere with you, man."

He turned to walk away, but Zack grabbed him. "Damnit, Darnell, quit being so damn," the fist stopped the sentence.

Only Zack didn't fall over. Instead, he punched back. The two traded punches before Zack finally caught a fist, twisted Darnell's arm behind his back and shoved Darnell's hand towards his shoulder blade. Darnell yelped and stopped struggling.

"Stop it! We aren't doing this! Now knock it off. If we keep this up, we'll both end up in that jail!"

He pushed Darnell away. Their breath labored.

"Screw you, Davey. I ain't playing in your fantasy."

"Fantasy? Some fantasy. I just traded punches with a convict. Who doesn't dream about that?" Zack wiped the blood from his lip. "Look, the cops probably already know you're out on bond, so they'll be looking for you. If what you said is true, how far do you think you'll get before you have an accident?" Zack saw that Darnell's expression changed. "They're going to come for you, Darnell. I don't care if you want to kill me, but you better trust me until this is over."

"And then what, Davey? My conscience is clear. I didn't do anything wrong."

"I know that. That's what I'm trying to prove to everyone."

"I ain't coming with you. Why the hell should I? Because we were friends before I went to jail? Screw you, man."

"Do you have anywhere to go?" Darnell was silent. "Then I'll have to do, won't I?" Zack waited, but Darnell still didn't budge. "All right. Give me three days. Just three days. If after that you still think you're better off alone, so be it."

Darnell wiped the blood from his mouth and nose. A county sheriff stared at the two as he walked towards the county jail. "I'll give you twenty-four hours, Davey."

Zack nodded. "Good enough. Now quit calling me Davey and get on the back of the damn motorcycle."

"You broke my damn nose."

"You ever punch me again I'll break your damn jaw. Now get on the bike and let's get the hell out of here."

"Like you could."

Zack eyed Darnell but smiled brief. "I'd rather not. I think I broke a bone in my hand punching that rock head of yours."

Darnell walked towards him. "I'm going to prove you offed your old man, Davey. That's the only chance I got."

Zack nodded as Darnell bumper his shoulder and walked past. He took in a deep breath. "My name is Zack."

* * * * * * * *

Andre Kitchell, the other half of the Dre-Zack Detective Agency, had been working long hours since Zack disappeared. This day was no different. Day three was long as he split his time on multiple cases. Business was good. Today he followed two different suspected cheating spouses before spending a few hours chasing leads on Katie Granders, the missing wife of Zack's last case.

He climbed the steps to the office well past dark; his heavy feet clomped on the stairs. The door was locked which meant Michelle had gone home. That was good. He didn't have the energy to deal with her and her incessant complaining about Zack, though he knew it was worrying.

He shut the door behind him and flipped on the lights, but only after he saw light escape beneath the door of Zack's office. That wasn't right. He put down a cup of Starbucks and removed his handgun. His was a simple S&W .357 Revolver. He crept to the door, took a deep breath and flung it open.

"JESUS!" He lowered the gun. "What the hell are you doing here?"

Julie Fletcher smiled. "Hi, Dre. Late night, huh?"

The gun went back into the holster he carried on his hip. "Julie, I could have shot you. What are you doing here and how did you get inside?"

"Research. The library kicked me out at eight."

"How did you get in? I know Michelle wouldn't have left with you here. Do you have a key or something?"

Julie smiled and returned to the computer.

Dre walked to the desk and saw her working on Zack's computer. "You have your own laptop, Julie." He pulled open the bottom left drawer of Zack's mahogany desk, removed a bottle of Glenlivet and a glass. "What's going on?"

She leaned back in the chair, grabbed several sheets from the printer tray and handed them to Andre. Her smile was gone. "What is this all about?"

He looked over the printouts. Copies of newspaper articles from some sixteen years earlier from a small town in Northwest Indiana about the killing of a man named Frank Staechel.

"Looks to me like these are newspaper clippings about the murder of a man named Frank Staechel."

"Don't play with me. I've had a really long past two days." She grabbed the glass and filled it with the aged Scotch.

"So have I, Julie. So have I." He slid the papers onto the desk. "Zack isn't going to like that you're drinking his prized Scotch."

"You are."

Andre smiled. "He's my boy."

"Where is he and why would he be investigating this?"

43

Andre nodded. "Jules, the man you love, is the man he is. That's all there is to it. I haven't talked to him since he left, and he didn't tell me where he went."

She let out a deep breath and slid the strap of her bag over her shoulder. "Semper fi, right?" She walked past him and stopped at the door. "I just hope you can forgive yourself when this whole thing goes south."

Andre watched her leave and grabbed the glass of scotch. He swigged it and picked up the papers. He shook his head and knew she played him. She was fishing for information and expected him to give up his best friend. He swigged again. He inadvertently gave her enough.

He put the print-outs back on the desk and thought. Maybe there was something he could do. He picked up the phone and dialed a number. "Hey Michelle, did I wake you?" He laughed at her response. "I need a favor. Who do we know that can get a copy of a police file from about seventeen years ago?" He ignored her next insubordinate answer. "No, not from here. From a city in Northwest Indiana." He swigged the drink. "Yep, that's the one."

"Why? Don't you trust Zack?"

"No, that's not it at all," Andre rushed. "Look, he's my boy, and we three always worried this would come back to haunt us. I want to know what they know; maybe they are hiding something. Maybe they aren't. But I want to know everything there is to know about the players involved so we can help our boy, Ok?"

"I have a friend in the FBI."

"That Ronald dude that wants to get in your pants?"

"Gross, Dre, but accurate. Maybe he can help us somehow. Not sure how since it wasn't a federal case, but they have agents in the area. Maybe they can make something up to get a look at the file buried in the cellar of that police station."

Andre nodded. "That would be a good thing. Get on it and get back to me."

Andy Gruse
STACKED CASE

CHAPTER 7

"You need stitches for that, man."

The butterfly Band-Aid didn't quite do the trick to stop the bleeding from the split on Zack's cheek. He put a second butterfly perpendicular to the first on the wound and eyed Darnell in the mirror.

"So does your nose."

"I know. You want to go to the hospital and explain who we are and what happened?"

Zack flashed a quick smile. "You're learning."

"You mean not to trust anyone?"

"That's exactly what I mean."

"That includes you, whitey."

Zack walked from the small bathroom, put a handful of ice in a washcloth, placed it on his cheek and sat down on one of the beds. "Do me a favor and quit your complaining. It's pissing me off."

Darnell disappeared into the bathroom and reappeared several minutes later with the same type of poorly applied first-aid on his split nose bridge. He sat on the other bed.

"You got a plan, whitey?"

"Whitey? Are you a racist?"

"No white man ever done me any good. I ain't expecting you to be the first."

"Well," he sighed, "that's better than Davey."

"What's your plan?"

"I have to make a few phone calls."

"What? Are you gonna call your mommy and tell her you came home? Or maybe you want to introduce me to your new step-dad."

That earned a look.

"That's right. I know who married your momma after you done offed your dad."

"Small world, huh, Darnell?"

"Yeah, some small world. I'm surprised you haven't called your new daddy since you're home."

Zack let out a deep breath. "I wouldn't worry too much. I think he'll be in touch before too long."

Darnell moved off the bed. "I swear to God, Zack, or Davey, or whoever the hell you are, you try to do me wrong again, I'll kill you!"

Zack lied back on the bed. "Relax, Darnell," he dismissed. "I'm tired and need to think. Your threats aren't helping. You may not trust me or like me, and I don't care. But it is in your best interest to lie low, here with me, until we figure this thing out. Just lie down and shut up, would you?"

Zack closed his eyes. He didn't want to have to fight Darnell again. He wasn't worried about losing; he was worried about getting hurt.

"Don't talk to me like I'm some punk you can tell what to do."

"Whatever, Darnell."

"That's your last warning."

"Duly noted." Zack realized he wasn't going to get any sleep. "What were you doing when you got busted?"

"Visiting my uncle's church."

"He a dealer?"

"Man, don't be talkin' 'bout my family like that! I'll bust you up."

"Why did the cops drop a bag of cocaine? Why not a gun? Or weed?"

"How the hell do I know, man? I've been locked up for the last few years, remember?"

"Was it at night?"

"Yeah. So, what?"

Zack sat up. "What were you doing at night at your uncle's church?"

"Looking for a place to stay, man, is that Ok with you?" Darnell leaned forward. "I ain't got no family left, man. My uncle is it. I was out of money and needed a place to sleep."

"Why were the cops there?"

"Why do you think?"

"I know that, but what I'm saying is why were they there? There must be some other reason or else it would simply look like they were following you. Warren isn't that stupid."

"How do you know how smart that honkey is?"

"He's Chief of Police. That didn't happen by accident."

Darnell didn't have a comeback. He blinked and looked at the ground. Zack could see he was thinking.

"Tomorrow morning, I want you to show me the neighborhood." Darnell was silent. "You ever do any recon work? Tail anyone?"

"Yeah," he scoffed. "We did that shit in the joint all the time."

"Well, you're going to learn. Get some sleep."

49

Andy Gruse
STACKED CASE

CHAPTER **8**

The new day never looked so hopeless. Julie Fletcher pulled her hair back into a ponytail and rubbed the tiredness from her eyes. She didn't sleep at all the night before. Zack hadn't tried to call her, and she didn't try to call him either. They never, after their first date, had gone this long without talking. She didn't know whether to be furious or worried. She was both. And now, her head swirled with questions.

As she splashed cold water on her face and stared into the mirror, she realized what she had to do: investigate. After all, it was her job, her instinct, her livelihood. The same thought frightened her; a shiver swept through her head to toe. What if what she learned would put Zack in jail?

She left the bathroom and stuffed clothes and items quickly into a bag. She grabbed her computer, her phone, and charger, purse and locked the door. Minutes later she steered her car west. She was heading to Indiana. One way or the other, she was going to find out the truth about Zack and his connection with the murder of Frank Staechel.

* * * * * * * *

The air was heavy that morning, full of humidity. Unseasonal was what the weatherman said. To Zack, it felt more like home in

Baltimore in the summer. Riding on the motorcycle made the air cooler, but the heat wasn't the problem. Yet. It was only seven in the morning.

Darnell clung to the back of the bike, trying hard to make sure he didn't touch Zack at all. Zack wondered how long the bike would work for transportation for him and a black man. It would draw looks.

He stopped the bike on the side street beside his former house and took off his helmet. He turned off the bike and stared at the house. It was empty now. A two-story gray house with shaker siding, many falling off or missing, several windows broke, others covered with plywood. The large white oak in the side yard had been unattended to in years and branches drooped low to the ground; sticks and debris littered the unkempt yard beneath it. The fence he had assembled out of chicken wire, wooden posts and zip ties to keep the family dog inside was still there but lying on the ground. It was sad to see what his childhood home had become.

When he was little, the neighborhood comprised of middle-class families of Germans, Poles, Italians; all were Americans but with strong heritage links. They worked the factory jobs at the steel mills, the railroad, the industries that littered the lakefront and it's towns because of the proximity to water, railroads and later interstates. They called it the Crossroads of America for a reason, and industry thrived there for decades.

Zack's father had grown up one block over, but that once proud neighborhood too had succumbed to depression and decay. First, it was the steel mills that began to lay off workers and some closed. Then the industries that fed off the steel shuttered their doors. Even the railroad struggled. What was left during the recession and oil embargo were retirees living off their pensions and social security. The younger families were forced to leave to find work. That, in turn, brought in a lower class, those dependent on welfare or those that could not find work and were forced out of better neighborhoods. Soon after, not long after a young David Staechel left town fearing for his life, the neighborhood and the families that kept the lawns mowed and houses nice simply left and fell apart. The jobs left, the people left. The jobs never came back for most and the few that did? Well, the people that took those jobs didn't come back to this part of town. Zack thought that it was forgotten in a time warp.

"You done reminiscing?"

Zack didn't want to say anything. Darnell's childhood home, three homes down the road was only a hollow, burned out shell. "Where's the church?"

"Go right at the corner. It's down by the hilltop."

Zack remembered the hilltop. It wasn't as much a hill as it was just the end of the street before the valley where the river took over. On one corner was a bar called Hilltop, while kitty-corner from it was the church. In addition to the parking lot, there was an empty lot next to the church that they played pick-up baseball and football games.

He drove towards the hilltop. The neighborhoods were the same: dilapidated, run down, near empty. Zack stopped in the parking lot beside the church. The bar had long since disappeared and now was an empty, overgrown lot.

"Jesus, what the hell happened to this area?"

"When the mills closed, the jobs disappeared. This ain't no industry town anymore," Darnell said. He understood the look from

Zack. "My uncle sent me letters in the joint. It's nice that you cared so much after you left."

Sarcasm. How refreshing. Zack looked around the area. It was concealed with the church blocking view from one direction and vegetation blocking two others and with the valley ahead, a water plant below and nothing but a creek, well it was called a creek but even at this point a couple of miles inland it was still navigable, and trees around that.

"This where you were when the cops busted you?"

"Me and my uncle was talkin' closer to the church."

"What about?"

Darnell tilted his head. "He was saying how he might have to sell the church. The congregation ain't as giving as they used to be, and the city isn't as forgiving about past due bills, know what I mean?" Zack stared at the church. "Look, man, what the hell any of this have to do with shit? My uncle ain't involved in nothing; you got it?"

"You know I said ain't once in the Corps, and my drill sergeant made me run until I puked and pushups until I passed out."

"Your point?"

"You want to stay on the outside, start talking like you belong out here."

"Screw you, man."

Zack rolled his eyes. "Your uncle is the minister here?" Darnell nodded. "And he owns it?"

"It goes way back in my family. My great-great-grandfather founded this church, and a Whittaker has been minister ever since."

"That's kind of odd, isn't it? Don't most churches belong to the congregation, or the parish or whatever?"

54

"I don't know, man. All I know is that we were talking, it was past dark, after his last service. He was about to give me the keys to his car when five-o bust in here and slam my ass against their car. Some cop forces my uncle back inside the church and the other two drop a bag, slap cuffs on me and haul my ass downtown."

More than two cops registered with Zack. "What else goes on in this neighborhood?"

"My uncle says it's gotten bad. Some gang has been moving in; the old brothers are moving out. He says five-o isn't helping much. Look, man, why don't we just go talk to him?"

Zack fastened his helmet strap around his chin. "Save that thought for later. Let's take a drive around."

He rode away from the church and took in the sites along the streets through the neighborhood. There were few people, fewer cars and the few he did see Zack could tell in their eyes, even at twenty-five miles per hour, that there was fear and hopelessness.

He resisted seeing any old haunts and drove out of town back towards the motel to get something to eat. But his mind had questions. He just didn't know how they were going to get answered.

Andy Gruse
STACKED CASE

CHAPTER 9

"Pensive?" Zack laughed. He hadn't laughed for a while, and it felt good, but it did hurt since it forced open a split lip and put pressure on the cut on his cheek. "I've never been called that before."

"You've looked like that all day. What's going on?"

"It's what I do." Zack tried to sound cool or something but after he said it realized he only sounded like a prick. "We need information. And a black guy and white guy on a motorcycle are bound to draw some looks."

Darnell shrugged. "You have family in this town. Shit, you had like five brothers and sisters. One of them must have a car we can borrow."

Zack shook his head. "No. I'm not talking to my family."

"Why not? I mean, I can see not wanting to talk to your step-dad, but your momma and siblings? Damn man, that's wrong. The family is the only thing a man has when everything is said and done. You can't go your whole life without them."

"You talk much to your family, Darnell?"

"Cancer took my momma when I was in the joint."

Not much else needed to be said. His father left when he was about twelve; Zack remembered so Darnell didn't know anyone on his father's side. His older brother was killed in a gang-related shooting

57

when Darnell was fifteen. His mother swore and made Darnell promise he'd make something out of his life. Zack heard that promise many times. Two years later, convicted of killing Frank Staechel broke his mother's heart. Once again, Zack felt like a prick for opening his mouth.

"Sorry, man. I didn't know."

Darnell looked from the ground right at Zack. "You only have one life, Davey. Or in your case, two. If this is your second chance, you should include your family. You only get one of them."

"You should be a minister like your uncle," Zack deadpanned. "And the answer is no."

"Why not?"

Zack exhaled through his nose. "Because I said."

"You are going to have to do better than that."

Zack exhaled again. "Ok, dumbass. Since you and your now dead lawyer screamed frame and said that David Staechel was the most likely person to have killed Frank Staechel, his father, what do you think would happen to me if I announced I'm still alive and now in town?"

"Why did you leave if you didn't do it?"

Zack thought. Another story for another time. He hated reliving it. "I didn't kill my father, Darnell. I found him dead, but I didn't kill him. And I can't announce that David is still alive. And before you ask me why just think about Zachary Stack and the life he has and what happens to that. End of story."

Darnell paused as if it finally hit him. "Then what are we going to do?"

Zack couldn't help but notice that Darnell could turn on the slang/street talk when he wanted to show some type of attitude and turn it off whenever he wanted to. The longer they were together Zack wondered if Darnell was getting more comfortable.

He didn't have an answer to that question though. "What did you do in the joint?"

"What?"

"What did you do? Lift weights and trade cigarettes for anal sex, or read, study, take a class or something. What did you do?"

For a moment, Zack thought Darnell was going to want to fight him again, but he smiled. "I never did any man sex, either, whitey so don't believe what you see on HBO about brothers in the joint."

"You're smarter than you want me to think. Why is that?"

"I studied my ass off. I made a promise to my momma and even though I was locked up, I knew I wouldn't always be, so I figured when I got out, I was going to become something."

"What?"

"I wanted to be a lawyer. Criminal defense," he said.

Zack smiled.

"What's so funny?"

"Nothing. I guess there's irony in there somewhere."

"Yeah, like if a racist, idiot white man hadn't been defending me in the first place, you and I may be trading places right now."

"So, you studied law?"

"I read as much as I could. No ex-con is ever going to pass the bar though. The last thing the white man's justice system wants is a black lawyer who was wrongfully imprisoned."

"You're probably right." Zack looked at his watch. "I'm going for a ride. Want to come along?"

"Joy ride?"

"No, not exactly." Zack tossed Darnell the helmet. "You better wear this. Where we're going, you're more likely to be recognized than I am."

* * * * * * * *

The two watched both perched on the bike as Chief of Police Warren Sapagio exited the police station. Two other officers were with him; they laughed and talked like they just shared a good joke. Zack wondered if he knew what that joke was.

Warren pointed the remote at his black Cadillac Escalade; the headlights and taillights lit, and the vehicle started. He opened the door, slid inside and buckled himself inside.

"Nice car for a pig," Darnell said.

The other two drove away in their police cruisers. At a distance, Zack followed on the motorcycle.

"Don't get too close."

Zack kept an eye on the side-rear view mirror and the other eye on the enormous SUV. After two turns, they drove south on Franklin Street, the main strip through the city. They turned again on Eleventh Street where the railroad tracks that an electric passenger train occupied split the road in two.

"Where's he going?"

Eleventh merged with Michigan Boulevard. They waited at a stop sign. Zack was about ten cars back. Warren drove onto Michigan Boulevard at the next opening. Zack waited his turn and followed. He stayed as far back as he could but noticed that Warren was slowing down. And he noticed a familiar car behind them. Warren hesitated at the next stop light, allowing two cars to pull around him before he moved forward.

Zack crept forward and turned right at the light.

"What the hell man? I thought we were following him?"

Zack had an idea of what part of town Warren was heading and raced the bike through the side streets. If the cops were being cautious, they would have used their radios. And then they would be looking for a motorcycle with two people on it with out-of-town plates.

The side streets offered cover not likely to be had on the main thoroughfares. But they were slow. It took twenty minutes before they drove outside the southeast side of town when Zack pulled over a hill on a country road and stopped the bike at the edge of a hedgerow. To the east was an estate. A fifty-acre parcel with a mansion, a horse barn, four-car garage and another building which, Zack guessed by the overhead door, housed a coach bus and still big enough to put in a boat, a couple more cars and still have room to have a party.

A white wooden fence surrounded the entire property and lined the long drive-way. To the rear of the horse barn, also enclosed in a separate white wooden fence was a pasture enclosed by an electric fence and inside that stood three horses that chomped the bluegrass at their feet. Zack could tell who ever lived there had money. It smelled of money.

Two cars were in the roundabout driveway in front of the large Tudor style home. One looked like a Lexus SUV, silver, and the other a Mercedes 300 class coupe. A neatly trimmed and full blooming line of Magnolia trees lined the driveway and grew in the roundabout amongst other perennials, annual flowers and a water fountain of an angelic figure flying, water cascading from her hands.

"Where are we? Who lives there?"

Zack pointed at the street in front of the house. "Take one guess. Recognize that vehicle?"

Warren Sapagio turned the SUV into the driveway. As it was concrete, there was no dust. Zack listened and waited. No dog, either. That made sense. His mother hated dogs. She always called them smelly, dirty animals though she allowed the kids to have one most of their lives growing up.

"He lives here?" Darnell whistled. "Holy shit. How does a cop make enough to live here?"

Zack had an idea how he got started. But that money would have disappeared quickly. Acquiring the land and building this would have taken most and his salary wouldn't have been enough to maintain it. Unless Lieutenant Barnes was full of crap about how much he made. Something smelled funny.

Warren stopped in the roundabout behind the Mercedes. When he stepped out, he was talking on a cell phone. Too far to hear. Looked too much like business. Is he being suspicious or doing his job and that car following was imaginary?

"How did you know he lived here?"

"Google search."

The front door opened. Two younger women walked outside. Both gave Warren half a hug as they walked to the Lexus SUV.

"Hey man, are those two,"

"Yeah. They are." Even at one hundred yards and not having seen them in seventeen years, Zack recognized Becky and Jennifer Staechel. Becky was only one year younger than he was while Jennifer was almost four years younger.

"What are they doing here?"

"Looks like they're leaving."

"Let's follow them and ask some questions. They might know what the hell that pig is up to."

Zack started the bike. "No. Not yet. They can't know about me, either." Zack started the motorcycle. "We should get back to the motel. Tomorrow is going to be a long day."

Andy Gruse
STACKED CASE

CHAPTER 10

A car door slammed, and a passing siren awoke Zack. He sat in a sweat on the edge of the bed. He stood, looked out the window and saw the approaching dawn on the horizon. A haze of orange and red crept in on the blackness of the night.

Day four started. He told Barnes and Julie he needed a couple. He asked Darnell for three. He surpassed all the deadlines so far. He needed answers.

He hadn't talked to Julie and knew she would be upset. More like extremely pissed off. She hadn't called either, but he knew somehow that fact would be lost with her during the fight that was certain to happen. That thought scared him. He went to the small bathroom, shut the door and turned on the shower. Almost lukewarm. Perfect. Wouldn't get much thinking done in a cold shower. He washed and dried as quickly as he could but still had goosebumps cover his body.

"What the hell, man? It's still dark outside!"

Zack finished dressing and entered the bathroom to brush his teeth. "Not for long it's not."

"Man, I ain't going nowhere until I get my sleep."

"That's fine with me." He slid on his jacket, grabbed his wallet, phone, and key. "Don't go anywhere. I'll be back. And if you think about it, complain to the owner that we don't have any hot water in the shower."

"Where are you going?"

"Breakfast. I'll bring you back something white. Know how you love the color."

* * * * * * * *

At five in the morning on whatever day it was, nothing was open. The streets were empty. He hoped the cops weren't actively patrolling yet. Wasn't looking for anything but food would be good. Darnell was cranky when he didn't eat. And the guy liked coffee. No coffee today. Not a chance.

He followed the boulevard to Eleventh, turned left on Franklin and headed south down the main thoroughfare of town. Several stoplights, nothing but a straight street ahead of him, he passed the same businesses, gas stations and buildings he did on the way into town. Only when he passed the McDonald's on Franklin, since it was open, and his stomach growled, he entered the lot and went inside to get some food.

* * * * * * * *

Julie Fletcher's maroon Toyota Camry was sucking fumes; and so was she. There was a gas station in sight. She'd fill her tank before she filled the cars'. The rest at the truck stop just inside the Indiana line didn't do much to rest her, and she knew she stunk and felt gritty. While talking on the phone on the Interstate, she didn't pay attention where she was going and ended up over two hundred miles south of where she wanted to be. That delay didn't brighten her mood.

As the sun rose, driving into her destination was a relief. But it was time to get out of the car. Nothing was open, and she didn't know where she was going. She passed several hotels on the south edge of town, not far from the interstate highways but she didn't want to stay at them. She wanted to be closer to town. Where the action was. Where Zack was likely to be. Probably at a dive motel. He was cheap when he traveled.

The lit golden arches beckoned her. She recalled Zack complaining the few times they traveled how he thought it ridiculous to go to another part of the country and eat at a fast food joint. They went to New Orleans once. He wouldn't stop, and when they arrived, she was so hungry she just needed to eat. She made him stop at a McDonald's and almost broke up with him after the next two hours of lecturing she received for having a hamburger when she should have had Cajun food or Jambalaya.

This McDonald's would do just fine. And a cup of coffee would suit her just fine. But, she wasn't going inside looking like she did! Drive-thru will work. Two cars ahead of her at dawn. As she waited, already knowing she was going to scarf down two Egg McMuffins, a hash brown and maybe come back for pancakes, her head flooded with thoughts of Zack.

Since they had gone on their first date, they have never gone more than a day without talking to one another. She knew at first, he was playing it coy and going to wait three days after the first date, but she couldn't wait and didn't. She wasn't going to waste time playing stupid games. If he's the one, might as well find out as soon as possible. So now, five days after leaving him at the hospital and not hearing or seeing him worried and upset her.

Why was he here? Why wouldn't he call her and talk to her? They had a promise!

"Welcome to McDonald's. Would you like to try a bacon, egg and cheese biscuit?"

That sounded good. "Yes, I'll try one of those and give me two Egg McMuffins, two hash browns, and the largest cup of coffee you have."

She didn't hear the order repeated for accuracy or the total. That was a lot of food. "Oh well," she said aloud. "Zack always says when you buy food here, you're really only renting it."

She pulled ahead to the window. Waited and finally was at the pick-up window. She looked inside as she waited. A man left on the other side.

"OH MY GOD!"

She was handed her food and wanted to peel out of there to get to the other side but the car ahead of her didn't pull far enough ahead, and she was trapped. "Damnit!" She honked her horn. "I don't care if you are waiting for food, MOVE!"

The car ahead of her slowly inched forward and gave Julie enough room to squeal her tires and race to the street. She had to stop as a truck passed. She saw a motorcycle heading north. That HAD to be Zack!

She zipped between the only other two cars on the road and raced after him but then her excitement turned to fear and hesitation. The deep-fried smell of the food didn't even smell good. *What if he doesn't WANT to see me?*

She slowed and tried to keep an eye on him, but he was good on that thing and hardly any other vehicles on the road, he'd spot her. *If he's looking, but he won't be looking for me!*

Uh-oh. The light turned red. He stopped. She slowed. That would look obvious. Maybe he won't notice. Should I turn? No. He'll disappear. "Shit!"

She drifted into the lane behind him and slowed more. The light turned. He turned right at the light. She saw the street sign. Barker Street. She turned. He had to be way ahead by now.

Suddenly she felt empty. There was no sign of him anywhere. At first, she let off the accelerator but then stepped on it. She raced several blocks. Nothing. He was gone. *How the hell does he do that?*

A half-hour later, Julie found Washington Park. A beautiful setting on the shores of Lake Michigan, she recognized it as a place that would be swarming with people when it warmed. For now, only a couple of joggers, three roller-bladers and a dozen fishermen were present. The sun speckled off the gentle waves as the gulls screeched for a handout about the parking lot.

She parked and ate her food. It didn't taste as good as it smelled. She watched a pair of terns resting on buoys in the harbor. Zack would know. Common or Caspian? She didn't know the difference. She read the article she printed in Zack's office again. The implications didn't escape her. She felt a convulsion. She was getting sick.

Ten seconds later, the food she just ingested rested in the parking lot. She wiped her mouth, sipped coffee, rinsed her mouth with it and spit it out. Three gulls circled above. "Have at it. I won't be re-eating that." She then left.

CHAPTER 11

Zack entered the motel room and found Darnell dressed and waiting.

"What took you so long? I figured you told your friend cops to come pick me up."

Zack tossed a McDonald's bag at him. "Your welcome."

Darnell opened the bag and ripped into the McMuffin sandwiches. "What? These are the same? No bacon? Man, this brother likes bacon!"

"I'll try to do better next time." He entered the bathroom and checked the cuts and bandages on his face. Not looking any better but at least they weren't bleeding.

"What's the matter with you?" Darnell watched Zack walk to the window and stare outside. "You expecting someone?"

Zack wiped his forehead and turned around. "Just planning on expelling the renters."

"What?"

Zack smiled. "Nothing. Inside joke."

Darnell took the third and final bite of the sandwich. "See, man, that's where you're wrong. You can't have no inside joke when it's just you and I in the room. No one else gets it. Now," he swallowed, "I'm thinking you're making fun of me."

71

"I'm not. Relax, Darnell."

"Then what the hell is wrong with you? How many days have I spent with you and you're acting like you saw a ghost or something."

Zack turned and looked at him. "Finish your breakfast. Let's go see our old haunts."

* * * * * * * *

Zack parked off the street, three blocks north of the Eleventh and Michigan merge and watched. The bike sat in a lot between several used cars.

"What are we waiting for? Why are we here?"

"I don't know." Zack leaned against one of the cars. "Something is a little fishy around here, don't you think?"

"Duh, but what is parking here going to do for anything?"

"Let's just wait and see."

Within fifteen minutes two police cruisers raced down Michigan Boulevard and turned into the old neighborhood. Another two crept past the lot slowly, Zack and Darnell hid behind the cars and watched the cruisers also turn into the neighborhood. Two unmarked cars also entered the area.

"What the hell? Something going on?"

Zack shook his head. They waited and then saw a black SUV turn off the main road onto a side road. Four houses down, the SUV turned at the next block and stopped just as it turned.

"What the hell? Is that the police chief's vehicle?"

"No. This one is unmarked police."

72

"What the hell is going on?"

Zack shrugged. "Almost as if he doesn't want anyone to see. We need to see what he's doing."

Darnell agreed and ran across the street. Zack followed. "No," he caught Darnell and led him between two houses. "We can't go on the street. They'll see. This is called tailing someone. Your first lesson."

Darnell followed Zack between the old houses, into an unkempt backyard with a large willow tree with branches touching the ground.

"Perfect. We stay here."

"But we can't hear him."

"I know. We'll have to guess." Zack knelt in the knee-high grass on the edge of the canopy the willow provided. Branches and whips from the willow obscured their vision but kept them hidden.

"Now what?"

"We watch."

It didn't take but a couple of minutes before a tricked-out four-door El Dorado appeared from the north, drove past the SUV, turned using a driveway down the street and then stopped next to the SUV.

"Brothers?"

"That vehicle is for a gang-banger. That's the leader of whatever gang is running this part of town," Zack deciphered by the markings on the rear window.

"Or a Five-O pimped out to trick us brothers, so they can jack us around."

Zack smiled. "I'm sure the cops would go through that much trouble."

The side windows of the El Dorado rolled down before a door opened. Zack could see four people in the car. The man in the passenger front was probably the leader. He had his right-hand man driving and two bodyguards in the backseat. The passenger, the presumed leader, got out of the front seat and walked to the passenger window of the SUV.

"What the hell? Are those Mexicans?"

Zack moved a branch. "Sure as hell are."

"What the hell is a spic banger doing in the brothers' hood?"

"You don't like whites; you don't like Latinos. Who do you like?"

"Screw you, man. You don't know what I know."

Zack ignored him and watched closely. The man's back was to Zack and Darnell, so he couldn't read the body language. He wore the stereotypical white wife-beater, as Zack called them, and stuck his hand inside the window of the SUV. He pulled out a large manila envelope that looked full.

"What was that? Did he just hand him something?"

The gang member walked back to the El Dorado, got inside and the car pulled away. It turned on the street and drove past the yard where Zack and Darnell hid. They ducked. The police SUV wasn't far behind on its way out of the neighborhood. And immediately after he pulled away, the many police cars returned to the neighborhood. Both Zack and Darnell dove to the ground to not be seen.

"Why are they back?"

Zack could only think one thing: "He doesn't want to be seen."

"Why wouldn't he want to be seen? I mean, he could just be doing civic duty or some shit like that."

74

Another cruiser crept past. *Civic duty my ass!* "That's what I intend to find out."

Thirty minutes later the two returned to the motorcycle.

"Davey, what was that? What just happened?"

Zack put on the helmet and turned the key. The bike fired with a push of a button.

"Zack," Darnell grabbed Zack's arm. "What was that?"

"The Chief of Police just handed the Mexican gang-bangers what looked like an envelope. That's what that was."

"What? What do you think it was? A payment? Payment for what? Why would the chief pig be giving the Mexicans money?"

"That is what we're going to find out. Get on. I have to make some phone calls and want to be away from here."

Andy Gruse
STACKED CASE

CHAPTER 12

Michelle Borman sniffed in every last awakening scent from the fresh Kona bean coffee. She had them shipped from Hawaii and charged it to the company. Zack blew a gasket that day. He was cheap at times. But she loved that coffee! Three long nights in a row made it difficult to wake in the morning and the weather, already humid and warm, didn't help her lethargy.

She looked at the phone, already three messages. She listened to them. All three were bill collectors. Where was their money? Well, they would have had it yesterday if Zack hadn't used everything they had to bail out the ex-convict he insisted he could save. Damn him. Dre wasn't very happy when he found out he wasn't getting a check on Friday. At least not until they get payments from the last batch of invoices she sent out. Good luck. She was getting tired of sending the lawyer to small claims court.

People. What was wrong with them?

She sipped the coffee and savored every flavor and how it excited her taste buds. If Zack returned, they were going to talk about his refusal to allow coffee in the office. Who the hell did he think he was anyway?

Besides the boss?

Damn him for leaving. Damn him. The phone rang as she engaged in another sip. Against her instinct, she answered it on the fourth ring.

"I can smell the damn coffee from here!"

"Goddamn you, Zack!"

"That costs us money, Michelle!"

"Seriously?"

"Michelle, Please!"

"We're broke thanks to you!"

"Relax, I'll take care of it. It will be all right," he said.

"I've heard that before."

Darnell smiled. "I like her."

Zack put his hand over the mouthpiece and gave him a dirty look. Butt out. Why he let him listen, he didn't know, but Darnell wanted to learn.

"Who was that?"

"No one. Look, Michelle, I need you to do that thing you do and get me some information."

"Now you want my help?" She dripped with sarcasm.

"It is what I pay you for."

"HA! That's funny."

"Michelle, Goddamnit, are you going to help me or not?"

"I'm surprised you're still alive. Has anyone figured out who you are yet?"

"No, and that isn't going to be a problem."

"Really? You should read the paper more then."

He shook his head. "Why? What did I miss?"

"Darnell Whittaker was released on bail. I managed to block to whom before the press got it and the lawyer we have on retainer who is going to want payment slapped a court order on it, so the name of Zack Stack won't be released. For now."

"Wow. You're good."

"You're damn right I'm good! However, the police are searching for Darnell and whoever bailed him out in fear that he'll leave the area."

Darnell put his hands to his side as if to ask, "what the hell did I do?"

"They are looking for you and your new friend, Zack."

"I know that, Michelle."

"Well, the dead lawyer was adamant about David being the real killer. Sapagio is blowing that off, but since David just disappeared, if you read the papers you would see that in one of the last statements the dead lawyer made before his fatal boating trip, he suggested that David left town, changed his name and has been quiet and once Darnell is released he expected him to return. Sapagio is saying that's all fabricated lies intended to slur his name, and his lawyers are going after the newspaper reporter, but it is out there. Someone is bound to follow up on that."

"How astute."

"I'd say prudent." Michelle paused and took a deep breath. "Someone also asked if the supposed accident that killed the lawyer could, in fact, be a murder committed by the real killer. Zack, I warned you! I told you to leave it alone and not go back. Nothing good can come from this, do you understand this?"

"Clearing the name of an innocent man is a good thing, in my opinion."

"For Christ's sake, all he had to do was behave, and he was free. Now," she stopped. She was too irritated to continue. "Damn you! You know what I've been dealing with ever since you bankrupted our agency?"

Darnell leaned away from the phone, initially pleased that someone else was yelling at Zack but now was uncomfortable.

"Just stop, all right? Look, I need you to get any financial information you can on Warren Sapagio. He must have bank accounts, brokers, accountants, something somewhere. I need you to find out."

A long silence. Zack knew. Next one to speak...

"What am I looking for?"

"You'll know when you see it. Oh, and since he's the Chief of Police," he started, but she interrupted.

"I know. He's not stupid. I know who he's married to. I'll search her name, too. Do me a favor, Zack and answer your GODDAMNED PHONE!"

The phone went dead, and Zack looked at it to verify the connection had been cut. He looked at Darnell and raised his eyebrows before shrugging. "Someone isn't happy with me," he said and put the phone in his pocket.

"Dude, are you bangin' her?"

Zack shook his head no.

Darnell laughed. "Don't bullshit me. I heard her voice. That chick cares for you man, and no chick is gonna care for some dude like you unless you're knockin' that ass. I ain't stupid." The street voice returned.

"I'd appreciate if you talk about her with a little more respect."

"Sorry, man." They walked back to the motorcycle. "So, is she hot? You did her, right? Come on; you got to tell someone. Might as well be me. After all, the way I see it, we both gonna end up shot and dead before the week's out. What's up?"

Zack tossed Darnell the helmet. "You wear it. You ever been inside the library before?"

"Is that a poor, black man joke?"

"No. A legitimate question as I don't know how to access the archived files."

Darnell shook his head. "Dumbass white man. Now fess up, you are or were banging that ass, weren't you?"

Zack tensed. "Last warning, Darnell. One more and I'm knocking your ass out!"

"Fine." He held up his hands. "But you can answer the question."

Zack got on the bike and started it. "We dated for a long time. It was serious. Now we're friends."

"And you care about her, or you wouldn't be all guilty and shaking and shit."

Zack rolled his eyes. Darnell was better at reading people than he let on. "I'm shaking and shit because you're right: we're probably going to be shot and dead by the end of the week."

Andy Gruse
STACKED CASE

CHAPTER 13

Michelle stared at her desk, the computer monitors to her left stared back, but she couldn't focus. She sipped from her coffee mug and grimaced as the room-temperature liquid burned down her throat. She heard heavy footsteps and the door slam. She thought she heard talking. A large hand shook her shoulder.

"Michelle, what's the matter with you?"

She focused and looked at the large black, man beside her. "Oh, I'm sorry Dre." She rubbed her face as he sat across from her. She could see the look. "You're in early. What's wrong?"

"Ahh man, you wouldn't believe it! I closed the case. The biggest dog-napping ring in the history of Maryland and I freaking solved it!"

Michelle forced a smile and sipped from the mug again. "Will it pay well?"

"These dudes were so stupid. I can't believe they got away with it for this long." He sat on the edge of the seat, rested his arms on her desk and beamed. "Ok, so this lady loses her Freakin' Cheesy, right,"

"You mean Bichon Frise."

"Whatever, man. So, she offers us this huge reward. Talks about how this dog came from this pedigree of champion dogs that have bred Winchester champions,"

"Dre, you mean Westminster."

"Whatever, 'Chelle, quit interrupting! So, I start thinking, and I put an ad out saying I have this Cheese Biscuit dog to breed, champion lines, right?"

Michelle finished her drink.

"So, I get this call, right?"

"Dre, I don't want to be rude, but can you cut to the chase?"

Andre sat straight, disappointment on his face. "I go to see the Bichon Frise and the idiots show me the dog. I tailed the one idiot and followed them to some land they have in the middle of nowhere where they had about fifty dogs. They were stealing purebreds and breeding them. Then selling the puppies back to the owners. Last year the idiots cleared over a half million! Can you believe that?"

"Congratulations. Get the paperwork to me so I can bill her." Michelle lifted a bottle of twenty-five-year-old Glenlivet and poured some into her mug.

"Chelle, what the hell are you doing? That's Zack's private bottle. He only opens that on special occasions."

Michelle swallowed a gulp and topped the mug again. "You mean the fact that it's only ten in the morning doesn't bother you?"

Dre smiled. "Not if it's because you wanted to celebrate my solving the case."

"Sorry to disappoint."

"Well, today is special, Dre. We're broke, and Zack is probably going to get killed or go to jail very shortly." She took a swig again. "He's not going to drink it, so I might as well."

Andre stared at her. "Relax, 'Chelle. This will work out."

"Don't protect him just because you are Marine buddies. There's a bigger picture, and he's not seeing it because of his stupid ego and pride."

"Maybe he just feels a need to help this man."

"This man was released from jail and then busted for possession within seventy-two hours. That's called stupid. Goddamn him!" She filled her mug again.

Andre grabbed the bottle from her. He leaned back, and a reminiscent look covered his face. "Look, 'Chelle, you know Zack. He's prone to do things that don't seem right when his conscience gets the best of him."

"Well, why is his conscience getting the best of him now? I thought I knew all about him."

Andre laughed. "You do. But our boy is evolving."

"And he's going to end up in jail or dead, and we will go down with him!"

"He won't."

"How the hell can you even think that?"

Andre smiled. "Look, me and him have been best friends for fifteen years. I know him probably better than he knows himself and he knows me that well. He wasn't lying to you. If anything, he was protecting you."

"That's supposed to make me feel better?"

"It's supposed to make you quit being so goddamn selfish." Andre leaned back. "We've seen some shit together. I mean, we went through everything together. We've been everywhere together. Even beat up a bunch of German skinheads together."

"You must be proud."

Andre smiled. "We were on a three-day leave in Germany. The broad he nailed wasn't to his liking, so he and I saw some sites. I wanted to do something fun, live it up and cut loose. He talked me into going to see the concentration camps. Well, typical Zack, he got all worked up about it, and when we were at a beer hall that night, some skinheads came in and started showing their swastika tattoos even though it's illegal. So, Zack gets in their faces and the next thing I know he's fighting about a dozen of them. I had to get in there to help, but we managed to knock out every one of those punks and get out of there before the police busted our asses. That wouldn't have been good." Andre shook his head and sipped the Scotch.

"He slept with a woman over there?"

"Yeah, she was hot, but he said she wasn't any good in bed. Which is odd 'cuz we were told those European women know how to get it on if you know what I'm saying."

"Yes, Dre, I know what you're saying."

"After he spent the night with her, he called me the next morning and told me he ditched the bitch and wanted to do something. So, we did."

"You two speak so colorfully sometimes; it warms my heart."

Andre ignored the sarcasm. "Look, our boy is there for a reason. He's not going to do anything stupid."

"Are you even aware of what is going on and how this could affect him and us?"

Andre put his drink down. "I know. I know about the guy he got out of jail. I know why he feels compelled to save him. And I know Zack will be just fine."

"Then tell me because I sure as hell don't understand why he's willing to sacrifice everything he has and probably end up in jail if not dead over this guy!"

"When he tells me I can tell you, I will."

She shook her head. "He's going to get himself killed at worst and thrown in prison at best, and you're worried about some goddamn code of loyalty. Unbelievable."

Andre grabbed her drink and the bottle. "No. I'm worried about my best goddamn friend. And I'm going to protect him however I see and however he asks. You got to separate your feelings for him from this job, Michelle. You know that. Now take a damn nap and clear that head of yours."

They were silent. Michelle closed out her email. "What about the business? We have bills that need to be paid. I need a paycheck. And we have nothing."

Andre sipped the scotch. "I'll call the bacon and cheese biscuit lady and see if we can't get that reward as an advance before we get our additional payment as well. We'll be fine, 'Chelle."

"You sound like Zack. I wish I shared your optimism."

"He's going to be pissed when he finds out that you're drinking his scotch." He looked at her. "What about Julie?"

"She drank it, too. The last time she was here. Remember?"

"I mean, have you heard from her?"

"Why would I? She's probably in Indiana trying to save him."

87

"He doesn't need saving."

CHAPTER 14

"I need a change of clothes, man. I've been wearing the same shit for three damn days, and they stink. This ain't," Darnell stopped, "I mean this isn't right."

"Would you quit your damn complaining? I'm no better off."

"You have a change of clothes at least!"

Zack stopped and faced Darnell before they entered the revolving entrance door to the city library. "All right. When we finish here, I'll take you shopping. Would that make you happy?"

Darnell nodded. "Yeah, it would."

"Jesus, you're like a fourth-grade girl!" Zack turned around and entered the revolving door. Darnell smiled, waited and entered behind him.

Zack took off his sunglasses and smiled at the librarian. "Where do I go to access archived newspapers?"

She pointed and explained the process, but Zack stopped listening. That was Darnell's job. Three minutes later, Darnell sat in front of a computer. "I'm only going to show you this once. I ain't your nigger."

"Do me a favor and get over yourself, all right? As soon as we figure this out and call the cavalry, you can go back to whatever you plan to do, and I'll go to whatever lies ahead of me. Until then, just cut the racist bullshit, all right?"

"What cavalry? The white cavalry?" Darnell scoffed. "Good luck with that. They won't be riding in to save no black ex-con."

"Don't be so sure. People sometimes have a way of surprising."

Zack wasn't computer-illiterate; he was just impatient when it came to research. He hated it. That's what Michelle was for. Well, at least until today. Who knew what would happen if he got back and that's when he stood straight and realized he said if.

"All right, look here, man," Darnell pointed to the screen. "They got all these on microfilm. Technology obviously hasn't caught up with this place." He wiped his mouth and Zack could tell Darnell knew what he was doing. "Lucky for you it's all chronological and categorized. So, you'll have to plug in search words and then check out every article. It's going to take a while."

"No faster way, huh?"

"Only if they computerized this shit so you could just google it or something. What are we looking for, anyway? I already know all about my trial and conviction."

"I'm interested in any talk about that side of town. Gang activity, city planners, anything. Did you notice the different colors of paint on some of the streets?"

Darnell thought. "Yeah, come to think of it. What was that all about?"

"That's what I want to know. They wouldn't re-do the roads or sidewalks or infrastructure for that neighborhood the way it stands."

"With those damn cucarachas running the streets, who the hell would want to try to develop anything there? I'd go closer to the lake or south, out by the interstate."

"The water is right there." Zack slid into the chair as Darnell got out and started typing search words.

"They already got rid of the projects for a damn casino and more shopping malls, which reminds me, I need new clothes."

The "projects" was the term the locals used to describe the low-income government subsidized housing that had housed poor people. The people were all black, and that part of town quickly deteriorated and filled with crime. Once there, it was unlikely there was a way out. As the jobs in the area left so did any hope of leaving the cavern of poverty. The crime and drugs circle increased and took hold of many of the residents in the small city. The police were slow to respond to any calls and when Zack left the area the expected lifespan of a black male from the "projects" was to the old age of 29. It was sad and an embarrassment to the city.

Eventually, the city officials decided that the placement of the low-income housing was too near the lakefront and along the navigable waters of Trail Creek. After the steel mills recession and the industry slowly and painfully withdrew from the area, the last chance for the city was tourism. And that meant the "projects" had to go. Ultimately, the city dozed the area, relocated the inhabitants out of town and developed it.

"You're relentless; you know that?"

"Yeah, well. I don't know how the hell any of this bullshit is going to help me get closer to proving that I didn't kill your old man.

What about that, huh? Is that why you don't want to talk to your family? Because you offed the dude and feel guilty?"

Zack leaned back in the chair and let out a deep breath. "Darnell, Goddamnit, I can't talk to my family! Don't you get that? They aren't my family anymore. Julie, Andre, Michelle and Ted Barnes are my family now. That's it."

Darnell shook his head. "No, that's not it! Blood is your family!"

Zack stood tall. "Please give it a rest, Darnell."

Darnell had the look of contempt in his eyes. Zack readied. "Look, man, what the hell? You have to tell me what is going on. This shit isn't gonna help me clear my name."

"Just be patient, all right? Something isn't right, and we're going to find out what it is."

"Something isn't right is an understatement! You're not right! Tell me what the hell we're doing here, or I'm walking right now."

Zack sat behind the desk. "All right. We saw who we think was the Chief of Police give something to the head of the Latino gang that is running that part of town. We believe it was a payment. Payment for what?" Zack shrugged. "We saw where he lives and it's a huge ranch. I know what he makes, and there's no way he could afford that."

"Maybe they got that from the insurance money from your dad's death."

Zack smiled. Darnell was thinking. "Maybe, but my dad wouldn't have had that big of a life insurance policy back then. We could barely afford to eat and heat the house in the winter, just like you, so there's no way he could have had a big life insurance policy."

"Ok, so you're thinking he's making money on the side somehow?"

"He has to be. And if he's in cahoots with the cucarachas, as you call them, there has to be a reason. And I think it has to do with that side of town somehow."

"Like how? There's nothing worth anything over there. The houses are dumps; most are abandoned. The only thing partly kept up is my uncle's church."

Zack nodded. "And if you weren't lying about the cops placing the drugs on you,"

"I wasn't!"

"Then we have to ask are they trying to implicate your uncle with drugs? Why would they do that?"

"Maybe they want the church."

Zack leaned back. "Why would they want a church?"

Darnell shook his head, but Zack was silent. "Maybe they want it gone?"

Zack smiled. "Precisely what I'm thinking. Now we have to figure out why they want it gone."

"The land values in that part of town are worthless. I mean," Darnell did mental calculations, "hell even a lot over there can't be worth much. You could probably get one for less than five grand."

"Right. Whereas a few blocks away on the other side of the tracks, houses are ten times as much. So, we have a de-valued market and the Chief of Police possibly paying the gang-bangers to cause problems."

"Which would only continue to de-value the market."

Zack saw the light come on behind Darnell's eyes. "So why would he want that? What is over there that they would want? That they could profit from?"

Darnell sat on a chair. "All right. You have my attention. Do your research."

Zack concentrated on the pages in front of him. He typed in names of people, streets, and businesses that used to be in the area. Nothing. He found the names of the city council and planners and tried those. Not much. Time-consuming. *God, do they have a Pepsi machine around here?*

"I have one question though, Zack." Darnell waited until Zack looked at him. "How does this have anything to do with clearing my name of your father's murder?"

Zack leaned back and sighed. "Directly, it doesn't."

"Then why the hell are we wasting time here?"

"Because indirectly it might. I don't know, man." Zack looked defeated and knew he sounded it too. "But the thing is this: you were followed, and they planted drugs on you. There must be a reason they want you behind bars. There must be a reason your lawyer turned up dead. I don't believe in coincidences, and deep down I believe they are tied together somehow."

"So, you think that if you can get them to roll over on the drug charge that will exonerate me on the murder wrap and get that ex-con label off me back?"

"I'm hoping something like that."

Darnell shook his head. "Flimsy at best. Very flimsy."

"Until we come up with something better, it will have to do. I need a Pepsi. Go see if you can find me one."

"This is a damn library. They don't allow any food or drink in here. What's wrong with you, man?"

Zack inhaled slowly and let it out loud through his nose.

"Fine, give me some money. I'll go get us one."

Zack opened his wallet and searched for a small bill.

"What? Give me the damn wallet! You think I'm going to rip your ass off?"

"Crossed my mind." He found a ten and handed it to Darnell. "You better come right back."

"Yeah, like I'm worried about you finding me." Darnell laughed. "Besides, my shit is back at the motel, and I'm not walking that far. I'll see you in twenty minutes."

Zack stared at him. A warning stare.

"What? You want the change, too?" Darnell laughed. "Lighten up. I want to be with you when you get your ass killed."

He left, and Zack returned to the screen. Noon. Painful. This was painful. He didn't know how much time lapsed as he scoured over archived newspaper articles and city planner meeting minutes. His eyes were feeling strained. He felt a headache. Blood sugar was low. Where was Darnell?

A hand slapped his back, and a liter plastic bottle of cold Pepsi slammed on the table next to the computer.

"There you go, man. Don't get caught. The librarian lady was looking at me like I was trying to steal something into this place, so she's gonna come 'round and check it out!"

"What took you so long?"

"Thought I'd try my luck at gambling with all that money you gave me." Darnell waited until Zack looked at him. "What do you think? I had to walk, and there isn't a convenience store within a mile of this place. Plus, Five-O was parked outside, so I had to wait until they left."

Zack's focus returned to Darnell. "What?"

"Donut sale or something. Chill out, dude."

* * * * * * * *

Julie Fletcher entered the Public Library at eleven in the morning. She hadn't slept, showered, or changed clothes since she left Baltimore the previous morning. Her hair pulled back in a ponytail and her sunglasses hiding the fact that she wore no make-up and looked like hell, she approached the help desk with confidence and a smile. A quick check of her breath, even after buying a bottle of water to brush her teeth in the parking lot of a convenience store, followed before she spoke.

"Hi, have you computerized archives of your city newspaper and any legal reports, like court proceedings, things like that?"

"Yes, of course," the lady said. "Well, we're not quite done updating the information. Some are still on microfilm. How far back do you want to go?"

"About seventeen years ago," Julie answered. She adjusted the strap of her bag on her shoulder.

"Perfect for you. We're only up to about twenty-five years. It's a slow process. Are you new here? You have an accent."

Julie smiled. She didn't think she had much of one. At one time she had hopes of being a news anchor. She trained to lose the typical east coast accent she developed through life. "I'm not from here." An idea. Maybe this librarian could reduce the search time. "I'm actually from the east coast. New York area." A little white lie. "I'm an investigative reporter, and I'm doing a report on wrongful imprisonment."

"Oh?" The librarian perked with interest.

"My editor saw a report about a man claiming he was wrongfully convicted and."

The librarian's eyes brightened. "You mean Darnell Whittaker? The boy who killed the white man so long ago? Of course. That's been in the paper lately. Right this way."

The boy who killed the white man? Had Julie not been tired, dirty, hungry and ornery, she would have taken offense. But that spoke volumes. She wondered if race played into the conviction. Was that the card the prosecution played?

"You know, it's funny. We almost never have anyone interested in seeing the archived material here, and already today we've had two!"

Julie didn't care to talk with this woman. She formed her opinion quickly. "Really?"

They reached a computer station. "Odd couple really. Dirty, smelly, men. One of color," she added as if it were a problem. "We've had incidents in the past with colored people, both black and brown. I'm always worried when they enter."

Narrow-minded bigot was what Julie wanted to say. "Well, thanks, I can find it from here."

"Ok, if you need help, please ask me. I'd be happy to help with your investigation."

Julie hesitated to tell her off. She could come in handy. "I might take you up on that. In fact, is there an inexpensive motel around here? I traveled all night and could use a room."

"Well, there's a hotel nearby. And you must have passed one on the way into town."

"I know." Julie was thinking of Zack. He wouldn't stay in some place expensive and nice. "I'm on a tight budget. Like really tight."

"Well, there are the budget motels on the east side of town. The airport was supposed to be out there years and years ago so many popped up thinking they could take advantage of it, but when the city decided to move the airport to the south side of town by the interstate, which makes more sense, they were left dry. But a couple are still open."

Julie smiled. That's where Zack would be. "Thank you. When I'm finished here, the first thing I'll do is get one."

The lady finally left her. And within seconds, she was reading articles about the murder of Frank Staechel, the investigation, arrest, trial, and conviction. She found it all easily.

She took a break from investigating and opened her email in the hopes that Zack may have emailed her. She was wrong, but the email from Michelle surprised her. It was the police file on the murder of Frank Staechel. Julie's jaw dropped. *How the hell did she get this?*

She read it thoroughly. Saved it on her computer and an urge to discover more filled her veins. What was Zack up to and why he was here was becoming clear to her.

And then she found family photos of the Staechel's and the oldest son David stared back at her. The black and white photo didn't do it justice. She searched and found a high school yearbook. He was in the senior class but noted that he disappeared before graduation. Those eyes she had seen before. She had gazed into them before and told them how much she loved him. She felt sick again and rushed to find the bathroom.

Andy Gruse
STACKED CASE

CHAPTER 15

Zack's stomach rumbled. It was more like thunder. He looked up, and a college-age girl seated fifteen feet away looked at him. He feigned a smile and looked at his watch. It was after six in the evening.

"Jesus." He looked at the chair Darnell had occupied. He was gone. His head swiveled all around. No Darnell. He had finally found something he could use but where the hell was Darnell.

"Your friend left a while ago," the college girl said.

"Excuse me?"

"You're looking for your friend, the gentleman you were talking to earlier, right?"

Zack couldn't remember talking to anyone, let alone a gentleman. "What?"

"The black guy. You two were talking. I assumed you were friends the way you talked."

Zack nodded. "What were we talking about?"

She blushed. "I'm sorry, I wasn't eavesdropping, but he spoke kind of loud for a library."

She was right about that. "That's ok. Frankly, I don't remember. What did we say?"

"He was asking you about your family, like if you were going to see them or something. Then he sat down for a while and then left."

"How long ago was that?"

"I don't know. An hour maybe?"

Jesus. "Thanks." Zack left the computer on and headed out. The motorcycle was still there. "Sonofabitch. He bailed on me. Damnit." He made another quick check inside the library, not seeing another man in the place anywhere. Outside he got on the bike and went to the only place he thought he might find Darnell.

* * * * * * * *

Darnell was tired of waiting. Tired of watching Davey, or Zack, or whatever he wanted to be called look at newspaper articles about a neighborhood that no one cared about anymore. Was that really going to help him prove who really killed Frank Staechel? Or did Zack not want to help him find out?

Darnell sat on the cushy chair and watched Zack zone on the screen like nothing else mattered. The dude was intense. But what was the deal with his family? He had tried talking to him about it. It made sense.

He has three sisters and a brother all living in town and another brother that lived not far away in South Bend. They might know something. They should know something. Davey left town. He had fled like a coward. Arrest, arraignment, trial, conviction all in record time. Where the hell was Davey?

Two of his sisters were at his momma's house. Talk to them. If something is dirty about the pig, ask them! Only Zack didn't want to. Why wouldn't he?

Darnell watched Zack rub his forehead and continue his stare at the screen. To hell with this. He won't even notice.

* * * * * * * *

Darnell walked out of the library and smiled at the late afternoon weather; sunny, light breeze, about eighty degrees. Perfect. And Zack was oblivious. He needed transportation. One place to get that.

A half hour later, after hugging his uncle and promising he was going to be all right, he left the church. Walked into the parking lot, unlocked the door of the 98 Chevy Malibu, checked under the passenger seat as his uncle said and then drove away. No time to waste.

Someone killed Frank Staechel, and it wasn't Darnell Whittaker. That much he knew. Time to ask someone who might know. He did learn something from Zack. Google searches can be very informative and as he drove south, the information he gleaned, in fact, the address of Rebecca Staechel Comier, was going to become very useful.

As was the credit card he lifted from Zack's wallet. First for new clothes. The retail stores at the north end of town were all right, but that was shit with defects and stuff. No, he was going downtown where the fancy high-end stores were. Then find some answers.

* * * * * * * *

The house was dark. No movement behind the windows and the house was full of windows. Nice house. A huge Colonial in the rich part of town on the south side called Edgewood, this house reeked of money.

103

The yard was well manicured, and better yet, there were no dogs. At least going off what Zack said about a yard. The trouble was going to be when she came home. If she wasn't alone, the gig was up. And if she was, he had to hope she would cooperate.

At long last, a silver Lexus SUV drove down the street and turned onto the driveway. This was it. If there was any chance of talking to her, this had to be it. He lowered himself in the shrubs beside the driveway.

The SUV pulled in slow. She was alone. She parked the vehicle and turned it off. She fiddled with something in the passenger seat. She wasn't looking. Now's the chance. He moved and crept low. She opened the door and stepped out.

It was dusk; visibility was bad. Even if neighbors were watching, it was far away from anyone who could see. This was the opportunity. He moved quickly behind her; she sensed someone, turned, he grabbed her. One hand went around her mouth; the other jabbed the object into her back.

"Becky, I'm not going to hurt you. We need to talk, and I'm not taking no for an answer, and we can't do it here."

She wanted to scream, but he kept her mouth covered tight.

"We are going to get into your vehicle, and we're going to drive off, Ok?"

She didn't move, but she was scared. Her breath quickened, her body shook.

"OK?"

She nodded.

"I swear to you, Becky, I'm not going to hurt you. Just get in, don't do anything stupid. I will use this." He jabbed the object into her lower back harder.

She nodded and got back into the SUV. He pushed her aside and made her climb into the passenger's seat. He kept one hand on her and quickly hit the locks as soon as he shut his door with the other hand. He started the car and backed out of the driveway and out of the neighborhood.

* * * * * * * *

Zack returned to the motel after sunset; he wouldn't find anything but trouble after dark. It was indeed a long day, he thought. Exhausted and famished, he opened the motel room door went inside and not seeing Darnell, fell on his bed completely spent.

The research was fruitful, but not the way he hoped. Darnell was right about the degradation of the neighborhood. Its decline was well chronicled. The transition of the demographics was easily explained.

The neighborhood became predominantly black as the wealthy moved out. And as Zack learned and knew from his youth, it wasn't even wealth. It was middle-class wealth. The working-class. And when the work disappeared, so did what little wealth there was. The middle class that worked so hard to keep up the looks of their houses and properties moved out in search of work, and the lower class moved into the repressed area as it was affordable.

Only that didn't last long either. Gangs, drugs, guns, alcohol all took their toll on the neighborhood, and the city didn't seem to care.

Welfare, disability, and unemployment didn't pay enough to keep up the neighborhood and offered little hope for the people dependent on it or abusing it. It all spiraled into more crime. The police seemed ineffective. The houses which were built with pride so many decades ago now fell apart and were not cared about at all. And the city didn't care, and if they did, there was nothing they could do about it.

Zack wished he had the bottle of scotch in his desk drawer with him as he wanted a drink. What did it all mean? How was Warren involved and could in any way he connect it to his father's death?

The value of the area had become so inconsequential that anyone with some money could buy up lot after lot with little investment. Whereas city lots in other parts of town undeveloped were selling for over thirty grand, lots in this neighborhood with a broken-down house would sell for maybe thirty, sometimes less. Unless the entire area would sell, there was no advantage to buying individual lots. It could take years before someone could own it all and turn it around to make some money.

Zack covered his face with his forearm, too tired to turn out the light. What was Warren doing in that neighborhood and why did he meet with the gang bangers? And why were the Mexican gang bangers running around in that part of town? And as Zack felt his stomach turn into knots, he had to ask himself what any of that had to do with why he was back in town and if he was just fishing for hope. He wondered if Michelle was right.

* * * * * * *

The information she gleaned Julie knew was conjectural at best. On the surface, it did look like Zack or David; she was uneasy calling him either, should have been a suspect. The fact that he disappeared immediately after the trial was incriminating. To a point. She reasoned with herself all the reasons why Zack, she forced herself to stick with that name, would disappear.

It made sense. But all the evidence on Darnell was circumstantial at best as well. Julie saw how almost twenty years ago in a small Midwestern town the police force would not suitably handle a murder investigation. Rarely were they handled correctly in big cities, as she was aware. It looked to her like the police singled out Darnell Whittaker and never considered anyone else; especially Zack.

And then it hit her: two men entered the library asking about newspaper archives. They had been there! She missed him again! "Damnit! He was probably there the same time I was!" She punched her steering wheel and laid on the horn while she screamed.

Maybe they were in it together, and Zack bolted when Darnell didn't get off, afraid he would talk. But then after so many years of no one listening, Darnell gets a lawyer that listens, they scream frame and name David Staechel as the real killer. David, now Zack, returns and the lawyer ends up dead. Next is Darnell.

But why would they be together? Why go to the library to investigate? Why would he bail him out? And the lawyer turned up dead when Zack was still in Baltimore. So that didn't hold much water. Or did it?

Julie's head swam. She still hadn't eaten anything that stayed in her stomach, and even the water she was sipping was making her feel nauseous. She had to find him. There's a story here. A damn good one. People will pay for this one. Where would he be?

Then it clicked. She knew exactly where to find him. She started the car, left the library parking lot and followed her GPS.

CHAPTER 16

Darnell stopped the vehicle in a dark lot near a park in the center of town and flipped on the dome light. He spun Becky to see her face. "You don't recognize me, do you?"

She wouldn't look.

"LOOK AT ME!"

She looked. Her eyes widened. He saw the hate, the anger, and the fear.

"I'm not who you think I am," Darnell offered as conciliatory as possible.

"You killed my father."

"No, I didn't."

She was silent.

"Becky, for Christ's sake, I slept at your house! I ate at your table. We were friends. Do you really think I killed your father?"

She was silent.

"I need to know the truth, that's why I'm here. That's why I grabbed you."

"You mean kidnapped."

Darnell shook his head. "He said, she said."

"You're an ex-convict that just got arrested for possession. I think they'll believe me first."

"Typical white town."

"Let me go. My husband and children will be wondering where I am."

"No one was home waiting for you. Don't play me."

"They'll ask questions and make phone calls."

Darnell thought about that. "Call your husband and tell him you'll be late."

"What are you going to do?"

The fear in her voice made him feel guilty. He only wanted to know what she knew. Why Davey wanted nothing to do with his family. "I just want to ask you some questions. I swear that's all."

She stared at him.

"Call your husband now. Tell him you'll be late." Darnell saw the terror in her eyes. "Becky, I swear to you, I swear to God, I am not going to hurt you."

"You have a gun."

"No, I don't," he said with a smile. He pulled a Snicker's bar out of his pocket. "I have a candy bar."

She looked confused.

"I needed to persuade you to come with me. If I had asked, you would have said no."

"What are you doing here? Why did you kidnap me? What do you want?"

"I want to talk to you about your father's death." He stared at her, and her face softened. She believed him. He smiled. "Now call your hubby and tell him not to worry. You'll be home soon." She was slow to react. "I promise."

Darnell watched her make the phone call. It was simple and sweet. Made him wish he had someone that cared about him. He lost out on that part of his life. Thanks to Zack. Seventeen years. Sonofabitch.

She closed the phone and slid it into her purse, but he grabbed it. "Sorry. I trust you, Becky, but I have to play it safe." He turned the phone off.

They used to play at this park when they grew up. Basketball courts always had nets and Davey was fascinated with the trains that traveled tracks on one side of the lot, and the birds in the swampy woods beside them. Darnell knew he was flirting with trouble because when they were kids, the cops would frequently pull in the park to try and catch teenagers making out or drinking. But if they did pull in, he could exit the park and disappear on the other side of the tracks and into the bordering cemetery if need be.

"What do you want?"

"I want to know what happened when your father was killed."

"I was at school," Becky offered. "Junior year. I was called out of the office and given a note by the principal to go to Aunt Barbara's instead of going home after school. I didn't know why."

Darnell frowned. "I know you didn't do it. What about your brother?"

"David? What about him?"

"What was he doing?"

"He was a senior; you know that. After school, he went straight to some practice. Then it would have been basketball practice. It was a Wednesday. I'll never forget that."

Darnell struggled with a line of questioning. How could he find out what she knew? *What she suspected?* What did she think? What would Zack ask?

"You were arrested, Darnell. The police said you killed my father."

"I didn't kill anyone! I was home that day because I had the damn flu! I didn't leave my house!" He shook his head. "My momma had to work so that we had money to buy food and clothes and pay for the damn heating bill! That's why I didn't have no one to corroborate where I was."

"If you didn't do it then who did?"

"That's what I need to find out, Becky. That's why I'm here. I think you know something that can help me."

"Like what?"

He noticed her attitude softened the longer she was with him. He wasn't sure if she was just playing the part to ensure her safety or because she remembered they were once friends. But he was going to play it out either way.

"Tell me what you know. Your mother married Warren Sapagio, the cop who arrested me. How long after your father's death was that?"

Darnell, even in the dark, could see the expression of her face change. This was disapproval.

"About a year," she said at length. "Yeah, it was about a year. I didn't want her to marry anyone. Especially so soon, but,"

"What?"

Becky was slow to respond. She didn't want to answer.

"What, Becky? This could be important?"

"I think she was having an affair with Warren before my dad was killed."

Motive. "Did Davey know about this?"

"I don't know. You hung out with David," she said. "Didn't he ever say anything to you?"

Darnell thought. Never. Hung out was a strong word during the school year. They saw each other on weekends, typically after the game as they went to different schools and would talk then, but that was about it. During the summer they were closer and would go to the park together to play basketball or sometimes just hang out with a group of friends.

"David was always the black sheep of the family. I think it was the OCS."

"What?"

"Oldest Child Syndrome." Becky shrugged. "He butted heads with mom and dad a lot. But by senior year he seemed aloof about it all." She looked like she was thinking. "Maybe he just was planning to get out and saw it was so close." She waved her hands in the air. "I don't know."

"Butted heads? What do you mean?"

"Oh, typical stuff. I have two children of my own, and the oldest always seems to be pushing the envelope, testing the waters, you know? Just trying to see how far he can go before he gets in trouble. I'm sure it's common stuff, especially after thinking about David."

Darnell saw more than just motive. "Did he talk to you after what happened?"

"Not really. Why do you ask?"

Darnell knew she was getting close to putting it together. The question was did she know anything. "Look, Becky, I need to know."

Becky moved back in her chair. "It's because your lawyer said that David should have been questioned and is the most logical suspect, right? You think my brother killed my dad?"

He exhaled. "I have to explore the possibility."

"Not a chance! David wouldn't have done that. No way."

"He disappeared right after I was convicted. What does that tell you?"

She was silent.

"Look, maybe I'm wrong, but maybe I'm not. And my life has been ruined because of it. Finding the real killer is my only chance."

"What about the arrest for possession of drugs? Was that David's fault too?"

Defensive. Don't push it. "You wouldn't believe me if I told you."

"Tell me what?"

"That was planted."

She was silent.

"I swear. I've never done drugs. That stuff was all over in prison, but I never touched it. I made a promise to my momma that I'd make something of myself and I knew that when I got out, I'd do it. The cops dropped that bag by my feet and said it was mine."

"These cops aren't dirty. That's my stepfather you're accusing!"

"I know. I don't like it either. But that's the truth. Here's what I'm thinking. David knew about your stepdad having an affair. It pissed him off. Being poor pissed him off. He used to complain about the other

114

kids in school not knowing a damn thing about life because their parents handed them everything. He was mad at your old man because he lost his job at the mill. When he found out about your mom and Warren, he snapped and killed your dad."

Becky shook her head. "That's ridiculous. Why would he do that? That doesn't make sense! And then frame you? You were friends," she laughed. "Look, Darnell, I can understand why you're pissed at him, but there's no way he killed my dad."

Darnell thought. Maybe it wasn't plausible. "What about the life insurance?"

That made her stop. He was onto something. She was thinking about it.

"If he killed my dad for the life insurance, why would he have left? He didn't benefit from it at all. I didn't talk much to him, but he didn't do it. I used to be able to read my brother, and if he did something wrong, it showed on his face. He didn't do it."

Darnell was frustrated. "Who else did he talk to? He had to hang out with someone after that."

Becky thought. "If he wasn't at school or basketball or following the trial, he was with his girlfriend. Sara Eckhart." She nodded. "He spent more time with her after that. She even snuck in the back and spent most weekend nights with him. I still say there's no way he did it but if he talked to anyone it would have been her."

Darnell committed the name to memory. Of course, she'd be married now and have a different last name. Heck, might not even be in town. "Do you know if she's still Sara Eckhart and living in town?"

"Yeah, she's still living here in town. After David left, she kind of went into a funk. I talked to her for a while but then she disappeared. Rumor was she had a baby, and in this town, that's pure sin. I heard she left town for a while, was living with relatives and put herself through college. She just moved back and now has an optometry business. Or was it dentistry? I don't know. I haven't talked to her, but her business is on Barker over by Woodlawn."

Nice part of town. He'll talk to her next. "What about the kid?"

"Junior in high school. The rumors were true."

"Who is the father?"

"Some guy she had a fling with after David left. She's single. That's all I know."

Darnell realized he had gotten as much from her as he was going to. She knew nothing. Now, time to get her home, so he didn't lose her trust. Parole violations were not excusable. Kidnapping was pretty serious. He started the vehicle. "Thanks for the information, Becky. I'll take you home now."

CHAPTER 17

Ten o'clock. Zack got off the bed and walked outside. Half of the lights on the overhang above the walkway outside the door were missing or not working. His was not working. He stepped forward and looked up at the sky. The stars at the far-east end of town, away from the city lights, were out in full force. He recognized many of the constellations. To his right was nothing but swampland and forest. He heard the whoo-hooing of a Great Horned Owl and thought of Julie. One of their first dates he took her to a wildlife refuge outside Baltimore and stayed well after dark until they finally heard the owl. He was pretty sure he'd never see her again after that date. He forgot mosquito spray, and she had close to fifty bites on her arms and legs. She wasn't happy.

But she called him the next day and asked if he wanted to go again.

She wouldn't be happy about this, though. She was in town investigating. She was going to find out. And he'd have a hard time explaining it. She wouldn't see it as he didn't lie to her, though technically he never did. Where was Darnell? What was he doing? He couldn't wait around any longer. He grabbed his stuff, hopped on his motorcycle and headed into town.

* * * * * * * *

Darnell parked the car a block away from Becky Staechel's house. A dark street, little lighting. He wasn't going to drive down that street.

"I'll get out and let you drive home alone from here," he said.

"How will you get to where you're going?" She looked puzzled. "Where are you going?"

Darnell had thought enough about it to want to see what Zack was up to. Maybe give him another chance to prove himself innocent and see how he was going to prove Darnell innocent. Maybe Becky was right; she sure seemed adamant enough about her brother not killing her father. But if it wasn't him, who?

"I got a room on the other side of town. It's a bed."

She nodded her head. "Darnell, you aren't lying to me, are you? You didn't kill my father, did you?"

He laughed and shook his head. "Why is it so hard to believe? Because I'm a black man? Get out of here." The disgust dripped from his mouth. He got out of the car, but Becky got out on the other side.

"I'm sorry! Please, don't be upset. I don't know what to believe. I never wanted to believe you did it, and I'm sure David didn't either. I'll believe you, just look at me and tell me the truth."

She grabbed his arms. He didn't understand her need to believe, her caring for him. It didn't make sense. He looked into her eyes, couldn't see much as it was dark but stared at them.

"I swear to you and your entire family; I did not kill your father or anyone. I did not break into your house that day, and I never stole a damn thing from your house or your family. That's the truth. What you do with it is up to you."

She held his arms for a moment and then smiled. She embraced him in a hug and pulled away. "I believe you. If you need anything, you know where to find me. Just knock on the door next time." With that, she got in the truck and disappeared.

* * * * * * *

Julie Fletcher ducked as the car turned and raised her head after it passed. Then she saw what she expected. A man got out of the vehicle. It was dark, she couldn't tell who it was but knew it wasn't Zack. At least he was smart enough not to do that! Then, inexplicably a woman got out of the other side. She guessed that the woman was Becky Staechel, David's younger sister. She smiled. Her hunch paid off; but only after she drove to his mother's home and realized he couldn't get in there anyway.

That must have been Darnell. Did Zack send him there? For what? He's onto something. Julie drummed her fingers on the steering wheel, happy that her instinct to park a block away on the only other exit street in the neighborhood paid off. The old Malibu did not belong in the neighborhood. Zack taught her that patience paid off. He was right again.

She watched the woman hug Darnell, get into her SUV and drive away. Darnell watched the truck disappear around the corner and walked to the Malibu. He never looked to see if there were any other cars around. Mistake number one. Now it was as simple as following him. She was betting that he would take her straight to Zack.

119

* * * * * * * *

Darnell felt good about what he did. He wasn't sure if he was starting to like Zack, but he needed closure on his life, and he had to talk to that family. They knew something and what the sister told him helped. He thought then how he wished she was single because she was hot. He wasn't sure that Zack offed his old man any longer, but there still was a chance he did. Either way, they had to get to the bottom of it. There was some sinister shit going on. And before this was over, he was going to make sure Zack met with his family. He had to.

And he wasn't being followed. Didn't know how Zack kept picking up cars when they were on the bike. He is probably just paranoid. And he's probably hungry. And pissed. Ditching him at the library probably wasn't going to earn his trust, and he was going to be mad. *Don't want him to punch me! My jaw still hurts!*

He drove down Franklin Street towards that pizza place Zack ranted about every time he saw it. That will make him happy. Bring him some food. No one would recognize him in this car anyway. If he had a phone, he'd call it in. Didn't matter. He'd order inside and wait. The place was always busy that time of night, even when they were kids, so no one would think twice about him and no one would recognize him.

He pulled into the parking lot and had to circle it twice before he found a parking space.

Zack didn't even ask for his credit card back. Was it trust or is he a dumbass? He ordered what he felt was appropriate, was told it would be twenty-five to thirty minutes and decided he'd wait outside in the car.

120

The Malibu had a decent sound system, so he listened to some rap. Didn't like Kanye West too much, TI was all right though. And then there was tomorrow. What did Zack have planned? Another field trip to the library? *What the hell is going on in that dude's head? What is he thinking?*

He went back inside, had to wait another five minutes and left with the two pizzas, a box of tacos and two hot submarine sandwiches. That would be enough for tomorrow, too. Planning ahead, that's all.

* * * * * * * *

Darnell didn't see the Camry across the street. He wasn't looking. He pulled onto Franklin and headed north. Julie Fletcher waited and was about to pull out to follow him when she watched two unmarked police cars drive past.

She drove behind them, managed to keep an eye on Darnell and the cops. This didn't feel good. He turned on Eleventh, heading east. They followed. He went down the hill past the old and majestic Lutheran church, and that's when the lights went on. She wanted to stop but knew it would look obvious. Instead, she turned off on the street previous, turned around, turned off her lights and watched from a distance at what looked like wasn't going to be an ordinary traffic stop.

* * * * * * * *

"Sonofabitch." He pulled to the side of the road. "What the hell? No way they could know. No way. Just stay cool, Darnell. Just stay cool."

The words he told himself offered little peace of mind. He put both hands on the steering wheel as the cop in the unmarked car that he didn't even see behind him approached the vehicle. A flashlight in one hand, his other hand on his gun. His partner was in a similar position on the other side of the car.

The window rolled down. "License and registration, please."

"What seems to be the problem, officer?"

"I asked you a question, sir, now license and registration."

"Officer, I just would like to know why you stopped me. I have that right."

Both flashlights turned off. "You don't have no rights, nigger."

Before he knew what had happened, the cop pulled him through the window of the car and threw him to the ground. A nightstick hit his rib cage. Another smashed into his arm as Darnell tried to deflect any blows.

The other grabbed his foot and dragging him away from the car, towards the darkened parking lot of the empty church. He saw the lights of the cop car turn off. This was it. They were going to kill him.

Away from the street in the dark, one of the cops grabbed his shirt and lifted him off the ground.

"Who got you out of jail? Huh? Who is hiding you?"

A punch in the gut. Another punch in the gut. They wouldn't drop him. "We can do this all night so speak up."

Darnell had a decision. He knew the right one. "You're going to kill me anyway, so screw you, pig."

He remembered being slammed into the pavement. He remembered the kick to the head. He hoped it would be quick. There was no chance to fight back, and there was another squad nearby. He lost consciousness soon after that. Death would be a relief.

The two cops stood above the unconscious and bloody Darnell Whittaker. The other patrol car drove off and disappeared. They looked at each other.

"What do we do now?"

The other looked around. "We can't leave him here." He turned and looked at the church. "Let's drag him to the church and leave him in the bushes by the door. No one will see him for hours."

The first cop nodded. "Ok. I'll park the car in the lot, so it doesn't look out of place."

The two did what they agreed.

On a side street in clear view, Julie sat in her car, her hand over her mouth, her eyes wide and she shook uncontrollably. She couldn't believe what she just witnessed. She wanted to run but knew she had to stay still, no lights, nothing. She couldn't be seen. One patrol car left, and she watched the two remaining cops drag the limp body of Darnell into the shadows and dump the body, either hoping he'd die there or because he was already dead, she didn't know. They moved the car, got into their unmarked car and took off into the dark.

"What do I do, what do I do, what do I do?" She said aloud, the battle to not panic wore her nerves thin. She dialed Zack's cell number. "Come on, Zack! Answer! I need help!" She said as it rung. "COME

ON!" She screamed and cut the connection when his voice mail answered.

She thought about getting him but worried the cops would come back and catch her. But she couldn't leave him. She knew that man was important. And if he wasn't dead, he needed help.

"Damn it!" She said. She started her car and drove into the parking lot and stopped by the hidden body. She opened the door and ran to Darnell. He wasn't moving, but he was breathing. "Darnell," she said, "come on. We have to get you out of here."

He didn't respond, and she grabbed his arms and dragged him to her car. He grunted.

"Get in the car, Darnell!" She urged as she struggled to get him into the back seat of her sedan. "PLEASE! MOVE!" She hunched to her knees and lifted his upper body onto the seat and fought to get him inside. She got out the other side, ran around and lifted his legs into the car. He was crumpled, but she finally got him inside. She shut the door, got behind the wheel and looked at his car.

Darnell grumbled something incoherent. She couldn't help herself and drove beside his car, looked inside and saw the food. She got out, grabbed the food and put in the passenger seat and looked in the car again. Zack's credit card was beneath the pizza boxes; her heart stopped when she picked it up and read it.

"Oh my God! They didn't look!" That made her do a quick search of the car. She quickly found the Glock under the seat but nothing else.

* * * * * * * *

The cops drove off and called the chief right away. There was no answer immediately, but as they drove down the boulevard away from the incident, the chief called back.

"What?"

The two cops looked at each other and smiled at the Chief's disposition. "Hey boss, we thought you should know we found the Whittaker guy."

There was a brief pause. "Yeah, and?"

"Well, we, uhh, interrogated him and worked him over pretty good as you said."

"Did the bastard say anything?" The chief asked. "I hope to God he did."

"No, he won't talk."

The chief let out a noticeably loud breath. "OK, take him to our cell, and we'll talk more with him tomorrow." There followed a long silence. "What? Is he alive?"

"He was when we left him," the cop replied.

"YOU DID WHAT? YOU LEFT HIM?" The chief screamed through the phone. "What the hell were you thinking? Why would you do that? What if someone finds him and he talks? What is wrong with you idiots?" He yelled more. "Go get his ass and take him to our cell! NOW!" He slammed down the phone.

The two cops looked at each other and feared the repercussion of the chief over this. They turned the car around quickly and accelerated. "We are so dead!"

"Don't worry," the other said, "he wasn't going anywhere."

They turned onto 11th and sped towards the church. A car passed going the opposite direction. The cops took no notice and raced to the parking lot. They reached it, and the car remained where they parked it. He stopped by the church, got out and walked to where they left Darnell.

"Oh shit!"

"What?"

"Look around, he ain't here!"

"OH SHIT!"

CHAPTER **18**

The streets were empty, and most of the street lamps were burnt out or busted. The headlight of Zack's motorcycle was the only light in the neighborhood. He stopped the bike and flipped the visor to see clearly. No one was around. There was no movement, no traffic, nothing. Like it was deserted. That's what Zack hoped. He closed the visor and drove slowly towards the church.

Looking for Darnell had proved to be fruitless. But he hadn't checked the church yet. He drove past the church, saw dim lights flicker through the stain glass windows but did not stop in the church parking lot. If the cops were looking, they'd see him there. He steered into an abandoned lot and tucked the bike behind tall grasses, shrubs and sucker trees that exploded through the cracks in the blacktop driveway beside the dilapidated shack on the lot.

Zack knew there was no reason to think Darnell was inside that church. Even Darnell would know that the cops would look there first. But Zack thought that his uncle might be inside, and despite an empty parking lot, the lights inside suggested it was not empty.

He crept around the outside of the lot, near the lot line and out of any light. The corner in front of the church had one of the few working street lamps and was powerful enough to shine into the lot. But Zack kept to the shadows and the dark. He reached the side of the church and

127

expected cop cars to race in and cuff him as they had done to Darnell. But there was just silence.

The first door in the rear of the church was locked. He sneaked alongside the church, wary of traffic, movement, even the gangs, reached the side entrance for the congregation and gently pulled the heavy wooden door. It opened.

Zack entered and thought of pulling his gun but did not. He let the outside door close gently before he opened the door to the inside of the church. It was unlocked, and he entered.

The flicker of oil lamps along the walls gave off an amber glow to the inside of the large, expansive, poorly lit church. It was like the Catholic Church he had attended when he was little. Wooden pews lined the main hall and on two small wings. Stain glass windows imported from Germany arched high towards the expansive ceiling. The altar rested on a stage, higher than the congregation and despite it not being a Catholic Church and Zack having not attending any Christian ceremony in many years, his presence affected him. He felt both awe and humility at once. He saw a large statue of Jesus Christ hanging on the crucifix against the wall behind the altar: His solemn eyes staring at the assembly, imploring them, almost begging them. Or was it different than that? Was He looking at Zack and saw all of his sins and faults and was waiting for Zack to confess and pray for forgiveness?

Zack stepped away from the door, remained in the shadows as he walked along the outside wall and approached the altar. He felt a presence. This was real. Someone else was inside.

"I wouldn't take another step unless you want to personally meet the Lord right now," said a voice from in front of the altar.

Zack stopped.

"You have no right in here, and you best turn and leave before there's any trouble," said the man.

Zack saw the shadow of a man rise from the second pew on the left of the main aisle. Zack moved his arms to show he was unarmed and walked across the front aisle to the side of the church on the right side of the aisle. The man moved forward, and Zack saw the unmistakable shape of a double-barrel shotgun pointing at him.

"I'm not here to cause trouble. Are you the minister?"

The man was silent but kept the gun aimed at Zack.

"I'm looking for Darnell. I believe you're his uncle."

"What do you want with Darnell?"

"I'm his friend. I'm here to help him."

"He doesn't have no friends. Take off that helmet."

Zack removed his helmet but was still between two lamps; the shadows kept his face hidden. "Was he here? Do you know where he is?"

"I ain't telling you nothing."

"Look, Mr. Whittaker, I know he was set up by the police. They don't want him out, and I don't know why but I'm going to find out and help him. I'm the one who got him out of jail. Now if he was here and I think he was, and you helped him somehow, you need to tell me, so I can find him before the wrong people do."

Zack waited for Mr. Whittaker to move or say something but there was only silence. "Sir, I give you my word, I'm not here to cause trouble or hurt anyone."

"Step out of the light so I can see you," he demanded. The shotgun cocked. "Now."

Zack dreaded this moment. What if he was recognized? He stepped into the light.

"You're a white man." The disapproval was obvious. "No white man ever helped Darnell or my family. Just get the hell out of this house of God now!"

"The God I believe in sees every man as the same color." No response. "As equals made in His image." Still no response. "I got him out of jail and intend to prove he's innocent of everything he's been accused of. I need you to give me a chance and put down that weapon." Zack had seen combat in the Gulf and elsewhere during his twelve years in the Marines, but he never was afraid to get shot until now. Darnell's uncle did not relent. His stare was strong and didn't budge. The gun didn't shake or move away from him either.

"You're one of them damn lawyers the cops keep sending to me. You're here for my church, don't deny it! The Lord doesn't forgive you for lying in His house and neither will I."

"I swear to God, I'm only looking to find Darnell, so I can help him."

"Don't blaspheme! Now get out of my Church!"

"I will; I will!" Zack raised his hands higher. "Why are they sending lawyers here? Why do they want your church?"

"You think I'm stupid?"

"No. I'm not from here. I don't know."

130

The old man stared at Zack and either sensed the fear and knew Zack wasn't a threat or believed him for a moment. The shotgun lowered. "You aren't from around here, are you boy?"

Zack did not respond.

"This Church is the only thing left in this neighborhood. They may have chased away all my congregation, but they still come and keep this house strong. But they want it, and they keep trying to take it."

"Why do they want it?"

"Take a look around you, man! Are you blind? This is valuable property. See what's across the street?"

Zack knew what was across the street: more poverty. But down the hill was the river. "What?"

"Opportunity for the white man to make more money and chase the people who built this town away. That's what it is."

"What opportunity?"

He shook his head. "They can't develop with this Church in the way. No one will build a casino next to a church. They won't build their fancy shopping malls and their fancy restaurants in this neighborhood as long as this church is here, and my people are coming to it. And that's what they want. They want to tear this symbol of faith and hope down and build nothing but excess and hedonism."

"They want to develop this part of town."

"That's what I just said! But they can't as long as this Church stands strong and it will as long as I'm alive and as long as Darnell is free. That's why they came and arrested him. They got to keep him in jail! He can't inherit this church if he's in jail."

Zack nodded. The reading he did on this part of town which they called the Triangle was anchored by the Church. The river was one axis, the railroad tracks and the boulevard the other two axes which formed the triangular piece of the city which was the giant slum Zack once called his childhood home.

"If they've offered you money, why don't you just take the cash, sell the Church and build a new one on the other side of town where the people are?" Zack tried offering a solution. If his suspicions were right, the Church was not going to last.

"Boy, this House of God is gonna stand strong! God doesn't believe in no wealth. The poor and the meek shall inherit the earth, not the crooked officials looking to profit from the destruction of this place of worship!"

"Sir, maybe selling and relocating the Church would allow for new urban development, create some good paying jobs. The kind of jobs the people in your congregation need. Maybe this could be a win-win situation."

Mr. Whittaker raised the gun again. "If you believe that, you're one of them and you're here to trick me. But you don't get it. It doesn't work that way. Not for me, not for Darnell and not for the black people that live around here and come to this church."

Race was a constant theme no matter who he talked to or what he read, Zack realized. It bothered him. It shouldn't be that way.

"Mr. Whittaker, Sir, I promise you I am not one of them. I'm here to help Darnell, and if I can, I'll help you. I just need you to lower that weapon."

"You afraid of an old black man with a gun?"

"Sir, I served in the military and saw action. I don't care if you're black or not. But I know enough to know that at this range with that gun if you fire it I'm not walking out of here."

Mr. Whittaker lowered the gun. "You served in the military?"

"Yes, sir."

"What branch?"

"United States Marine Corps, sir. Two stints."

Mr. Whittaker smiled. "Hoorah! I served two tours in Nam in the Corps. Semper fi, brother."

Zack smiled and nodded. "Semper fi."

"I should have known you're a jarhead. Any other man would have pissed his pants already."

"It crossed my mind," Zack laughed. "Sir, do you know where Darnell is?"

"I don't know."

Zack took a deep breath. "You're the only family he has left?"

"That's right. His mother, God rest her soul, was taken by the Good Lord in a cruel way. Maybe to punish her because her children done her wrong. Now he and I are all that's left of the Whittaker name. If you ain't got family, you ain't got nothing."

The old man stared long and hard at Zack.

"You look familiar. Have we met before?"

Twenty years ago, they ate corn on the cob at a Whittaker family get together. Zack sat between Darnell and the uncle that day. "I get that a lot. We've never met."

"So, you think you're going to help Darnell?"

"I'm the only one who can." Zack nodded and headed for the door. "I'd lock these doors, sir. That shotgun may stop one person, but the people that break into churches late at night travel in packs. Thank you for your time."

Zack was just as careful as he left the church and sneaked onto his bike. He fled the area quickly. As he rode through the neighborhood, a feeling of dread crept through him. Something didn't feel right. Maybe it was one of the last statements he heard: if you ain't got family, you ain't got nothing. Another theme he kept hearing.

CHAPTER 19

Zack watched the sun come up that morning while sitting on his bike at the lakefront. 'If you ain't got family, you ain't got nothing' went through his head over and over like a skipping record. Seeing his two sisters earlier only made the thoughts worse, especially with Darnell bombarding him with comments about seeing his family again.

He couldn't go back to his family, though.

So why did he come back? Michelle was adamant about getting him to think it through, and he hadn't. Why did he come back? Because of Darnell. Ok. Why because of Darnell? Because he was put in prison for a crime he didn't commit. Michelle's voice echoed another question in his head. *So why should you ruin your life to save him? It wasn't your fault he's in there. You, Zack, didn't convict him! The jury did.*

Her voice reverberated, and he squeezed his eyes shut to force it out of his head. But he could hear her reason to him again: with him gone, there's no point in helping him. If he doesn't want your help, Zack, you're wasting your time.

He took a deep breath and watched a Common Tern fly along the edges of the lake and decided he'd pushed his luck long enough. He still needed answers. Then his phone rang.

"Hey, Dre', what's up?"

"You sound down, man. What's up with you?"

135

Zack took a long breath. "I lost the man I came here to save."

"What do you mean you lost him?"

Zack shook his head and watched a couple of joggers go down the beach. "He ducked me yesterday, and I haven't been able to find him."

Andre was silent. "What are you gonna do?"

"I'm not sure."

"Well, I got news for you. Are you sitting down?"

"Should I be?"

"I think we found the missing Mrs. Kate Granders."

"Really. Good. Did she pay us yet?"

Dre hesitated. "I don't think that's gonna happen."

"Why not? She owes us money."

"Yeah well, here's the deal Zack. She was found face down in a swamp just outside of town." He paused. "She's dead, Zack."

"Sonofabitch." His mind swirled with thoughts; none made sense. "What did she die of?"

"If I were to guess I'd say drowning! She was face down in a swamp. But we don't know for sure. We just found the body late last night."

"Shit. In a swamp? How long was she there?"

"Looked like a while. It was pretty grotesque."

Zack thought. "Are you sure it was her?"

"Well, here's the deal, Zack. She had ID on her." Dre paused. "And your business card was on her person."

"What?"

"Zack, the police want to talk to you."

Zack rubbed his head. "Sonofabitch. They think I did it?"

"You're a person of interest. You need to get back here now."

"What the shit?" He took a deep breath. He thought about what was going on where he was and summed it up quickly: nothing. He didn't want to leave, knowing that he saw Julie the day before and Darnell was missing. This needed his attention, but he knew he couldn't stay. The longer he stayed away from Baltimore, the guiltier he would look.

"Zack, Lieutenant Barnes keeps calling Michelle and me. You can't stretch this out. He's going to call you."

"All right. Have Michelle book me a flight out of Chicago O'Hare. I'll be at the airport in about two hours. Make sure they know I'm carrying. I'll call when I land in Baltimore."

"You got it, man. I'll pick you up here."

Zack stared over the lake one last time. The stench of rotting fish filled the air. It was still calm. The winds always picked up a little later. But he would be gone. He put on the helmet, started the bike and rode towards Chicago.

* * * * * * * *

The hooting of the Great Horned Owls startled her. But the sound was clear, and it reminded her again of the man she loved. Julie folded her arms as if to ward off the cold, but the early summer night was warm. She had stayed at the motel with the injured Darnell all day. When he was finally cognizant enough to let her know where the motel was and which room he was staying, she got him there and inside.

137

Her medical skills were limited to applying band-aids and rubbing alcohol, but she knew nothing was broke in Darnell. But he looked bad and wasn't going to going anywhere anytime soon. The whole incident confused her. It made no sense. The questions raced through her head, and she had no answers. Why did they do to Darnell what they did? Why didn't they search the car? How close was she to being caught as she saw them return only moments after she left the parking lot? She trembled and clutched herself tighter.

She leaned against the post anchored to the ground and the awning above the walkway outside the motel room doors. She watched the night time bugs circle below the lights in the walkway that still worked and heard the buzz of a mosquito in her ear. A quick swat erased that threat.

A light breeze blew, cooling off the night and made her squeeze more tightly. Where was he?

Darnell slept most of the day. She made sure he was comfortable, and he did eat a little and drank fluids, but he was sore. Anyone would with the beating Darnell got.

She looked at her watch. Midnight. She took a deep breath, frowned and turned to go inside. She locked the door, looked at the sleeping Darnell and designed a plan for the following day.

CHAPTER **20**

Darnell stared at the woman. "Who the hell are you anyway?"

Julie smiled. "Zack's girlfriend. We went over that already." She sat on a chair across from him. "Do you remember anything?"

"I'm hungry."

Julie smiled. Darnell was typically hungry when he was awake. "There's plenty of pizza here. You bought it the other night."

He rubbed his forehead. "Five-O pulled me over and tried to kill me. Did you save me?"

"No one saved you. They didn't try to kill you. If they had, you'd be dead right now. What did they want?"

"I don't know, lady. Who the hell are you anyway?"

"I'll tell you for the last time. My name is Julie Fletcher. I'm Zack's girlfriend. Do you know where Zack is?"

"Last I saw he was sitting at the library. What is today anyway?"

"Thursday. You last saw him on Tuesday. Did you run from him?"

"What is he doing with a fine-looking woman like you?"

Julie smiled. "Darnell, focus. I need to find Zack."

"I don't know where he is. I ditched him at the library because I was tired of sitting around. I was on my way back here when the cops caught me. I wasn't planning on ditching him for good."

"What was he doing? Was he looking for something in particular?"

"Yeah, he had some thought in his head that my uncle's church was the reason for all the shit going on. The harassment, the city being a dump over there, the gang running the locals out of the neighborhoods. He thinks it's all tied together or some shit like that."

"Tell me what you remember from the other night. I need to know everything. Where you went, who you talked with, what that person said, everything."

"Who the hell are you again?"

She stood from her chair and moved to the bed next to him. She sat and faced him. "Look, Darnell, you may find this hard to believe coming from a complete stranger, but I'm here to help you. So is Zack. Something is going on, people are dying, and we have to figure out why. Now think."

"I can't."

She stood, walked across the room, grabbed a box of pizza and a warm can of soda, took it to him and sat again. "Yes, you can. Now I know you met with his sister. What did you talk about? Think, Darnell. We may not have much time."

"Yeah? Well, think of this, little lady. If they think you're helping me, you don't have much time either."

"Duly noted. Now tell me what you remember?"

Thirty minutes later she left the motel room. And she decided to go to a few places. On the list was to see the woman Darnell was going to see next: Zack's high school girlfriend. Then the county coroner. The death of his lawyer was bothering Darnell, and the more Julie thought about it, the less it sounded like a coincidence. After that, to talk to Darnell's uncle, Gerald. And if she were lucky she'd find Zack, have dinner with him and force him to tell her what the hell is going on. But first, she wanted to confirm that the man she loved was really David Staechel. His mother would confirm that.

* * * * * * * *

The GPS system in the car was a Godsend. Without it, she'd have been lost. The driveway was as long as any she'd seen in Maryland. Actually it was longer. The trees and shrubs were different than back home, but they were still impressive. And the house was more of an estate than anything and would hold its own alongside any estate in the ritziest neighborhoods in Maryland around Baltimore or DC.

The driveway was empty, and Julie stopped her car in front of the house. She took a deep breath and exited her car. She walked up the several colored and stamped concrete stairs, finished to look like granite, and stood before the oversized steel doors that were finished to look like wood. She found the doorbell and pressed the button.

Several seconds later, a woman opened the door. She had graying hair, some dark remained in streaks and looked to be in her early fifties. Julie recognized Mrs. Staechel-Sapagio from the pictures in the papers. Sixteen years treated her well. The woman stared at Julie with a quizzical look.

"Hello. Are you Mrs. Staechel-Sapagio?"

"It's just Sapagio. Who are you? How can I help you?"

Julie saw a little of David in her face. Perhaps in the eyes but not much else resemblance. She flashed plenty of jewelry: large diamond earrings, a gold necklace with a diamond stud in a heart-shaped pendant around her neck; a silver wrist bracelet that hid her entire wrist and flopped up and down her forearm when she moved her arm and wore rings on several fingers, including a diamond on her ring finger that Julie guessed was five carats.

Her clothes were all designer, and the first impression of this woman was that she had money. And a lot of it.

"My name is Julie Fletcher. I'm a reporter working a story, and I wanted to talk to you about,"

"I don't know anything about whatever story you're working on, and with my husband being the Chief of Police, I couldn't answer anything anyway."

Julie re-grouped. "I'm not working with a paper." She tried to smile to make Mrs. Louise Staechel-Sapagio more comfortable. "I'm interested in your son."

Mrs. Sapagio lost her smile. "Which son? I have two."

Julie noticed the hesitancy and uneasiness already. "You mean three, don't you?"

"Oh, well of course. But David has been gone for such a long time."

Julie thought it odd that she would dismiss having a son so easily. "Your name is Louise, right? May I call you that?"

"Of course. What do you want?"

"Louise, I've been following the Darnell Whittaker case, and recently his deceased lawyer alleged that your son was, in fact, the killer of your first husband, Frank."

"Yes, I'm aware of those accusations."

Julie waited for more. Louise Sapagio stared at her. Then, as if social etiquette protocol finally entered her mind, she gasped. "Oh my, where are my manners? Won't you please come inside? Would you like a cup of coffee?"

"Oh, thank you, Louise. I'd love some."

Julie entered the house and tried to hide her awe. The inside was more opulent than the outside. The marble floors, high ceilings, elaborate hand-carved woodwork around the doors, floors, and ceilings along with red-satin drapes surrounding the magnificent original paintings from artists Julie did not recognize but thought for a second that Zack probably would, all smelled of money. He never left her thoughts.

A hand-carved cherry railing lined the wide stairwell in the center of the grand foyer. The wide steps were covered in a deep, red carpet and must have been at least twelve feet wide. She had seen similar railings and stairwells in movies, particularly ones that were about the grandiose estates of the south back in the days before the Civil War. She imagined Scarlett dashing down the stairs.

"Please, let's sit in the breakfast nook."

Julie thought about the breakfast nook. She didn't know what one was.

"The morning sun is shining through the windows, and it has a lovely view of the gardens. It's lovely this time of year."

143

Julie smiled and followed her through the house, trying to look into every room they passed which included a large dining room, a den, and the kitchen. They entered the room. "It is lovely," Julie commented as Louise motioned her to a chair which did not face the windows.

A silver tray with a silver coffee pot with two cups, a sugar dish and a small dish which Julie figured had cream or milk or something in it.

"They're Zona beans. They're hard to find here in Indiana, but we have them shipped from Hawaii. They make the best coffee."

Julie smiled. She knew of those beans. Michelle had them shipped once a year and Zack had a fit because they cost so much. And somehow, she got the company to pay for it. "It is good coffee."

She was poured a cup.

"Would you like any cream or sugar?"

"Oh, thank you no. I like it black."

Louise looked for a moment like she didn't understand that concept as she scooped sugar and poured cream into her coffee. "Please, sit down. Now, you said you were investigating the murder committed by Darnell Whittaker?"

Interesting phrasing. "Yes, the death of your husband."

"Former husband. That marriage has been annulled."

Julie tried not to look appalled by the lack of emotion, how she nonchalantly disregarded her first husband, the father of her six children.

"I know this must be hard for you, but I'd like to talk about that day, and what happened and the subsequent disappearance of your son, David." Saying David pained her every time.

"There isn't much I could tell you. I was at the supermarket," Louise sipped her coffee, hesitated with the liquid in her mouth and savored the flavor. "You see, I got home early from my job as a waitress to help make ends meet, and Frank was at home, of course," the sound of disdain resonated to Julie, "and he was working on another pipe-dream of his in the basement."

"Pipe dream? What do you mean?"

"Oh, Frank had the craziest idea that he could invent something or other and that it would be the answer to all of your problems."

"Problems?"

"I'm sorry, who do you work for again?"

Julie stammered. "Actually I'm an independent. I saw the story while cruising the wire last week and saw the story of Darnell Whittaker and his lawyer's claims and decided that I wanted to pursue it."

"Do you sell it then?"

Julie smiled. "If I'm lucky." She sipped her coffee. It was good. *Why did I quit drinking it?* "You were saying about the problems?"

Louise looked over the gardens filled with iris's, rose bushes, daisies, lilies and a host of other annual and perennial flowers that Julie didn't recognize. "Well, Frank, well, he wasn't that much of a provider. And with six kids there was never enough, and instead of trying to find a decent paying job, he spent his time chasing those dreams he had."

Julie could imagine what those fights were like. Her parents had those, too.

"So, you came home from work?"

"Yes, and Frank had decided to drink that day, so he told me to go to the supermarket to get him some Pabst Blue Ribbon, the beer he

145

drank, and of course with what little money I made that day in tips I was getting some food for the children."

"You were at the supermarket then?"

Louise watched something flit from flower to flower and then fly to an orange feeder hanging from a branch. Julie followed her eyesight and recognized the hummingbirds.

"Yes," Louise paused to sip her coffee. "And when I came home, there were police cars in front of the house."

Julie remembered the police report she got from Michelle. So far, no mention of Detective Warren Sapagio who was the first on the scene based on a phone call from a neighbor and the "sighting" of a person running down the alley.

"Where was David?"

"David?" She paused again. "Well he was at school of course, and from school, he went right to basketball practice."

"How can he be a suspect then?"

"Well, there was someone," Louise hesitated and looked uncomfortable, "someone of color," there was another pause, "who claimed to see David come home early that day. I don't know how that would have been possible though."

"But you were at the store, so it is possible that Za, David," she corrected herself, "came home and somehow participated in the murder of your husband?"

"Former husband." Louise sipped her coffee. "I suppose it's possible."

"Mrs. Staechel, I mean Mrs. Sapagio,"

"Louise."

"Louise," Julie smiled, "if the lawyer's accusations are true, can you think of any reason why David would have shot and killed his father?"

Louise shook her head. "Oh, I never really believed that." A sip of her coffee. "I mean he was the oldest, so it seemed that they fought a lot. As David got older, he seemed more defiant, and he and his father were always yelling at each other. I guess I never really looked back, but David seemed troubled now that I remember."

Julie cocked her head. She had to ask herself if she just heard correctly. "Troubled?"

"Oh, I don't know. Looking back I guess there were signs that I never realized. Never saw. I had five other kids and a husband that couldn't provide for us, so I had to work as many part-time jobs as I could to get by. Perhaps this was all my fault."

"Your fault?"

"Oh, as a mother I guess I should have paid more attention to his friends, who he hung out with, who he was dating. Perhaps I would have seen that he was troubled or maybe if he did kill his father, maybe I could have prevented it."

Julie set the cup on the table in front of her. She heard correctly. "Was Darnell Whittaker his friend?"

"We were neighbors, so they were. Played basketball together all the time in the summer."

"Why would Darnell kill your husband?"

"Former husband. I don't know. I know he and David fought earlier in the week because David's team beat Darnell's team the week before. There must have been something else, they were yelling and

147

might have wrestled. I didn't see it, only heard from his sister Rebecca. The police said he stole something from our house and was planning on selling it for money. They were as poor as we were. Maybe worse."

Julie wished she had a tape recorder going. She'd remember this though.

"Do you think Darnell was guilty or that David could have done it and Darnell was framed as his lawyer claimed?"

Julie watched the facial expressions of Louise. Julie wondered how she'd answer knowing that her husband made the arrest and was the primary investigator. The newspaper articles suggested that the Whittaker arrest and conviction is what propelled Warren Sapagio's career.

"He was tried and convicted by a jury of his peers. A court of law found him guilty. I'm comfortable with the result."

Julie nodded. "David disappeared right after the sentencing. Did you ever hear from him again?"

She shook her head. "He just left one day. I don't know what happened to him and have not heard from him since."

"Was there a search? Anything?"

"Of course. The police searched and searched and followed every lead for the next few months, but it was like he disappeared. Warren speculated that he may have gotten involved with the wrong crowd and is probably dead. A John Doe and I'll never know."

Julie wanted to comment on the lack of emotion. "Why do you think he left? The Whittaker camp claimed he felt guilty about another man going to jail for the murder he himself committed. Do you believe that?"

148

Louise shrugged. "Who knows? Maybe they were in it together? I don't know. I wish I knew what happened to him though."

"You have no idea of why he just left?"

Louise shrugged again. "You know, David was flaky at times, he was having girl problems and was a lot like his father." She sipped her coffee. "Couldn't finish anything, couldn't commit to anything, spent more time dreaming than working. Maybe he was afraid of adulthood and the death of his father, whether he did it or not, might have scared him and he decided to avoid it and just left. I don't know. I've thought so long and hard about it I don't even know what is real any longer."

Julie nodded.

"I'm sorry, but I really must be going. I have an appointment in town pretty soon, and I don't want to be late. Rafael is the most exclusive hairdresser in Northwest Indiana, and if I miss this appointment, I won't get back in for three months. You must know how that is." Louise laughed.

Julie chuckled. She had no idea what that was like. Cost Cutters did her hair. "Of course. Thank you for your time. I'm sorry if I've inconvenienced you."

"Oh, that's quite all right."

They walked to the front door.

"So, will you be following up on this story?"

"I intend to." Julie stepped through the door. "I'll be sure to let you know if I find out anything about David."

"Thank you. I'd like that."

Julie went to her car and wasted no time leaving. She tried to compute what she was just told. Either David killed his father, or he didn't. But if a son had ever gotten thrown under the bus by his mother, she just witnessed Louise Staechel do it. She intended to find out why.

CHAPTER 21

The girlfriend David had problems with was next. The GPS helped Julie again and took her to an optometrist's office. The name of the office told Julie what she needed: Sara Eckhart-Robbins; Doctor of Optometry.

So, she married. The place was closed, and the lot was empty. It was only nine in the morning, so that seemed odd, but she had a name. And her phone's search feature would locate an address soon enough. And then, the GPS would take her to the house.

Ten minutes later she entered an area to the northeast of the city called Long Beach. She turned off the highway, crossed over a set of railroad tracks and immediately saw a cop in a driveway with a radar gun. She smiled as the cop watched her. She knew undoubtedly wondering why a stranger was in his part of town. Zack called cops like that Barney Fifes. But yet one of his good friends was Lieutenant Barnes in Baltimore. Contradiction, wasn't it? Her GPS spoke to her, told her to turn left and that the address was on the left.

She saw the number on the mailbox and slowed in front of the drive. She looked at the house and wondered why she didn't go into optometry. The two-story house was huge, brick covered in the neutral tan-brown mix with deep green shutters beside large windows with white trim. The yard was immaculate, and the concrete stamped driveway was

151

long.   She noticed the other houses and knew this area was where the money was.

She pulled into the driveway, collected her thoughts and walked to the front door. She pressed the doorbell, and besides the screaming Blue Jays in the oak trees in the front yards and an angry squirrel, she heard the chime of the doorbell. A simple four-note chime seemed to temper the yelling match between the jays and the squirrel.

The door opened. Julie stared at who she knew was Sara Eckhart-Robbins. She was tall and slender with longer than shoulder length black hair that looked naturally curly, but Sara wore it straight. Her brown eyes jumped from her, and the olive tone of her skin glowed. Julie saw why Zack would have been interested in her. And her body wasn't too bad either.

"May I help you?"

Julie smiled. "Hi, this is going to seem really strange, but my name is Julie Fletcher. I'm sorry to bother you, but I was wondering if I could ask you a few questions."

"I have to leave for work pretty soon; you can make an appointment."

"No, no, wait," Julie urged as Sara backed away from the door. "I'm not here about my eyes." She smiled. "I'm a reporter, and I was wondering if you could spare five minutes."

Sara eyed her up and down, perhaps comparing, and stepped outside, shutting the door behind her. "What do you want?"

Julie smiled. She noticed that Sara wore makeup and smelled of perfume. Not too strong, but strong enough. A hint of vanilla in the scent so it might have just been lotion. She wore navy slacks that fit her well

152

and a V-neck tee shirt, green. Probably wore a white overcoat at work. Not large breasts, but nice. Julie realized she was critiquing this woman because she had been Zack's girlfriend. She wiped the comparisons out of her mind but wondered if she was the one Zack lost his virginity to.

"I'm doing a story on a murder case that happened many years ago. Do you remember David Staechel and Darnell Whittaker?"

Sara's face turned white. She did. "Yes. Why?"

"What could you tell me about it?"

Sara shifted her weight and looked at the ground beside her. "You're only here because you know David and I dated, right?"

Julie nodded.

"I don't know what you're after, but I do know that David didn't do it. Some lawyer was asking me about that not too long ago. I don't know about Darnell. All I know is what the newspaper said. That's all I know."

"A lawyer was here?"

"Yes. He was trying to prove that Darnell Whittaker was innocent. I thought I saw in the paper that he drowned while fishing in Lake Michigan or something like that?"

"He's dead." Julie shifted. "How was your relationship with Za, David?"

Sara narrowed her eyes. "What does that have to do with anything?"

"Anything you can tell me about your relationship with David and anything he might have shared with you before or after his father was killed could be very important."

153

"Are you trying to find him guilty?" There was a pause. "Because I can tell you he didn't do it."

"How do you know?"

"Because I dated him all through high school and I know him." She paused and frowned. "At least I knew him before he disappeared."

So, he DID lose his virginity to this woman. "He never contacted you after he left?"

"After Darnell was found guilty of murdering David's father, I called him one day, and he was gone. He just left. I haven't heard from him since."

"Were you two having any problems? Relationship or otherwise?"

"What? No, of course not. Why are you asking me that?"

"You and he weren't having problems before his father was murdered?"

Sara laughed. "God no! Who told you that? I don't think we fought once all the time we dated. We definitely were not having problems."

Julie noted that in her brain. *These two were an item!* "Did you know Darnell?"

"Of course. We all knew each other. David and Darnell were friends, played basketball against one another. I was David's girlfriend." She blushed. "You know that school girl crush, your first love? Well, I watched him play and got to know Darnell."

"Do you think Darnell did it?"

Sara shrugged. "The cops said he did. The jury convicted him. He did his time. I don't know if he did or not. If he did, I certainly don't

154

know why. They both were poor, and David didn't have anything in his house worth stealing, at least not anything nicer than what Darnell had so personally, I never believed that Darnell would rob David like the police said."

Julie wondered why she seemed to open up so easily. That was good. Keep her talking. "The police said it was a robbery and Darnell got caught and then shot Mr. Staechel?"

Sara scoffed. "Yeah, that's what they said but I think, and don't tell anyone this, this isn't on the record, is it? You're not going to print what I'm saying are you?"

She retreated, and Julie realized that Sara was worried that her words could ruin her reputation, possibly her business, or was she afraid of something else? "No, no, I promise you. I won't use your name or anything you say in any story I do. I promise you that. I'm looking for information, that's all."

Sara eyed her up and down again. "It's just that I don't want to create any unnecessary attention for my son or myself, with my business and all."

"I understand, and I assure you you're safe with me."

Sara nodded. "Well, as I was saying, I think the police don't know who did it but at the time, I think they just arrested a black kid who had no alibi and figured they'd play the race card to keep people from asking questions. I mean, Mr. Staechel used to play basketball with David and Darnell and their friends. He was a great dad to David as well to Darnell and the other kids. So, for me to believe that Darnell produced a gun and shot Mr. Staechel point blank while robbing a crappy small TV that didn't work is just too much of a stretch for me."

"Wait, it didn't work?"

"No. David and I used to watch it in his bedroom. One night we," she paused, "well, it went black and stopped working. Couldn't get it to work again." What Sara wasn't going to admit was that she and David were making love and her foot kicked it off the small table, and it broke. It never worked again after that.

"So why steal a broken TV?"

"Exactly," Sara said.

Julie changed gears. "Didn't Darnell have an alibi?"

"He was home sick that day. The flu. A lot of us were that winter. His mother was working, and no one else was home. No one was going to believe the word of a seventeen-year-old black kid over an up and coming white police detective in this town back then. Heck, I don't think they would now, either."

"What about David?" She felt odd saying David. He was Zack, wasn't he? She wasn't sure anymore. Who was the man she loved? "Did he ever say anything to you afterward? Did you spend a lot of time with him after the murder?"

Sara's face tightened. She crossed her arms. "He was confused. He didn't know what happened and didn't understand it." She paused. "He never really told me what happened. I know he found the body."

The body. The phrasing seemed cold, but Julie suspected that Sara was convinced that Frank Staechel was not killed by Zack, so the body was no longer Frank. And this also contradicted what his mother had told her. Why the lies? And why the hesitation? Julie suspected Sara was holding back.

156

"He seemed to withdraw from his family after the murder. I don't know what it was." Julie watched Sara fall into deep thought and suspected Sara's memories brightened yet she sensed bitterness. Or was it sadness? "He hated being there. I remember him telling me that once about the time Darnell was found guilty."

"Really? Why do you think that?"

Sara shrugged again. "I think it was because his mother was seeing that cop she married. I remember Becky telling me once, his sister; she was a year behind us in school, that she thought her mother was having an affair."

"She told you that?"

"We were close. As I said, I spent a lot of time with David throughout high school and at his house, so I got to know his family and Becky and I did things together when David was off doing his sports or hanging with his guy friends."

"Did David know that?"

"No," Sara chuckled. "He was naïve in a lot of ways. And I wasn't going to be the one to ruin his image of his parents." She held her arms tighter across her chest. Her gaze went to her lower right. She looked sad for a moment before snapping her head up and forcing a smile. "Is there anything else?"

"I'm curious as to why David just disappeared. You don't know why? And this was right after they sentenced Darnell to fifteen years?"

"They sentenced him to twenty-five, eligible for parole in fifteen because he was young. Some of the people in town wanted the death penalty. But no, I don't know why he left. We were talking college, both planning on going to IU and even talked marriage." She chuckled.

"Again, you know how teenage romance is. It was all silly. But after the death of his dad and the trial and conviction of Darnell, he wanted to leave. He asked me to leave with him. I said we couldn't leave; we have to graduate. I thought he was kidding." Sara frowned. "And then one day, he was gone."

Julie had to ask. "If you knew he really was leaving, would you have left with him?"

Sara smiled. "Yes."

"He never called, or wrote or anything?"

Sara shook her head no. Julie thought she saw a tear.

"And this was right after Darnell was sentenced?"

Sara's eyes looked up and to the right. "Yeah. It all happened so fast. We only had like a month until graduation. I knew something was bothering him, but he never told me. He said it was nothing, that he just missed his dad. But he was tense, and no matter what I did, it didn't help."

"Did he argue or fight with his dad at all?"

Sara smiled. "No. Why would you think that? He idolized his father. David spent more time talking to his dad than any other kid our age. They never fought."

"How about with Darnell? Did he fight with him after the game? Was there a game they played, and David's team finally won?"

Sara smiled more. "You've done your homework. Yeah, a couple of weeks before," she paused, "we played City and finally beat them. But Darnell and David didn't fight or argue. After the game, we all went out and had a good time. David isn't a fighter."

Julie nodded. "You really have no reason to think David would kill his father?"

"God no. It's ridiculous."

A car pulled into the driveway. Julie watched Sara's eyes and followed her look. An older model BMW 325, white, stopped, and a teenage boy got out. Julie looked back at Sara. Despite the smile, there was something about the way she held her body. Was she nervous? Was it the trip down memory lane?

The teenage boy, carrying a towel, wearing baggy swim trunks, a loose tank top and sandals smiled at her. "Hi," he said to Julie. He looked at Sara. "Hey, mom. What's for lunch? And who is this?"

Julie saw it immediately. She knew her face betrayed her, but the resemblance was unmistakable. He was tall, slender, blonde haired, blue eyed, athletic looking and the nose and smile were the same she had fallen in love with before: Zack's.

"Is this your son?"

Sara smiled and pulled the still wet son to her. "Yep, this is my son." She turned to her son. "There's some pizza on the counter. Are you staying home tonight?"

"I was thinking of doing something with Emma. Maybe a movie."

"You went to a movie last night with her."

"So?"

"Well, I don't want you rushing," Sara's voice trailed off.

Her son laughed and turned to Julie. "Can you believe that? I'm David, what's your name?" He extended his hand. An etiquette faux pas.

159

"I'm Julie." She shook his hand. David smiled at her and gently pulled her hand up while he bent over.

"Ahh, Julie. A lovely name for a lovely lady." He kissed her hand lightly. Ever the gentleman. And a fast-mover. Julie knew women would fall all over him.

"Thank you, but you're a little young for me." She joked, and the three laughed.

"Honey, the pizza is getting cold."

"You're not going to tell me who Julie is?"

"She's an old friend from college."

David turned back to Julie. "Really? Did you go to IU? Can you stay for lunch? Maybe come back for dinner after mom is off work? You two must have a lot to talk about, and I'd love to hear it all."

Julie smiled. This Casanova was hitting on her! "Unfortunately, I can't stay. And I'm already in a relationship as are you. But thanks, I'm flattered."

"Story of my life," David joked. "They throw me away with reckless abandon. If only they realized what they are missing." They laughed. "It was nice to meet you. Please don't hesitate to stop by." He winked. "Anytime."

David disappeared into the house. Sara closed the door, her arms crossed again over her chest, and she looked at Julie with a bit of discomfort on her face.

"He's a real ladies man. How does his father handle that?"

"Umm, we're divorced," Sara said.

"I'm sorry."

"That's Ok. You didn't know."

Julie knew that Sara wanted her to leave. "Listen, thank you very much for your cooperation. Again, I promise you I won't use your name or anything you said." She reached into her purse and pulled out a business card. It said simply Dre-Zack Detective Agency and had the eight-hundred number in the corner. She wrote her cell number on the back of the card. "If you remember anything that might be helpful, or if you just want to talk, please don't hesitate to call me."

Sara took the card. "I will." Julie turned and stepped down one step and heard the door shut. Sara was in the house.

Then the emotion poured through Julie. She rushed to her car. It was too much. That was Zack's kid! He was over sixteen. The math made sense. Did he bolt after he learned Sara was pregnant? Did he know he had a kid? She felt like a ton of weights were suddenly pressing against her lungs. She got into her car. She couldn't breathe. How could this happen? How could she not know? Did he know? What was happening? Then, she opened her car door, leaned out and what little she had in her stomach exited the hard way. She vomited.

Andy Gruse
STACKED CASE

CHAPTER 22

The County Coroner's office was located in LaPorte, the county seat. It took Julie about thirty minutes to find it and get inside the building. In Baltimore, they knew her well so when she entered the building they sent her right to the examining room, or wherever the chief coroner was. She didn't think some little burb in northern Indiana would grant such favors.

All she wanted was to look at the autopsy report for the lawyer that was killed in a boating accident. Connor Delvins. It took some relentless asking, but a guy at a desk finally let her through to the examining room where the coroner was doing another autopsy. It made her change her mind about the burb in Indiana. Apparently, people didn't care where they were when they killed someone.

The man looked at her. "Who are you?"

Julie smiled. "Well, my name is Julie Fletcher, I'm an investigative reporter. The officer out front was easy to flirt with. He let me come back here."

"What do you want?"

He didn't seem bothered any longer. Must have been her tight tee-shirt. Guys loved it when she showed off her modest breasts. They were all so easy. Put her sandy-brown hair in a ponytail and show off her neck like Zack loved so much and bingo. She smiled. "I'm curious if your office did an autopsy on Connor Delvins?"

"The lawyer that can't swim? Sure, I did one."

"He drowned?"

"Nope."

"I thought the official report said he drowned in a fishing boat accident?"

"The official report said he died in a fishing boat accident. He didn't drown though."

Julie waited. The man dropped the bone-saw he was using to carve open the corpse's chest and walked across the sterile, mostly steel and glass room to his desk. He dumped his gloves in the wastebasket and pulled open a drawer in a file cabinet.

"What's your interest in it?"

"I think it was murder."

The man smiled. "Who are you working for?"

"No one. I'm independent."

He flipped through the file and found the official paper. He read it silently. He frowned and looked around. "This has been sealed. I can't talk about it. It's under investigation. Order of the boss."

Julie smiled. "Ok, so how about if you tell me off the record?"

"You're a reporter, which means you're a busybody, and you're a woman which means you're about as bad as a lawyer and you can't be trusted with anything off the record."

Julie chuckled, made a seductive move with her chest, sticking it out slightly, without making it obvious and stepped closer to the middle-aged man. "Look, I know I'm fishing," she chuckled, "sorry for the pun, and I knew it was a long shot coming all the way here. But I can tell you this; I won't divulge any information. Not in an ongoing investigation. That could compromise you, and I wouldn't want that." She touched his arm. Usually, that did the trick.

The man's eyes lit up. "Well, perhaps we could come to some sort of an arrangement?"

"And what would that be?"

"You want something; I want something."

Sly. Real sly. She saw the ring on the man's finger. Pig. "How do I know what you want is worth the information in that file?"

"You want me to trust you? You have to trust me." His smile widened. He stepped closer; she could smell his coffee breath. That was yet another reason why she knew she should quit drinking the stuff.

His hands slid up her arms, onto her breasts and around her back. "Slow down, killer. You first." She winked.

She could sense his hormones racing. How quickly the mood changed, she thought. In a matter of moments, it went from alarm to her presence to a sexual opportunity. How was she going to get out of this one?

He stepped back, his breathing charged. "There was no liquid in his lungs. He didn't drown. There was a fire on the boat, and he was severely burned. Almost beyond recognition."

"So, he burned to death?"

"No. Without getting too technical, he had a heart attack before the fire, and that killed him."

"Wait. A forty-five-year-old lawyer dies of a heart attack?"

"Not uncommon. But I did the autopsy. He was fit, in shape, not overweight and had no history of heart disease in his family."

"Tox report?"

The man smiled. "Ahh, there's the rub. It's missing."

"What?"

"I sent one out. It's not exactly protocol, but I thought it was odd. A man on a boat, alone supposedly, has a heart attack and then the boat bursts into flames? Had there not been a boat of birdwatchers scanning the horizon for seagulls, the fire might not have been seen, and he would be missing. So, thinking suspicion, I sent out for a tox screen."

For some reason, the term seagull resonated in her head. Zack hated that term. Always said 'there's no such thing as a seagull!' "And?"

"And the samples disappeared."

"So, send out another."

"The body was claimed and cremated in the meantime."

"Isn't that unusual?"

"Of course, it is," the coroner said. "It usually takes forever to get a result back but losing one is very rare."

"Who processes those reports?"

"Hank LaRocco. Been there a few years. Nice guy. Just unusual to lose a sample."

"Why was the body cremated so quickly?"

The coroner shrugged. "I don't get into politics. I just say why they died."

"And what did you say about this guy's death?"

He shrugged again. "Case still open pending a tox report. Which is never coming so my lips are effectively sealed, and the brass will say simply he died in a fishing boat accident."

She recorded the name and nodded. She knew this was political bullshit. They were hiding something. She had seen it before. "You can't do anymore?"

He shook his head. "Nope. Now you got yours. Now, how about mine?"

He moved forward. His hands quickly found her breasts. He pulled Julie close.

"Wait. You think he might have been poisoned?"

"Something caused him to have a heart attack." The coroner's hands found her perfectly formed ass.

"Can't you just go ask him where it went?"

"We have to send it to Indianapolis, the state lab, to get that done. So, no, I can't just walk across the lab and ask. I've sent a couple of inquiries. It's gone."

Julie had her suspicions. But now, she had to figure out a way to get Doctor Horny from getting into her pants. He was moderately attractive and had she not been in a relationship with Zack, and if there a need for sex, he would do. But this wasn't going to happen. Of course, as his lips devoured her neck and his hands squeezed her ass, she wasn't so sure it wasn't going to happen.

"Wait, one last question. Are there heart attack inducing drugs?"

"Oh, hell yes there are."

"Are they hard to get ahold of?"

"Not for me. For you, yes. Look, we don't have much time, and that's all I can help you with. Now it's my turn."

Now would be a good time for a miracle!

CHAPTER **23**

Julie found a Starbucks and got a Carmel Latte instead of a simple large black coffee. Of course, the sizes confused her, and someone had to explain what a large actually was and by the time the explanation finished, she remembered why she stopped going to Starbucks in the first place. A large coffee is a large coffee. Why do they have to make it so Goddamned difficult?

After the thankfully shortened experience with the horny county coroner, interrupted by the arrival of another body, thank God for the timing of another death, the urge for a relaxing cup of coffee overwhelmed her. Then her phone rang. Michelle Borman calling her. Odd. She answered.

"Michelle? Hi. Why are you calling me?" Only after she said, it did she realize how bad it sounded.

"Zack wanted me to do some research, and I did it. It was more difficult than I thought it would be, but I got some good stuff."

"So why don't you give it to Zack?" The next sound was more of sigh.

"Because I know you're there and, well,"

Julie waited, but nothing came. "Well what, Michelle? I haven't heard from him for over five days, and I'm worried sick. Please tell me something!"

Michelle sighed again. "He's here Julie and if he knows I told you he'd kill me."

"What the hell is he doing there?"

"Lieutenant Barnes is questioning him for the murder of Katie Granders."

"What?" Julie almost fell off her chair. "What the hell is going on?"

Andre took the phone from Michelle. "Look, Jules. He's innocent, we all know he is. But he had to come back. He's worried about you and didn't know how to tell you, so I took it upon myself to make sure you know."

Julie was stunned. "Andre," she stopped as she didn't know what else to say.

"Jules, just do me a favor and be careful. Don't do anything stupid. Ok?" He gave the phone back to Michelle.

"Jules, me again," Michelle said. "Do you want the information?"

"First I have to know one thing. How much did you know?"

Michelle was silent. She stared at Andre, though Julie couldn't see that, and Andre nodded. "I knew."

"So, you knew about this? Did he tell you much when you met him and when you guys dated?"

"He told me exactly what he wanted me to know at first. But eventually, he told me everything. Andre, too."

"So," Julie was piecing together this chain of events. "You didn't know much about why he suddenly showed up one day in Baltimore?"

"Not then. But I learned."

There was a long silence, but Julie knew this wasn't the battle of wills the two normally had. This was genuine. "What did you find for me?"

"He asked me to dig up some financial info on Warren Sapagio. Well, I did. You know he married Zack's real mother about a year after his dad was killed, right? Well, Louise landed a nice fat life insurance check to the tune of two million dollars."

"WHAT?"

"Yeah. Two million."

"Poor mother my ass!" Julie heard Michelle chuckle when she said that.

"The policy was taken out about seven months before Frank Staechel died. No one bothered to ask questions about that."

"Two million?"

"Well, they did have six kids."

Julie shook her head. "What else you got?"

"Ok, well, I checked further. She also collected on a five hundred-thousand-dollar policy that was written when the Staechel's were married. But it was from a different company."

"Well, that's odd."

"I have copies of both signed policies."

Julie knew where she was headed and wondered how the hell she got hold of that. She decided that she'd be nicer to Michelle as Michelle seemed to be resourceful. "And?"

"The signatures aren't the same," Michelle announced. "I mean they are similar, but I know they aren't the same. Zack had me take a class, and I know the big one is forged."

"Ok. What are you thinking?"

"I'm thinking there is more to the murder of Frank Staechel than it simply being a poor black kid robbing the house, getting caught and shooting Zack's dad."

Julie knew it was much more than that. But how to prove it? "You think Zack had any knowledge of this?"

"No. Do you?"

"No."

"If he did, nothing after that makes sense. Nor does him going back there to help Darnell. None of it makes sense." Julie sipped her Latte.

Michelle wanted to agree to pacify Julie but decided that wasn't the right course of action. "Julie, it does a little. You'll see."

"I don't know what to think."

Michelle was silent not because it was the typical battle but because she knew Julie was hurting. She felt bad for her. "Zack wants you to be careful. He'll find you as soon as he takes care of the stupid business here."

"He's never done this," Julie trailed off, and there was silence.

"I wouldn't worry."

Julie wondered if Michelle still had feelings for her boyfriend. She wasn't sure how to take that, but she'd deal with that later. "All right. What else do you got?"

"Well, step-dad has some investment ties with some shady companies. You have to dig real deep to find the connection, but it's there. There are some unusual deposits in his bank accounts that then get transferred to an overseas account in the Caymans."

"Oh my God. The Caymans? How cliché!"

"He's not getting rich off them, but he has a nice retirement account. I think something fishy is going on there. And unless you're really good, no one is going to find those accounts or trace that money."

Michelle is good, and she wants me to know it. Interesting. "I agree."

"Well Zack did some remedial type research and sent me an email from an un-secured computer location, and I followed from there. There's a company called Ventures Unlimited. It's an investment group that buys land and develops it. Mainly casinos, hotels, business development, income producers, you know? Warren is part owner of the company. They were accused of some shady dealings in Atlantic City and then in Las Vegas. Sounds like getting in bed with politicians, greasing wheels, stuff like that. Nothing was ever proved, and somehow Warren's name never came up. Again, you have to dig deep to find his name. Well, I found meeting minutes from a closed-door session of some city councilmen. Ventures Unlimited made a presentation. Warren Sapagio sat in on the meeting."

"Really? That may be something." Julie sipped her over-priced caffeine hit and again remembered another reason why she stopped going there: she couldn't afford it. And then wondered why anyone would keep minutes of a closed-door session? Was someone covering their ass? Or using for blackmail?

"That's what I thought. There must be some property that they want."

Something clicked inside Julie. "Michelle, do me a favor and see if you can dig up anything else on that company. Find out what they are looking for in this town and if it has anything to do with a part of the city they call the Triangle." A term she got from an article she saw online at the library. At the time it seemed pointless.

"Will do. I also did some research on the Frank Staechel murder and the arrest of Darnell Whittaker. The prosecuting attorney at the time was Richard Cappalio. He was a young, white, attorney fresh out of some law school."

Julie had to interrupt. "You mentioned white for a reason. Why?"

"At the time, a reporter for the local paper questioned if race was an issue. White judge, white jury, white cops, a white prosecutor, white victim, a black man arrested in a predominantly white town. The reporter questioned the evidence and the quickness of the arrest and trial. Did you get the email I sent you? There's a file attached that has the actual police file from the case. It is interesting reading. No wonder they don't let anyone see it. It's so full of holes it's laughable!"

"Yeah, I got it. Thanks for sending it. I don't want to know how you got it."

"I won't tell you anyway."

Julie smiled. "Ok. What's the name of that reporter? I want to talk to him."

"Are you any good at a séance?"

"What?"

"He died of a heart attack shortly after raising those questions."

"Great. Dead end."

"Funny. Yeah, well, Richard Cappalio was the court-appointed attorney for Whittaker. From the notes I've seen, he did little for his client. He rebuffed the reporter's suggestions. He worked for the state for a while and seemed to move up the ranks with Sapagio. A few years back he went into private practice. In Michigan City. Surprised? Why move out of Indianapolis? Anyway, he doesn't do much criminal law anymore. But he is the family attorney for the Sapagio's as well as the lawyer representing Ventures Unlimited in the state of Indiana."

Julie thought about what she heard. "You think he was in on the crime?"

"No. I think he's a racist. But Sapagio does seem to be looking out for him. Rewarding him almost."

Yes, he did. But how did that tie to Zack? "You know Zack is Frank Staechel's son, David, right?"

"Yes. I did all along."

Julie was silent, and Michelle knew why, and Andre did as he listened to the phone call. She was the most important person in Zack's life, but yet he kept the biggest secret he could have from her.

"Look, Julie, I'm guessing you're pissed at him and want someone to blame. I'm not happy with what he's doing either."

"I need that information on the area they call the Triangle. Can you work on that for me?"

"Yeah, I'll put it on Zack's bill."

"Can you also dig up anything and everything you can on a guy named Hank LaRocco?"

"Who is he? Give me something to start with."

"State forensics lab in Indiana. Works toxicology. Smells funny to me."

"I'm on it."

Julie disconnected, stared out the window and smelled the aromas of a nearby bakery. She could smell the cinnamon and vanilla scents and the always alluring smell of fresh dough of a nearby bakery. It reminded her she was hungry. But she needed to find out what to do next. She raised far more questions than she had when she started. Her first thought was Zack. She had to figure out what happened the day his father died.

CHAPTER 24

The flight was uneventful. Three o'clock in the afternoon and Zack stepped foot in the town he now called home. He met Andre in the baggage claim area and headed to the office.

"I asked Barnes to meet us here. I'm not sure what their plan is, Zack. That's why he agreed to meet us at the office instead of coming down to the station."

"You know damn well I didn't kill her, Dre."

"I know that. But you've been gone five days, and she's been dead over a week. At least that's the preliminary findings. The story is that you were the last person to see Katie Granders alive." He looked at Zack again. "And those bruises on your face aren't going to help your claim."

"Whoever killed her was the last person to see her alive. What about Doug Granders and the bitch he was hosing?"

Dre stopped the car in front of the office. "The good lieutenant is already here. I'll let him tell you."

The two walked inside. Zack paused outside the door to admire the weather and the scenery of Fells Point. People walked around the square, gulls flew over looking for free food, and the weather was perfect. He wondered what waited for him upstairs but wondered more what was happening back in Indiana.

Finally, he climbed the stairs to the office. He entered the main office and saw Michelle staring at him, a look of disapproval and angst on her face while Lieutenant Ted Barnes sat in a chair sipping coffee.

Zack sniffed. "I thought I said no coffee in the office, Michelle?"

"Well when you're not here, that makes me in charge, and I changed the rules."

Andre laughed. Lieutenant Barnes stood. "Hey, Zack." He walked over and shook Zack's hand. "Let's go for a walk."

The two went outside into the square and walked. "I see you've been up to no good again."

"Just cut to the chase, Ted. What the hell's going on? You know damn well know I didn't kill anyone."

"Yeah well. It's not looking like that, Zack. You are tied to Katie Granders' dead body. A good lawyer could put you away for a long time on this one."

"What's it look like?"

"Her cell phone records showed you were the last person she called and the last number that called her. Two hours before the coroner put a preliminary T.O.D. on her. Your business card was on the body as was a receipt that she had coffee with you at a local café. The video showed you two together, and you left together. She was dead an hour later. And right now, you have bruises on your face which suggests she fought back. That's what it looks like."

They passed a bar. Zack wanted to go inside and get a drink. They walked past. "Are you taking me in?"

"No. I'm hoping we can come up with what really happened and I'm hoping it wasn't you, Zack."

"You know it wasn't." Zack saw a Franklin's Gull picking French fries off a table. "Andre said the body was face down in a swamp. If she was there over a week, in this weather, was she even recognizable?"

Barnes shook his head. "No."

"How did you ID her? Prints? DNA?"

"Neither. Fingers were missing. The mouth was mangled so we can't try to match dental records, either. DNA will take months. The state lab is so backed up it's just a joke right now. No," Barnes grabbed a handle of a doorway on a restaurant/bar and motioned for Zack to go inside. "Come on, looks like you need a drink."

"It crossed my mind. Aren't you on duty?"

"Yep, but duty calls for a drink right now."

"So how are you sure it's her?"

"Jewelry matches via photos, engravings. And she had her ID on her."

"What?"

"Zack, this is trouble." The two sat down at the bar and Barnes ordered two pints of a Sam Adams Summer Ale. "Do you have an explanation, alibi, anything? And tell me about those bruises. You've obviously been in a fight."

"Depending on the time, there's a good chance I was with Julie."

"Julie doesn't spend the night at your apartment. I checked that. She was at the paper filing a story the same time Katie Granders was killed. Your whereabouts I don't know. Now the bruises."

Zack drank a long, slow sip of the pint. "I was visiting a guy I used to know, and he was pissed at me. He took a few swings at me. Clearly a couple landed. End of story as they are not related to this. Look,

Ted, you know I didn't do it. After I left the hospital the last day I saw you, I went to the office, saw Michelle and left town. It wasn't me."

"Why did you leave town?"

Another long sip from the pint. "I have to take care of some old business in Indiana."

"You aren't going to tell me what's going on?"

"I'd rather not at this point, Lieutenant."

Barnes sipped his beer. "You only call me Lieutenant when you think I'm a cop. I'm your friend right now, Zack. And something tells me you're swimming in shit right now."

Zack smiled. "Colorful." He put his drink down. "Apropos, yes."

"You need to talk to me."

"Do you think I'm capable of committing murder?"

Barnes laughed. "Hell yeah, I do. The questions I need to answer are: did you, and if you did, why did you?"

"What about if I didn't who really did and why are they framing me?"

"I was getting to that."

Zack finished his pint quickly and ordered a second. "I can't spend much time here. What's your plan for me?"

Ted finished his pint. "Let's tackle one thing at a time." He ordered another pint. "We finish this pint and go to the morgue."

"Why?"

"Because I'm hoping you're being set up. And maybe you can identify the body."

"What about Doug and his girlfriend?"

180

"Released on bail and disappeared."

"WHAT?"

"Doug Granders has a lot of money and a good lawyer. He disappeared the day after he was released. His mistress was with him."

"Skipped the country. I bet Europe."

"What?"

"Tickets on the luggage at his house. They were to Amsterdam. Have Michelle contact her FBI boyfriend and check the surveillance at every international airport along the eastern seaboard the day they disappeared."

Lieutenant Barnes made a note on a small flip notepad and put it back in his pocket. "We can do that, you know."

"Michelle is better than the flatfooted pencil-pushers that man your office. They had to use a credit card to get the tickets. Using cash at an airport nowadays would have sent the nation into a panic. Have her check that, too."

"Why don't you tell her this?"

Zack smiled and lifted his pint of beer. "Because she can charge you after you tell her, and we need the money."

"Well, my swimming in shit friend, I can trump Michelle's FBI friend with an Interpol friend of my own." He smiled at Zack.

"What are they gonna do? Fine them for illegally downloading songs off the internet?"

Barnes shook his head. "Finish your beer. Prick."

Andy Gruse
STACKED CASE

CHAPTER 25

The church parking lot was vacant. Middle of the afternoon on a weekday and not a single car was around. The neighborhood, worse than Darnell described it, was empty. She parked her car on the street and looked, but there was no sign of life in any direction.

She had the feeling of something being off, or odd all day. The feeling exacerbated as she walked towards the main entrance of the church. The word eerie kept entering her mind. She checked her phone as she climbed the several wide stone steps to the church entrance, hoping she missed a call from Zack which would give her an excuse to not enter the building in front of her. Nothing.

The heavy wooden doors creaked open, and she entered a wide congregation area separated by another set of wooden doors that opened into the cavernous, dark hollows of the church.

Those doors opened smoothly. She stepped inside and saw that lanterns mounted on the walls was the only light save the colored and funneled sunlight blazing through the stain glass windows. She crept down the main aisle, long wooden pews in perfect lines on each side of the aisle.

Then, in the shadows ahead of her near the altar in front, she saw a humped mass on the floor. "Hello?"

She slowed her walk, but the form began to take shape as she neared. Still several steps away, she realized it was a body. A beaten body of an old man. She rushed to the man on the floor.

She knelt beside him and rolled him onto his back. An elderly black man tried to open his eyes. His face was bloody, swollen and unrecognizable. A bubble formed at his lips filled with blood.

"Oh, Dear God," she said. She checked his pulse, and her fingers managed to feel a faint beating in his neck.

The man tried to move, his labored breathing quicker, as if in a panic.

"It's Ok; I'm here to help you. I'm going to get help. Just hang on. You're safe now." She grabbed her phone, but his hand grabbed her arm. "No, I'm calling 911. I have to get help here."

The man moved his head from side to side. She dialed the number.

"Who did this to you? I'll need to tell the police who did this."

The man made a sound; she couldn't hear. She leaned forward but could only make out these words "no, no, the police, no."

Then the doors burst open.

"FREEZE! Don't Move! PUT DOWN THE WEAPON!"

Julie looked back and to her sides. Police, both uniformed and plain clothes, their weapons were drawn and pointed, charged her as she knelt beside the ailing Gerald Whittaker.

"No, it's all right. It's just my phone. I was calling 911!"

The police shouted at her to shut up and get on the floor, hands behind her head. She did. They were rough. One immediately yanked her arms behind her back and slapped cuffs on her, making sure they were tight around her wrists.

Another kicked the phone away while she was frisked, rather rough at that, too.

"He needs medical attention."

"SHUT UP! JUST SHUT YOUR DAMN MOUTH!"

It took several minutes before they lifted her off the floor, dragged her outside the church and threw her into the back of a police cruiser. As her car drove away, only then did an ambulance appear on the street heading for the church.

She sat there and wanted to cry. But she wasn't going to give them the satisfaction. Someone brutally beat Gerald Whittaker and the moment she entered the church the police charged and arrested her. This was a set up all the way. She knew it.

* * * * * * * *

Lieutenant Barnes opened the door to the coroner's lab. Zack and Andre walked through the door and saw the coroner look up from the body he was working on, frown, put down the saw he used and walked to a cold, steel wall filled with small doors big enough to slide in a gurney with a dead body and that was it.

"I presume you're here for the Jane Doe?"

Barnes nodded, and the three walked over. "Thanks for coming along, Dre. I know you've seen pictures of Katie Granders. I think it's going to take more than one set of eyes for a sight ID."

"Have you told them what to expect?"

"We've seen dead bodies before, Doc," Dre chuckled.

Smiling, the doctor responded only by opening the drawer. He pulled back the sheet and uncovered the rotted, half-eaten corpse.

"What the hell happened to her?"

The doctor nodded. "Well, snapping turtles I'm guessing feasted on a lot of her face. Add the array of maggots, leaches and other flesh loving insects, warm, brackish water, a little sunlight and a body will deteriorate rather quickly. There might have been some other animals clawing at her evidenced by marks on the torso and legs, but the bottom line is that she was dead before she went in the water and the killer," the doctor paused when he looked at Zack, "was probably counting on that. Do you recognize her?"

Dre stifled a gag. "There's nothing to identify!"

Zack stared at the body and tried to envision Katie Granders face on the decayed skull. He couldn't.

"What do you think Zack?"

He pulled the sheet down further. The rest of the front of her body was in a similar fashion. He could barely even tell it was a woman until he saw the groin. Nothing.

"You think it's her?"

"Roll her over."

"Help me," the doctor said to Zack.

"Hey, if I'm gonna be arrested for murder, I sure as hell ain't touching that!"

"Sissy." Lieutenant Barnes pulled latex gloves and helped roll over the dead body.

The backside was not nearly as bad as the other side, but it was still very bad. Zack stared at the lower back. "Hand me that magnifying glass." He studied the area. The other three men waited and looked at each other. "It's not her."

"What? How can you tell?"

"There should be some ink from a tattoo she had right about there," he pointed to the area directly above her buttocks. "Even bloated and stretched there's nothing. I can't believe sunlight would destroy all the pigment, so it's not her."

"He's right," the doctor said.

"What kind of a tattoo?"

"I think it was a phoenix, but it could have been a dragon or butterfly or something. It looked a little mystical." Zack nodded. "Yeah, more like a phoenix spreading its wings."

"Dude, how the hell would you know if she had a tattoo above her ass crack? You ain't supposed to be boning the clients!"

The doctor covered the body as Barnes chuckled and Zack shook his head. "She wore low cut jeans all the time. When I interviewed her for the case, she constantly got up and down off the couch to get pictures or something to convince me that Doug Granders not only was cheating on her but hiding a great deal of money from her. I'm a man. She has a nice ass. And the red thong she wore didn't hide much."

Dre slapped him on the back. Barnes clicked on the verb tense and felt a lot better about dealing with Zack. He had interviewed enough murderers that even when they denied doing the crime they used the past tense to describe the victim.

"So, she's still missing." The doctor closed the drawer and walked back to the table. The other three men stood there.

"At least she's not dead."

"We hope."

"Then where the hell is she?"

Zack looked at his watch. "Let's get out of here and tell me about Doug Granders. How did he get out of jail and how did he just disappear?"

Lieutenant Barnes sighed. "Let's get some dinner and figure this out." He guided Zack out of the room.

"I'd love to, Ted, but I have a flight to catch."

Lieutenant Barnes chuckled. "You're missing it. You try to leave this town on me before I get to the bottom of this, my captain will put me through a shit storm and then I'll have to do that to you. Got it?"

"Duly noted."

CHAPTER 26

Julie knew they were watching her. They placed her in an interrogation room; no one had bothered to come in to ask her anything in she guessed at least the hour she was there. She sat on a metal folding chair, her hands cuffed behind her back, her legs cuffed to the chair. A gray steel table and another chair were the only other things in the room. The wall she faced was all mirrors, and she knew they were on the other side watching.

She couldn't wait to get that phone call. Her lawyer was going to tear them apart. She knew enough of her civil rights had been violated already to know that someone would have some explaining to do.

It was warm in the room, too. Trying to make her uncomfortable. First, they'd come in and ask if she wanted a soda or something. Then, they'd get her one, perhaps turn the heat up a little more and keep her drinking while not really saying anything. Then, she'd have to use the restroom, and that's when they'd begin the interrogation. Make it uncomfortable as possible, put the detainee in as much discomfort and pressure as possible and try to coerce a confession. Police tactics 101.

The only problem was that those tactics made the entire force look like idiots once a good defense lawyer caught wind of it. And when the detainee was completely innocent it usually spelled lawsuit for the police. Lieutenant Barnes used different tactics precisely for that reason.

189

He was one of the good guys. She wished she could call him. But now, she could only wait.

* * * * * * * *

Chief of Police Warren Sapagio sipped a cup of coffee while he stood on the other side of the windows and stared at the beautiful young woman in the interrogation room. Two detectives stood beside him when a third entered the hallway carrying a file folder and handed it to the lead detective, Chet Manske.

"What do you got, Pete?" Sapagio asked the third detective. "We got anything on her?"

"No. Not a thing."

"What's her story, who is she?"

"Her name is Julie Fletcher. She's a reporter from Baltimore, Maryland. No priors. No history with this town and no connection to Gerald Whittaker. Or Darnell Whittaker. Why she was at that church is a mystery."

"That's it? You got her purse and her car, and that's all you can get?"

"We called the Baltimore PD, see if they have anything for us. She does a lot of investigative stories and follows the crime cases out east. Won some awards. Was really big into getting the stories of soldiers returning from the Gulf, shit like that."

Sapagio nodded. "We got nothing to hold her with?"

"We've got nothing. There's no way we could try to hold her on that beating. There are no defensive wounds on her; the only blood was on her hands where she said she rolled him over and checked his pulse. And she was connected with 911 when we busted in on her. She's clean, boss."

"If she's so Goddamn clean, what was she doing at that church? She knows something. We got anything else?"

"We found a business card for the Dre-Zack Detective Agency in Baltimore. That's the only thing out of the ordinary."

Another detective spoke. "She is an investigative reporter. Probably just a source for stories."

Sapagio nodded. "Probably. See if the BPD has anything on them, too."

"Will do, boss. What are you thinking?"

He looked at the detective. "It's a little odd that a reporter from Baltimore shows up one day at a church in the Triangle, don't you think? And only a few days after we lose track of Darnell Whittaker? Something is going on in my city, Goddamnit, and we're going to find out what it is and put an end to it before it gets out of hand. Now get on it."

"And her?" Detective Manske spoke.

"I'll deal with her."

* * * * * * * *

The solid metal door creaked open and in walked a large man in a cheap gray suit with the red power tie. He carried a cup of coffee and a can of Sprite. He smiled at Julie as he put down the cup and can. He reached into his pockets, removed a set of keys, walked around her and undid all the cuffs.

191

Julie had seen way too many movies where the detainee immediately rubbed his wrists where the cuffs had been but resisted the urge and put her hands on the table.

"Miss Fletcher, is it?"

She stared at the large smiling man. He was imposing, and she could see how he could be intimidating.

"I'm Chief Warren Sapagio. I'm sorry you've been in here so long. We've been trying to figure out what we have here." He sat on the other side of the table.

"I could have saved you a lot of trouble. You got nothing. You're currently wrongfully detaining me. There's absolutely no evidence that suggests I did that to Gerald Whittaker and you know it. When do I get to call my lawyer?"

Sapagio smiled and pushed the can of soda closer to her. "Oh, Miss Fletcher, Julie, can I call you Julie?"

"No, you may not."

He chuckled. "Miss Fletcher, there's no need for all of that. I know you're not guilty of the murder of Gerald Whittaker."

"What?" Her face went white. "He's dead?"

"I just got the call a few minutes ago. Internal injuries were too severe for someone his age."

"Oh my God," she whispered. She thought of Darnell.

"There's no way someone of your stature could do something like that to him. Quite frankly, I'm leaning towards you having nothing to do with it at all."

"Then you can let me go and find out who did it."

192

"Well, you were the last person possibly to see him alive, after whoever did that, and I just want to know what you know, why you were there, things like that." He pointed at the soda. "You can have that if you'd like. I know it's warm in here. The damn thermostat is broke and with the budget cuts," he waved his hands like there was nothing he could do.

"Like I tried telling Detective Meathead, or whatever his name is, I entered the church looking for Gerald Whittaker. I saw him lying on the floor. I rushed to him to see if he was all right and as I tried to dial 911, you guys burst in, manhandled me and carted me off. That's it."

"Did he say anything to you?"

Julie remembered Gerald saying 'no, no, the police, no' but it meant nothing to her at the time. Her paranoia crept in. "He was mumbling, but it was incoherent."

"You couldn't make out any words he may have said?"

"No. I tried to listen to him, but I couldn't make out anything." She knew it was bothering the Chief that she wouldn't take the soda.

"Miss Fletcher, why were you there?"

"I felt like praying."

Sapagio smiled. "You saw no one else? No one leaving, nothing at all?"

He's fishing. "No. The neighborhood was empty when I stopped in front of the church. There was nothing."

"Why were you there?"

She already answered but clearly, he didn't like her sarcasm. But she wasn't giving in. Not in this cell. "You can't hold me here. This is a violation of my rights."

Sapagio smiled his disarming smile. "You're free to go whenever you'd like, Miss Fletcher. But knowing that you're a reporter, I'd think you'd be interested in getting to the bottom of this. Finding out the truth. Isn't that what you do?"

"It is."

"Tell me why you were there?" They stared at each other. "Look, we can go to my office if you'd like but I'm figuring we might as well just talk here so you can go on your way."

"I'm doing a story, and I wanted to talk to Gerald Whittaker."

"Really? What about?"

Her mind raced. She couldn't give herself away. If she told the truth, she'd never get out of that room. "The declining membership of Churches and how Christianity seems to be in jeopardy here in the US."

"You expect me to believe that?"

"Yes."

Sapagio smiled, sat on the edge of the table, grabbed the soda and drank from it. "Miss Fletcher, you're a liar. You know how I know that? Because it's my job and because I know that you talked to my wife earlier. Perhaps you should choose your lies more carefully."

"Bravo, Chief. You got me. I talked to your wife. Still not a punishable offense so let me go."

"You were asking questions about a case that has been closed for years. I know because I investigated that case and solved it myself. You are asking about Darnell Whittaker. Why don't you just tell me what you think you know. I'm all for justice, Miss Fletcher. Talk to me and let's put all this nonsense to rest."

Julie thought for a moment. She was bound to lose no matter what. She decided to play the game. Zack wasn't in town. She was all alone and decided to play as she knew how. "Well, I know that Darnell Whittaker was just released from prison, his lawyer claimed he was wrongfully imprisoned and then turned up dead."

"His lawyer was foolish enough to somehow start a fire on a boat he was on alone in the middle of Lake Michigan. And Darnell was tried and convicted by his peers. There's no story here, Miss Fletcher."

"Really? Do you have the coroner's report? I'd like to see it."

Warren shook his head. "Miss Fletcher, I've seen a million of people like you who want to be the next Woodward and Bernstein. It isn't going to happen here. Sometimes accidents just happen."

"Yeah, that's quite an accident." She waved it off.

"Anything else you'd like to tell me?"

Julie wondered how far to push it. He was fishing for a confession of some kind. She decided to go a different direction. "You're married to the widow of Frank Staechel, correct? Darnell was imprisoned for the murder of Mr. Staechel, right?"

"Miss Fletcher," he smiled and chuckled. "Ok, let's see where you're going with this. Yes, to both."

"Darnell's lawyer claimed that a person of interest that should have been questioned but was not was David Staechel, the oldest son. Was David ever a suspect in the case?"

"There was no reason to think he was. We arrested the guilty party."

"David disappeared right after the trial, correct?"

"He did."

"Did anyone ever look for him? Ever an investigation or anything?"

Sapagio laughed. "I can't believe I'm getting interrogated in my own interrogation room."

"Is it possible that David came back to silence the parties that might know the truth?"

Warren's smile left. "My wife, David's mother, has spent many, many sleepless nights hoping and praying that her oldest son comes home alive and well someday. No one knows why he left, where he went or anything about his disappearance. As a police officer, we sent out a missing person's report to every agency in the country. We got nothing."

"You think he's dead?"

"I don't think anything. I support his mother and hope he someday at least has the common courtesy to send a postcard or something to his poor mother. A parent should never have to grieve over a child."

"On what basis was Darnell Whittaker arrested for the murder of Frank Staechel?"

"Miss Fletcher," Sapagio smiled again, "this is my interrogation. You don't get to cross-examine me. What aren't you telling me? Are you involved with Darnell Whittaker somehow? Because if you are, you're in big trouble. He is now in violation of his parole and has failed to meet a court date about his drug possession charge."

"Which he claims was planted."

Sapagio's face tightened. "I hope you're not suggesting what I think you are because my police force does not do anything of the sort.

And if you are harboring or aiding a fugitive in any way, you'll be spending a long time in a cell someplace."

"I don't know Darnell Whittaker and have never met him. But I read all the reports his lawyer filed. I was hoping to find him, so I could interview him and see what he has to say."

Sapagio stood. "Miss Fletcher, why do I feel you're lying to me?"

She watched him turn and walk to the one-way windows, cross his arms and turn again to face her. "My guess is because you're a police officer and it's your nature not to trust anyone."

He walked back to the table and sat down. "And after thirty years of dealing with criminals, I got a pretty good feeling about when people are lying and when they aren't."

Julie stared at him. He was very imposing and intimidating. Maybe that's why Zack ran. "Yeah? What's your feeling about me?"

"You're a tough one." He stared at her, but she didn't blink. "We found a business card for a Dre-Zack Detective Agency?" He pronounced is wrong.

Oh shit! She thought for a moment. "Yeah, so? I'm an investigative reporter. They sometimes give me leads for a story."

"I guessed you'd say that."

"It's the truth."

He stared at her. "You were in the wrong place at the wrong time. That concerns me. You aren't being honest me, that concerns me as well. I'm perplexed as what to do with you."

197

Julie understood his threat. *Oh shit!* "Chief Sapagio, I have done nothing wrong. There is a killer loose in this city. I think I'm the very least of your concerns."

Sapagio chuckled. He stood, put his hands wide on the table and leaned forward. "You're free to go, Miss Fletcher. But let me give you some advice. You're dangerously close to interfering with a police investigation, and I don't like it. Some Edward J. Murrow wannabe coming into my town and snooping around where she shouldn't be can lead to judges throwing cases out of court, people getting hurt, criminals getting away. That pisses me off. So, my advice is for you to get your pretty little ass in that foreign car of yours and get the hell out of my city. I won't ask you again."

She stood and stared at him. "Duly noted."

CHAPTER 27

"**No, Michelle, that won't work.** I need a plane back to Chicago now. Find one." Zack hung up and finished dressing. Andre took Zack back to Zack's apartment where Zack showered, shaved and packed another set of clean clothes. He exited the bedroom and saw Andre flipping through a Victoria's Secret catalog.

"Damn, Heidi Klum is hot! Why do you get these?"

"Look at the name on the label, dude. Those are Julie's."

Andre tossed the catalog onto a coffee table. "Speaking of Julie, have you heard from her?"

Zack stopped. "No. Have you?"

"You know she's there, right? She went there to help you."

"I saw her at a McDonald's."

"Did you talk to her? What happened?"

Zack tossed the bag on a chair. "I panicked when I saw her." He recognized the look on Andre's face. "I didn't know what to tell her. I don't know. I guess I didn't think that far ahead."

"Yeah, well, she's called me probably four times a day since she left town and I haven't heard from her today."

They were silent. "Then I better get there."

"I'm coming with."

"I appreciate the offer, but you know why I'm there. If this goes bad, you'll go down too."

Andre smiled and stood. "So what? You and Jules need my help. I'm up on what's going down there. I saw the shit Michelle dug up. You need my help. I'll get some gear, and we'll save your ass again."

He extended his hand. Zack looked at it and frowned. "Goddamn you, Andre." He shook his hand. "Fine. But you're not going to be on the front lines with me. We do this my way. And if things get shitty, you and Jules are getting the hell out of there, understood?"

"And leave my boy behind? That's not how we operate."

The knock on the door startled them both. "Zack, open up! It's Lieutenant Barnes."

The door opened, and Lieutenant Ted Barnes walked inside. He held a file, and the look on his face wasn't a happy one. "You have some explaining to do."

"What?"

Barnes looked at Andre. "Dre, would you mind waiting outside? I have to speak to the person in front of me alone right now."

"See you later, Zack."

"What about that leave your boy behind stuff?"

"Not this time. He looks pissed. I'll be outside."

The door shut, Lieutenant Barnes turned and fired a right cross into Zack's face. Zack fell over the coffee table, hit the couch and bounced to the floor.

"What the hell?"

200

"An hour ago, we got a phone call from the Police Department in Michigan City, Indiana. They were requesting any information we had on a Julie Fletcher."

Zack quit holding his throbbing face and stood.

"She was being held with the connection of the beating death of Gerald Whittaker. Obviously, she didn't do it. But she had your business card in her purse, so they asked if we had any information about your agency."

"What did you tell them?"

"Your good buddy Sergeant Crispin was more than happy to send them everything we have on you."

"Goddamn that Crispy Cream! Did he give them my file? Why don't you fire that fat-ass worthless flatfoot!"

"No, I stopped him. But my point is Zack that you and Julie are being investigated by the MCPD. So, I asked why and what came back was some information about a murder case some seventeen years ago involving a man named Darnell Whittaker."

Zack's body tension released, and he slumped.

"Me being a detective, I asked some more questions, did a little more digging and it's interesting what I found out."

"Do tell." Only Zack knew that the sarcasm with that answer wasn't getting him anywhere.

"You've been lying to me for the last four Goddamn years! Who the hell are you? And you better talk fast before I slam your ass through that freaking wall! NOW TALK!"

* * * * * * * *

Julie returned to the motel room as the sun began to set. She drove around town for two hours, stopped for gas, drove out of town, back into town on the southeast side and did everything she could to make sure she wasn't followed. She even stopped outside of town and searched her car for a tracking device, knowing that Zack and Andre had used one once to follow a cheating husband who was pretty slippery. But there was nothing and no tail

She was tired, hungry and dirty. She read the police file on the Frank Staechel murder case so many times she knew exactly where each misspelling was by the number of the word on the page. More questions appeared every time she went over it, but she was convinced of one thing: shoddy police work sent Darnell Whittaker to jail.

And she was sure that race did play a part in it, but that wasn't her fight for now. After it was all over, maybe. But Zack's story was bigger. And the more she learned about Zack being David Staechel she knew if the story was told that Zack's life would be over.

In the morning, she would visit a couple of people. The current District Attorney would be interested in learning what she had so far; the defense attorney for Darnell who happened to live in town and was on the Sapagio payroll warranted some questions. And if those panned out, she'd have to find Zack, talk to Michelle to see if she had anything else and put it all together.

Darnell was in his bed when she got back. She wasn't going to tell him about his dead uncle. She wondered what spin the police would put on it. Who would they blame? It made sense to her after she left the police station: Gerald Whittaker did not want her to call the police. The only reason she could determine was that they were responsible. How else could they have been there so quickly after she arrived? The Mexican gang-bangers that Darnell despised probably would take the blame, but they had absolutely nothing to gain. More questions. Cold pizza and a shower would probably do some good.

Andy Gruse
STACKED CASE

CHAPTER 28

"You look like you got your ass beat again, dude. You should quit that. It takes years off your life."

Zack held the glass of ice water against the side of his face at an airport bar. "I guess I had that coming from Barnes. I suspect I'll have to go through it again with Jules."

Andre laughed. "I told you when we started this that you better 'fess up. We both knew it could come back to haunt you."

"Let's just hope it stops haunting me now. If it goes much further, I'll be calling you and asking for a conjugal visit."

"You aren't my type, but maybe if I'm drunk enough." They laughed. "What happened with Barnes?"

"He released me to go back to Indiana to finish this thing. So, hopefully, we're good."

"Did you tell him everything?"

"Right down to the last detail. I got the feeling he understood."

Andre laughed again. "It took you eight hours to get him to understand! We're lucky to get on this flight."

Zack looked at his watch. "Damnit. There's no telling what we'll find when we get there."

"Relax. Julie is resourceful and smart. I'm sure she and Darnell are fine."

They heard the first call for boarding of their plane.

"Pay the bill, I'm going to the bathroom," Zack told Andre and left the barstool. Andre shook his head as Zack disappeared. Ten minutes later, they sat on the plane and waited to head to Chicago.

* * * * * * * *

The phone rang and woke her. The sun was bright coming through the opened shades, which meant that Darnell had opened them. The ring chimed again, a song Zack downloaded on it, U2's 'All I Want Is You.' She looked at the number. It was Michelle.

"Yeah?"

"Hey, jackpot."

Julie moved to rest on her elbow. "You don't have to try to impress me. I already am. What did you get?"

"Let's see how this fits into what is going on there. I have a friend who has the equipment and power to hack into just about anyone's computer. If they are online, he can get into their computer and wreak some havoc, and they won't even know it, right?"

Julie smiled.

"Warren Sapagio has a lot of encrypted files and passwords on his computer. Even for a police chief, he has a lot of protection on his computer."

"How do you know that?"

Michelle chuckled. "It's my job. Ronald is better though. And the good thing is that Warren is always logged onto his computer."

"What did you find?"

"Ok, the Triangle. It's a part of the city that is apparently a disaster area. I can't find the exact street names on it but the emails mention railroad tracks, some creek and neighborhoods owned, or rather being run by an out-of-town based Mexican gang. Does that sound familiar?"

"Do they mention a church?"

"Yeah! They do, how did you know?"

"Because I know exactly what you're talking about." Julie heard the toilet flush and the sink turn on. Darnell was obviously in the bathroom.

"That part of the city got its name because someone in the city thought it was cute to use it as a way to get Commerce, Tourism, and Environment together. And that's the city's goal there. Geographically it looks like a triangle, so the name stuck. Well, this Triangle is a very valuable piece of land if they can raze it and that group Ventures Unlimited can get vested in it. Apparently, the state and the feds are willing to put some serious coin into the area via the company designated to do the development. Part of the President's Urban Renewal Program."

"Sounds like a great area for mismanagement of funds if you ask me."

Michelle chuckled again. "That's exactly what it is. Nice acronym, too! The best part is that there is no watchdog group tracking these funds, so they'll end up in the hands of shady investment companies like Ventures Unlimited and generally nothing substantial gets done. Ever. But that's not the point. The point is that Warren is spearheading his company's desire to get this Triangle."

"How?"

"First, he has to get the city to vote that it's ruined, a disaster area, whatever term you want to use. Basically, they treat it like a single-family housing unit and condemn it. When they determine it's beyond repair based on things like crime rate, property values, percent habitation, quality of structures and a bunch of cost-benefit equations that no one understands, they vote to condemn it. Then the city appoints a panel, which this city already has, to find the proper company to develop the area. Ventures Unlimited is the only one being considered right now."

Julie smiled. "Well, that's interesting. Anything about the church?"

"Found one email that mentions only one structure worth keeping but that was being remedied," Michelle said. "That could be it."

"Could be. So, this is dirty?"

"Dirty as can be. There's no competition like there should be in any government award and Ventures Unlimited gets an obscene amount of cash. They did the same thing in Jersey somewhere. Awarded close to one hundred million but when someone from the state finally came looking for the results, a bunch of demolition had taken place, but then the company disappeared."

"Really?"

"Names change, addresses change, people die, it will never get resolved. In fact, other than passing tougher laws when awarding government contracts, nothing ever came of that, so Ventures Unlimited moves on."

"That's unbelievable."

"Yeah, so another email says that he thinks he has enough votes to condemn it. He was working on two other council members but said he had five bought and paid for, along with two members on the state panel and who knows how many others are collecting on this deal."

Julie whistled. This was corruption beyond her imagination. "Is any of this information legal?"

"You mean would it hold up in court? Hell no." Michelle laughed. "The best you can hope for is that you can convince a non-corrupt judge, if you can find one over there, to issue a search warrant before Warren deletes everything and wipes the hard drive clean."

"What is their objective? He already has money, already has power. What else is driving Warren?"

Michelle scoffed. "Money and power corrupt people into believing they can never have enough. They always want more. Maybe this is the last big payday Warren needs to disappear for good? I don't know."

"And this is legitimate?"

"Please, don't insult me. It's off the SOB's computer!"

"Try to get the names of those on Warren's and Ventures Unlimited payroll. See if you can connect any more dots to this thing. If there are other cops on the bad side, I want to know about them, and Zack will need to know about them!"

"Well, I already hit pay dirt with Hank LaRocco."

"That was fast."

Michelle shook her head. "Guess who was Sapagio's partner way back when the Staechel case was solved? Henry James LaRocco. A few years later he graduated from the small time and ended up in Indianapolis, and after some college and training, he is now the toxicologist at the state lab."

"Well, that's certainly within the six degrees of separation parameter!"

Michelle chuckled. "I'm still digging on him. I'll find more; I'm almost sure of it."

Julie thought about it more. She was ready to blow off her conspiracy thoughts but the more information she received, the more she believed in them. "Is Zack on his way back here yet?"

"He and Andre are on their way." Both were silent. "Be careful, Julie. I don't like anything that's going on there." The line disconnected.

CHAPTER 29

Warren Sapagio sat in his office and stared at the picture of his family, his wife Louise and her five children along with himself at some function years back. He glanced at the files on his desk that covered Julie Fletcher. The BPD had nothing to send on the detective agency. He looked at the police file on Darnell Whittaker. Something was going on in his town. He didn't like it. It was a lack of control.

"Pete, get in here."

The plainclothes detective entered. "Yeah, boss?"

"Put out an APB on these two people. If anyone sees them in my town, I want them locked up."

"Here?"

Sapagio shook his head. "No. Take them to our special place for special people."

"What's up?"

Sapagio exhaled again and leaned back in his chair. "I have my suspicions, but I want these two locked up first. I don't believe they are acting alone and I want to know what they are up to."

* * * * * * * *

"Last time I was at this airport we were still in the Corps, remember?"

Zack threw the backpack over one shoulder and watched the people around him, standing along the walls, buying coffee, fruit or a paper at the kiosks as they left the concourse.

"Well, yes, Andre, I do remember. Right before we went for cold weather training," Andre said in his mock-Zack voice as Zack was silent.

Zack still said nothing.

"Dude, if you're not gonna talk at least you can let me know."

Zack stopped. "Call Julie's cell."

"You call her."

"She won't answer me if she's doing something I wouldn't like her doing."

"Like what would that be?"

Zack walked again. "If she's there, she knows enough about what happened and my past to keep investigating and she's stubborn enough and brazen enough to ask the wrong questions to the wrong people."

Andre dialed the number and held the phone to his ear. "It's ringing. No answer. Went to voicemail."

"That means it's not turned off. Keep trying."

"And what will you be doing?"

Zack stopped in front of a car rental agency. "You hate my motorcycle, and we need a car. So, rent something half-ass decent and get moving. I'll be waiting at my bike."

* * * * * * * *

Julie recognized the number, but no way was she going to answer it. She knew Zack wouldn't approve of her plan for the day, so it reasoned that Andre wouldn't approve either and she knew she was getting close to an answer. The truth. The truth about Zack. More than anything, that's what she needed. Michelle confirmed the two were together which meant he was with Andre and talking to Andre meant Zack was right there listening. No way. She typed in the address into her GPS and drove away.

Convincing Darnell to stay inside the motel room was easy. He was healing and feeling better, but he'd draw attention. He'd be recognized. And he needed rest.

She stopped her car in front of the address she punched in and admired the colonial estate. The reddish-brown brick house with white shutters and window frames, and three large, white columns on the porch told her that his District Attorney was getting paid well. It seemed all the city officials did from what she saw so far. The DA in Baltimore would be jealous.

She took a deep breath, grabbed her press badge and notebook and headed up the long brick walkway towards the giant house. After climbing five wide marble topped stairs, she walked to the door and raised the knocker. She pounded on the brass door knocker three times.

Moments later, a man, late thirties maybe, not unlike Doctor Horny from the coroner's office, opened the door. He wore loafers, designer jeans, and a white button shirt. He was rolling the sleeves up to the elbows when he answered. His gold wire-rimmed glasses gave him a dapper appearance, but she didn't care for the slicked back, brown hair.

"Can I help you?"

"Are you District Attorney Alan Bentson?"

"Yes. And who might you be?"

"My name isn't important. Do you have a moment? I need a moment of your time."

"I might if I were to know who I'm talking to."

Julie frowned. "My name is Julie Fletcher."

He stared at her.

"Look, I'm a reporter, was working on a story and came across information I find quite disturbing. Are you familiar with the Frank Staechel murder case and the subsequent release and arrest of Darnell Whittaker?"

"Yes, and also of the bail bond and now his missing a court date and being a fugitive again. I'm aware of all of it. That's my job."

"Please forgive me; I don't mean to sound patronizing. But in my investigation, I found some irregularities."

The man smiled. A lady appeared behind him. "Honey, is everything all right?"

"Yes dear," Alan said to who Julie figured was his wife. "Just a fan wanting an autograph." She smiled and disappeared. Alan returned his attention to Julie. "My office opens at nine on Monday."

He went to shut the door, but Julie grabbed his arm. "This can't wait. A man's life is in danger." He looked at her. "Mr. Bentson, I'm sorry to bother you on a Saturday, but I have information that you don't, and I think you need to hear it."

He looked at her and frowned. "Darnell Whittaker's claim that the drugs found on his person were planted follows his conspiracy theory about his claimed wrongful conviction. I'm well aware of it all."

"Are you aware of the documents that show that the Chief of Police forged an insurance policy that paid the widow of Frank Staechel two million dollars after the death of her husband and proof that Darnell Whittaker didn't kill Frank Staechel."

He stared at her.

"I also have reason to believe that the former lawyer of Darnell Whittaker was poisoned so he'd have a heart attack and that the same poison was used on a newspaper reporter seventeen years ago who didn't believe the police arrested the right man." She stared at him. "That case needs to be reopened."

"Those are very serious allegations that if not correct will land you in jail. Chief Sapagio is highly decorated, well-respected and the city is seeing its lowest crime rate in years."

Julie could tell Bentson had no desire to listen to her any longer. "If you reopen the case you'll see that Darnell's fingerprints were not found at the scene, nor was any sign of a struggle. In fact, if you exhume the body and do an autopsy, you'll see that Frank Staechel was shot point blank by a .38, the same gun that Warren Sapagio carried at the time. No weapon was found, but the bullet is still in the evidence locker. If you do a ballistics comparison, you'll prove that it was Sapagio's gun."

"Ballistics reports are far from conclusive. Flimsy, circumstantial and you would be arrested for libel, and I would be jeopardizing my career trying to pin a near twenty-year-old crime on a very decorated police chief."

"Ok, how about the money he's paying the Mexican gang to ruin the old part of town and how the police planted the drugs on Darnell Whittaker to arrest him and get him back in jail, so he can't claim his inheritance if his uncle dies: The Church. Mr. Bentson, I know this sounds crazy, but there is too much at stake here for you to not reopen the case." She was grasping at straws. She wasn't sure that's what Darnell and Zack saw, but Darnell said that's what it looked like, so she went with it.

Alan Bentson studied her. "How did you get this information? Can any of it be corroborated?"

"Yes, sir, it can."

"How?"

"I can get copies of the documents that prove all that I've said. I know of enough evidence to put the Chief behind bars and to clear Darnell Whittaker's name."

"And what's in it for you?"

"What do you mean? Why would there be anything in it for me?"

Bentson smiled. "I've been doing this long enough to suspect that you are possibly trying to help someone or save someone, or both. Which is it?"

She breathed through her nose. "You don't believe in altruism?"

He laughed. "You're patronizing me again. Are you hiding something?"

Julie stood firm. "I'm protecting the very thing you swore to protect: the law and ensuring that it's carried out accordingly. Justice is blind, sir. I've given you enough reason to be suspicious. All you have to do is investigate yourself."

"Miss Fletcher, I am getting ready to take my eight-year-old to a soccer game so if you'll be on your way."

"Maybe you should investigate Ventures Unlimited." There was no change of expression on the lawyer's face. He was good. "I bet you'll find that they are behind the beating of Gerald Whittaker and the vandalism of that church. Your chief of police is a dirty cop, Mr. Bentson. If you can live with that, then perhaps I should be asking you what are you hiding?" She turned and left. That didn't go as she had planned.

She got into her car and drove off, not wasting time as Bentson was probably writing down her license plate number. Had she read him wrong? Then the possibility that she could have been giving information to a person on Sapagio's side hit her like a ton of bricks. *Oh Shit!*

* * * * * * * *

Alan Bentson watched the pretty reporter get into her maroon Toyota Camry and drive away. He pulled the cell phone out of his pocket and hit two buttons. The Chief was on speed dial.

"Hey Chief, good morning. You'll never guess who just visited me and what she had to say?"

Andy Gruse
STACKED CASE

CHAPTER 30

Richard Cappalio had a listed address which surprised her but what didn't surprise her was the neighborhood. Further out in the Long Beach area than Sara Eckhart lived, and Julie noticed they named it stops. Stop 2, Stop 14, Stop 26 et cetera. The further north along the lakeshore and higher the stop equaled bigger houses and more money. She found the lakefront house of Richard Cappalio and saw nothing but money.

He didn't live on the beach though; rather he lived on the lot across Lakeshore Drive on a hill that overlooked the smaller but still grandiose house on the lakefront. She could see containment walls and rock piles down where it looked like a beach used to be. Ahh yes, the ever-present man's love of water: build as close to it as possible and claim it as yours. Buy the best view of the lake, or ocean and enjoy it. And then spend the rest of your days spending money trying to keep the water from destroying your property. Man versus Mother Nature.

She stopped her car in the driveway.

When would man learn that Mother Nature isn't going to be stopped? She looked at the impressive view. She could see as far out over Lake Michigan as possible. It was stunning. She saw herself eating breakfast with Zack and their two children overlooking a body of water like that and realized that's why Mother Nature would keep fighting such battles.

The lawn was well kept. They probably hired a lawn care company to maintain it and all the shrubs, flowers and small ornamental trees that dotted the lawn and surrounded the property. The dogwoods were in bloom. She tried to remember what kind they were. Zack told her once how to differentiate dogwoods and thought how odd it was that he was full of such trivial knowledge. Certainly, the Marine Corps didn't teach him about dogwoods.

The trees were full of birds. She didn't know those either. Again, Zack entered her mind. How did he know birds, too? She walked up the limestone walkway that curled around a beautiful bed of roses and led to the front door.

She knocked on the door and wished she dressed fancier. Sure, she looked like a reporter but the house, a huge brick temple with large columns supporting a roof above the porch and windows taller than her surrounding the front demanded class.

The door opened. The outfit told her butler. He had a butler. *Screw being an optometrist. Should have been a lawyer!*

"May I help you, madam? Are you lost?"

Julie was caught off guard but smiled. "I'm looking for Richard Cappalio?" She pronounced it CAP-a-leo. The butler frowned.

"Mr. Cappalio isn't expecting company." He pronounced it cap-PAL-leo. *Embrace the culture, Julie!*

"I know he isn't. I apologize for my unexpected visit. Could you tell him that a reporter is at the front door? I'm doing a story that only he has information about."

The butler frowned again. He looked her up and down, the frown deepened. Apparently, he disapproved of her attire, too.

"Well madam, I'm sure he'd rather not be disturbed during his morning coffee. I'll tell him you're here and perhaps you could schedule an appointment."

This guy is a real dick! Ok, go for broke.

"Listen Jeeves, go tell Mr. Cap-pal-leo that a woman is here investigating the murder of Frank Staechel and subsequent trial of Darnell Whittaker and is wondering why the lack of credible evidence that convicted Mr. Whittaker was enough? Can you do that for me?"

The butler took a deep breath. "That's very rude."

"Fine, now go tell your master what I said. I'll wait outside."

The butler straightened his white jacket, refrained from saying anything else and disappeared after shutting the door in her face.

Nice Julie. Way to let that idiot bother you. Let's see if this cappalio dude comes to the door.

She waited for several minutes, turned her back to the door to admire the view and watched what looked like, if she remembered correctly, warblers flitting at the tops of the large oak trees in the front yard. The door finally opened.

"I'm sorry for my butler, miss…. I'm sorry. What is your name?"

Andy Gruse
STACKED CASE

CHAPTER 31

Zack emerged from the inside of the mini-mart gas station just off the interstate and sat on his motorcycle. Andre stopped the rental car, a Ford Fusion, beside the bike.

"If you drove a car, you wouldn't have to stop so often to get gas."

"Ten bucks and I'm full. You can't do that with your fancy car."

"Haha. The city's that way?"

Zack nodded. "Still no word from Jules?"

"She's onto us. Gotta be." Andre looked around. "Almost lunch time and I'm hungry. What's the plan?"

"We'll take the long way around town. Stop at the motel I stayed at. Maybe she's there."

"What about that Darnell dude?"

Zack shrugged. "If he's not in custody or dead, I doubt he's there."

Andre laughed. "If he's dead, we find Jules and go home. End of story."

"Agreed." He strapped on his helmet. "We'll get food after we get to the motel."

* * * * * * *

"Julie Fletcher." She extended her hand. "It's nice to meet you Mr. Cappalio."

"Please, call me Rich." He shook her hand, closed the door behind him and stepped onto the stone patio with her. He pushed up the sleeves of his cardigan sweater and motioned to her to walk. He wore leather slip-on shoes with white chinos. Looked freshly pressed and nothing had a wrinkle about him. He had a nice Cartier gold watch, a thick solid gold ring on his wedding ring finger and a gold bracelet on his right wrist. Nothing inexpensive about him.

"Jeeves said you had a question about a case long ago?" He chuckled when he said Jeeves. "I often want to call him Jeeves too, just to be funny, but he does such a wonderful job for me and my family that I can't bear to upset him and possibly lose him."

Julie smiled. "I suppose good help is hard to find nowadays, huh?"

"Yes."

They walked around the path to the driveway, down the driveway to Lakeshore Drive and down the street a hundred feet and crossed. He led her across the street and under a wooden archway that led to a stairwell down to the beach. She forgot the stop number written on the arch the moment she saw the long descending stairwell.

A good place to get rid of a nosy reporter and I bet the stiff, stuck-up rich snobs that live out here would never notice or care! I should have dressed better!

"Now what can I do for you?" They small talked as they walked down the stairs and onto the beach. He was investigating her as much she was him. Stalling. She wondered if he called Sapagio before he came to the door. Finally, he gave her an opening.

"Darnell Whittaker was arrested, tried and convicted for the murder of Frank Staechel. You defended him. At the time you were fresh out of law school and appointed by the state. Before he was released a week or so ago, his current lawyer said he was framed and played the race card. What do you think about that?"

"I think it's ridiculous. He was tried by his peers, and the evidence supported the conviction."

Same thing Sapagio said. They've rehearsed it. "A reporter for the local newspaper said at the time that the evidence was lacking, and he demanded the case be reopened. He later turned up dead. A heart attack at the age of thirty-three."

"Quite unfortunate, to die so young. What a shame."

She almost detected sincerity. "Odd though, isn't it, that someone that young would die of a heart attack when he started stirring the pot?"

"Are you implying something sinister?"

"It certainly suggests it, doesn't it?"

"Miss Fletcher, no it does not. It implies that a thirty-three-year-old man drank too much, smoked too much and ate too much red meat. It's unfortunate that anyone at such a young age dies, but I knew that man, and he was hardly a saint."

"What about his charges?"

"That the evidence was faulty and that I did not do my job?" Cappalio chuckled. "That wasn't my first case, Miss Fletcher. I don't like the implication there either."

Julie nodded. "What do you think about the case being more about race than evidence though? I saw the pictures. Darnell was the only black man inside that courthouse."

Cappalio laughed. "This isn't the Deep South in the fifties." They reached the beach and walked. "Racism is a vicious, vicious disease. He may have been a Negro without a father and a poor, poor, background, but he made his choice. And he paid for it. As did his older brother."

"Racism isn't a disease; it's a choice. A choice of acceptance. And from what I've learned about this town it was mostly white. Older white and that suggests,"

"Suggests nothing, Miss Fletcher," Cappalio said, his voice unnerved. "The evidence was the only over-riding factor there."

"What was the evidence?"

Cappalio shrugged. "That was a long time ago. I don't remember."

Julie smiled. "He allegedly broke into the house to steal, Mr. Staechel was home, they scuffled, and Mr. Staechel was shot point blank in the head and killed."

"In a scuffle, it's not unusual for the kill shot to be point blank."

Julie smiled again. "You were the defense attorney. Why didn't you use your position to ensure the jury would be balanced and not be all white? Weren't you concerned that Darnell wouldn't get a fair trial?"

"I had no reason to believe that. As I said, this isn't the Deep South in the fifties. The coloreds and the whites have been living side by side a long, long time up here."

"The reporter suggested that the evidence was lacking. He suggested that with a bullet wound like that there should have been evidence in the way the blood splattered that someone else was there. Apparently, he was ahead of his time. It also suggested there should have been footprints or something that actually tied Darnell to the crime. When Darnell was found, he was sick, in his bed, correct?"

"A classic misdirection."

"But no bloody clothes of his, or bloody shoes were found. In fact, the only evidence that actually linked him to the scene was an old television set that was in the basement that was never tested for prints. Is that right?"

Cappalio looked at her. "You have a lot of information. How did you get any of this?"

"Same place as you could have, the police file." *How did Michelle get this?*

"I don't like the way you're trying to impugn me or the Chief of Police, who was the lead detective on the case."

"I don't like the way this case was investigated or tried, so we're even."

Cappalio nodded. "Touché, Miss Fletcher. What's your theory?"

"Did anyone consider suicide?"

"Are you suggesting now that our Chief of Police, Warren Sapagio, the detective on the site didn't do his job?"

Julie stopped walking. "That's exactly what I'm suggesting."

227

Cappalio thought about that. "If you were to print those allegations without proof, as his lawyer, I'd be forced to sue you for libel. Are you prepared for that?"

She heard that from the DA. "I'm just trying to find the truth."

"The truth was that Darnell Whittaker, a little negro street kid without a father and living in poverty needed money. He broke into the Staechel house, attempted to steal items he knew he could sell on the street and when was caught, he produced a .38 handgun and shot and killed Frank Staechel, a father of six children. That's the truth."

Julie couldn't help herself. She knew the report better than he did. Or lack of it and that was the card she played. "An eyewitness to the scene said there was no evidence of forced entry and that there was no gun at the scene. In fact, no gun was ever found."

Cappalio took the bait. She knew he was rattled. "There were no eyewitnesses. Mrs. Staechel came home that afternoon from grocery shopping and found her husband dead. The door had been kicked open in the back of the house, and they were able to track the footprints and a trail of blood to Darnell's house."

Julie knew that wasn't true. She saw pictures of the scene. If there had actually been any evidence in the alley that led to Darnell's house, it would have been marked; the alley roped off. The newspaper reporter claimed that evidence was made up only after the fact to ensure Darnell's guilt and there were no pictures of bloody footprints anywhere.

"Look, I know in this day in age people love to embrace the conspiracy theory. It is very fashionable," he laughed. "We've all seen JFK, right? Well, forensics has come a long way since the mid-eighties, but I'm sure had we had the forensics then that we do now, it only would have made a stronger case against Darnell. I wanted to plea him down. Maybe get him manslaughter and have him sent to juvey for three years and then be on probation. He wanted nothing to do with it. If I remember correctly," he appeared to think, "Mr. Whittaker was quite uncooperative. He often said he didn't do it, but he never offered a reason why he couldn't have or suggested another suspect."

"Wasn't that your job?"

Rich Cappalio ran his hand over his slicked-back gray-streaked hair. They turned back towards the stairs. "Careful, Miss Fletcher. I think I've heard just about enough of your accusations."

"How long were you an attorney in the state's office?"

"Long enough to learn that life isn't as rosy as people like you want it to be."

She had struck a nerve. He wasn't as calming and smooth as he was when they first started to talk. He was close to giving himself up. She was pleased with herself for getting a lawyer rattled.

"Does your firm represent Warren Sapagio?"

"Yes, it does."

"How about Ventures Unlimited?"

"I'm not aware of any company by that name."

Julie smiled as they crossed the beach and headed for the stairs. "You were taught well. If I didn't know otherwise, I would have believed that lie."

"Are you recording any of this?"

"Should I be?"

"Listen to me, and you listen good, you're asking questions that have been answered already, and if you keep this up, you'll end up in serious trouble."

"Worse trouble than the innocent Darnell Whittaker is in?"

He stopped again, grabbed her arm and spun her to face him. "There are some people who are contributors to society, and there are some that are not. The Whittaker family and the people in that neighborhood were not contributors. They were drains on society as a whole. Just like that entire part of town. Those Negro's don't care about anything. Not their homes, their children, an education, a job, paying their dues and earning their keep. They didn't then. That's why over ninety percent of my cases were defending coloreds. If it wasn't enough that we had a problem with Negroes, then we had to deal with the Mexicans. Darnell Whittaker stole and murdered because that's the only thing he knew. That's what his father did, his brother did and what he was going to do. Getting him off the street saved lives and saved the taxpayers money."

"You mean the taxpayers paying to keep him in prison for seventeen years unjustly didn't cost us anything?" They stared at each other. "I wonder what the NAACP would do with this case? I wonder how much of taxpayer's money will be spent putting you and Sapagio and all of your dirty little guild behind bars?"

"That's enough! I've had it with you!"

He grabbed her other arm and squeezed. It hurt, and her face showed it. He let go of one arm and began up the stairs. She tried to resist, but he pulled her.

"Let go of me!"

"You and I are going to talk to Chief Sapagio, so you can tell him about your conspiracy theory."

He yanked her up the stairs, she jerked her arm back, he turned and smacked her with an open hand, but she didn't go down or quit. She had been taught by one of the best: her boyfriend. She stepped closer and shot her knee into his groin. His face turned blue, and he dropped to the stairs like a rock. She shoved him down the stairs. He rolled down five stairs and stopped on a landing, held his crotch and laid in the fetal position.

Julie ran up the stairs, three at a time, reached the top and sprinted down the street, up the drive, and into her car. The tires squealed as she pressed the accelerator and went in reverse. She skidded to a stop in the street and saw Cappalio limp and run down the street after her. She floored it and sped away.

* * * * * * *

Richard Cappalio ran into his house and grabbed his phone. She knew things, was making speculative comments that were dead-on and was asking the right questions. The Frank Staechel murder case was supposed to disappear. They all were supposed to walk away from it. No more questions would come, he was told.

"Warren, she was here. That woman reporter you put the APB out on. She just left my house."

"Don't worry about her. We'll catch her."

"Well, Warren, as your legal counsel, I'm telling you we should worry! She knows things she shouldn't. She's asking questions and making wild-ass guesses that are right on track! She knows about the reporter being poisoned to make it look like a heart attack. If she ties that with the negro lawyer in the boat, well,"

"RELAX and quit talking, damnit!"

"But, I'm telling you,"

"And I'm telling you to shut up! She knows nothing, and we will find her and find out what she knows."

"It just that she knows so much about the case. I think she saw the file."

"That's impossible. There's no way she could have accessed my computer. Let me worry about her. You just keep your eyes on the grand prize."

Warren hung up and rubbed his brow. *That little bitch has got to be shut up!*

CHAPTER 32

Julie felt the adrenaline pumping through her veins. The rush scared her, and her hands shook. She couldn't drive yet she drove the car down Lakeshore Drive, stopping every block for another sign, another stop. She tried to collect herself.

Had to think. Had to get off that street. She turned left and hoped she could find her way out of the area without getting pulled over. She was sure Cappalio would call Sapagio, and the cops would be looking for her. No doubt.

She forced herself to think. Where was Zack? Where was her phone? She found it in her purse and dialed Zack's number. It was busy. She felt the wave of panic, of nausea, approach.

Keep it together, Jules! KEEP IT TOGETHER! She dialed Zack again. Her phone beeped. Someone was calling her. Zack's phone was busy again. *How can it be busy?? Damnit!*

She had to get back to the motel. Ditch the car. That's how they'd find her. Darnell might know an abandoned lot somewhere they could hide the car. Then she could lie low, find Zack and figure this thing out before Sapagio and his goons found her and put her in that cell he talked about.

* * * * * * * *

Zack waited for Julie's voice message to play out and heard the beep. He took a deep breath. "Hey Jules, it's me." He paused and took another breath. "I know I have some explaining to do, but right now I need you to call me. I don't think it's safe here anymore. Please call me the moment you get this. Please!" He hung up and looked at Andre.

"That's all you can do, man. Now let's go find that chump of yours."

There were two entrances to the motel. The main one was old, faded blacktop still holding together but showing the tests of time. It was wide enough for a semi-truck to pull in and park along the front until the driver got a room. Then, he was able to drive around the back of the motel, circling it, then exit onto the highway on a one-lane dirt and gravel road that went between scrub-brush, sucker growth, and over-grown honey-suckle shrubs. The motel owned the land and had thought of putting in a pool, but once the airport moved to the south side of town, they let it grow wild.

Zack steered the motorcycle onto the narrow dirt-gravel path behind the motel, followed by Andre and pulled his motorcycle into a small clearing formed by years of having a campfire amongst the trees and shrubs and stopped. He readied his bike for a quick exit and got off.

Andre rolled around the window. "You want me to park here?"

"No. Go around to the front and if you see anything suspicious, like a cop car or an unmarked cop car, just keep driving. I'll hop back on and get out of here."

Andre did just that. Five minutes later, Zack appeared in the back of the motel and entered the main office. He came back outside, nodded at Andre, and they walked towards the room.

"Anybody in there?"

"I don't know. It's still in my name though and no one's checked out."

Andre shrugged. "Let's check it out."

Zack turned the knob, but it was locked. He stuck the key in the door and turned. The latch clicked, and he pushed open the door.

"Stop right there! I'll blow your head off!"

Zack ducked at the sight of the nine-millimeter pointed at him. Andre pulled his gun and dodged beside the doorjamb.

"Darnell! It's me, Zack! Put the goddamn gun down!"

"JESUS!" Andre added.

Zack put his Sig back in the holster, and Andre entered the room.

"Where the hell have you been?" Darnell yelled.

Zack shut the door and looked at Darnell. "What the hell happened to you?"

Darnell shook his head and got off the floor from behind the bed and put the gun away. "Man, you answer me first? And who the hell's the brother with you?"

"I had to take care of some business," Zack said as he looked around the room. "Where's Julie?"

"Business? You left your girlfriend and me here to fight your battle for your white ass, and that's all you have to say? And it looks like someone whupped your ass!"

"Where's Julie?"

"She left this morning, and I haven't seen her since. Who's he?"

Zack looked at Andre. "She hasn't called?"

"Not my phone. Did you check yours?"

He checked. Two missed calls both from Julie. He then realized they were calling each other at the same time. He dialed her again. Straight to voicemail.

"Straight to voicemail this time," Zack said to Andre.

Andre shook his head. "Doesn't mean anything. Maybe she's just processing things and needs a few to think before she talks to you."

"I hope that's all it is."

Darnell sat on the bed and looked at Andre. "Who are you, man? How do you know this honkey?"

Andre shook his head at Darnell and looked at Zack. "You dragged me back here to save this guy?"

"He only talks like he's from the ghetto when he's trying to be tough or something. Haven't figured it out." Zack sent a text to Julie.

"Well, he got his ass kicked, so I'm guessing his mouth didn't help him there."

Darnell watched the two talk as if he weren't there.

"Probably Warren's goons," Zack surmised. "Looking for me, you think? Or for Julie?"

Andre shook his head. "If it was Warren's goons and they didn't kill him, they were looking for you I'd guess. Julie will be a bonus."

"Yeah, that's what scares me. Damnit!" Zack checked his phone. "We have to find her. I don't think she knows what she's up against."

"We don't know what we're up against, Zack," Andre looked about the room. He saw her bag and moved some stuff. "She packed light when she drove here."

"Are you two gonna tell me what's going on? And who the hell he is?"

They looked at Darnell. Zack spoke. "How do you feel?"

"Like hell. I got my ass kicked by two cops."

"Tell me about it later. Where is Julie?"

"I don't know, man. She said she was gonna investigate some things, ask some questions, shit like that. She told me to stay here, and she'd be back. That was like at eight this morning. Now you gonna tell me who the big-ass brother is with you?"

"You've been here the whole time since I left?"

"Yeah, I got busted up pretty good. I'm feeling better though."

Zack looked at Andre. "What do you think?"

"We can't stay here. Time to pack up and leave. Surprised they haven't been here already."

"Or they have been and are waiting for Julie or me." Zack grabbed Julie's bag, zipped it shut. "Get your stuff, Darnell. We're leaving now."

Andre cased the room, grabbed a towel from the bathroom and wiped all the surfaces while Zack checked the beds, drawers, table, and counter for items left behind. Darnell stared at them.

"HOLD IT!" The two stopped and stared at Darnell. "Please tell me who he is?"

Zack smiled at the return of Darnell's normal voice. "Darnell, meet Andre. He's my best friend. We served in the Corps together and now run a detective agency. If you still think I'm a racist or have been lying to you, ask him. He knows everything. And I do mean everything. Now get your shit and let's go!"

Five minutes after Zack turned onto the highway and headed east, away from the city, two police cruisers came from the west, turned into the main entrance and entered the motel's main office. They didn't ask for permission from the owner. The rooms were busted into and searched, but they found nothing.

CHAPTER 33

She slammed into the wall from the force of the smack across her face. She fell to her butt and stared at one of her abductors.

"Where are they?"

Julie refused to rub her sore face. "Screw you."

The man rushed her, grabbed her off the floor and cocked his arm.

"HOLD IT!" Another voice yelled from the doorway. "That's enough. Let her think about it," the man said. "If the boss finds out you've been slapping her around, he might not be so happy about it. We'll keep her locked in here and find them on our own."

The first man stared at Julie, rage, and anger radiated from his eyes, his breath heavy. He relaxed his grip but shoved her into the wall. "We'll be back, sweetheart, but next time the boss won't be so nice."

He turned and left. The second man hesitated in the doorway then shut the door. She heard it lock. She was trapped.

She was less than a half mile from the hotel when a city police cruiser, off-duty, happened to spot her car. She tried the back roads to get out of town. It almost worked until the off-duty cop radioed the site and before the next intersection spun her into the ditch.

They didn't take her to the police station. She was handcuffed and blindfolded. After a short ride in the back of an unmarked cruiser, they dragged her into a room that looked to her like an abandoned warehouse but modified for the specific purpose of retaining people against their will.

The room was about twelve by twelve, wooden walls that were solid and no ceiling. The walls extended upwards about fifteen feet and opened to the room, so it did have light from the many windows along the roof of the warehouse. And one solid door that after she guessed she was alone, she kicked and struggled with, but it didn't budge.

She sat on the floor, cupped her face in her hands and cried. Bad cops. She knew that. One she recognized from the police station which meant that the Chief of Police, Warren Sapagio, was as dirty as the day was long, and her suspicions were true. She only wished she could hear the truth about her Zack from Zack, but that didn't look like it was going to happen.

* * * * * * * *

"I'm starving, man," Andre deadpanned.

"Yeah, so am I," Darnell added.

"Should we just go through a drive-thru and get something?" Andre leafed through the yellow pages looking at restaurants.

"That'd be cool with me!" Darnell was salivating.

"They're looking for us, Darnell. There aren't a lot of options out there for us," Zack tempered.

"Maybe not for you two but no one is looking for me," Andre offered. "And I need something to eat. You can stay here with him, and I'll drive into town to get something. Give me some cash."

Darnell nodded. "I like this guy. Give him some cash, crabby!"

Zack shook his head, pulled out his wallet and flipped it to Andre. "Where are we anyway?"

"About five miles out of town. This is just an abandoned farm that civilization hasn't found yet. We used to come out here and drink and stuff back in high school." Zack closed his eyes.

"You never told me about this place."

Zack shrugged at Darnell. "It was more for guys to bring their girlfriends and we never dated." Zack smiled. "It's about forty acres owned by a family that moved out east and never sold it. All I know is that we're safe here for now."

Darnell pointed at the street. "Until they come in the driveway."

"There's a trail that leads across the forty right onto a highway. We're fine." Zack looked back at Andre. "She's not answering her phone. Something's wrong."

Andre nodded. He looked at his watch. Four hours had passed since they left the motel. "We'll find her, man. You gotta eat something. We all do. Just stay low and keep your phone on. If I get lost, I'll call."

* * * * * * * *

"What do we got on the girl?" Warren Sapagio stood behind his desk and waited for an answer.

"She's not talking. Says she doesn't know anything. I believe her. I don't think she knows where they are."

Warren chuckled. "She knows. She damn well knows. Her purse have anything in it?"

"Motel key but there was no sign of anything at the motel. We've checked the rest. They aren't in this town."

"What about her car? We have that, right? We didn't leave it in Long Beach for them pretty boys to impound?"

The one cop smiled. "No, we have it. Other than telling us where she lives, which we already knew, it had nothing. An old piece of shit Toyota. We did her a favor by destroying it."

"Could be in LaPorte," a third man suggested. "We could call them?"

"And tell them what?" Sapagio snapped and turned his back to them. "That we're holding a female reporter against her will in an attempt to find the fugitive someone bailed out of jail before they find enough evidence to expose us? Yeah," he snorted, "that's a great idea."

The two men were silent.

"What else did she have on her?"

"Just the usual. Cell phone, car keys, stuff like that."

Warren smiled. "Then get me her damn cell phone, you idiot. That's why I'm the chief!"

CHAPTER 34

Darnell finished picking bits of chicken from his teeth while leaning against the rental car, now parked far from the main road and out of view from passing cars. He looked for Zack and Andre and saw the two about one hundred feet away discussing something. He didn't know what. Probably a plan or something.

He liked the two the more he was around them. Zack having a black man as his best friend was tough to swallow at first. Darnell wanted to believe that David Staechel was a racist like the pigs that arrested, tried and convicted him but he couldn't find any evidence of that at all. He gained respect for Zack. Made it easier to believe his story.

He sipped from his giant cup of soda and thought of his own plan. How was he going to get out of this mess? Zack's best answer was to prove he was set-up. That seemed to be going nowhere.

The thought stopped when Zack's cell phone rang. He looked at the caller ID. It was Jules.

"YO, Zack! You better take this!" He grabbed the phone and ran towards Zack.

Zack walked towards the Darnell and his ringing phone. "What?"

"Dude, it's Julie!"

Zack grabbed the phone and pressed the green button. "Hello?"

He heard nothing but breathing at first. He looked again at the screen. It still said Jules.

"Hello, Zack."

The voice stopped him in his tracks. His breathing stopped, and a shiver went down his spine. He felt a cold sweat cover his body as the color left his face.

"Who is this?"

The man laughed. "You know who this is, and I know who you are, and you're in trouble."

"It seems this must be a misunderstanding. This phone is my girlfriends, and you aren't anything to me which begs the question, who are you and why are you using my girlfriend's phone?"

The heavy breathing through the phone made Zack shake. "If Zack is your real name, I suspect that you have someone I want. In fact, he is in violation of his parole, and you are harboring him which puts you in serious trouble as well. I strongly recommend to you that you, Zack Stack of the Dre-Zack Detective Agency in Baltimore, Maryland, bring back the person you got out of jail, and maybe I'll go easy on you."

Zack struggled to stay calm and think, to not give anything away. He wondered if he had anything left to keep. This pig had his Julie. "How did you get Julie's phone?"

"How did you hide Darnell Whittaker from me?"

"I don't know what you are talking about. Answer me. Why do you have my girlfriend?"

"I'll do you one better. I'll answer everything you want but face to face. How about that? We should clear the air, don't you think?"

Warren Sapagio winked at the subordinates with him. Inside his mind, he was suspecting much more. But he wanted to play his cards right.

"Where's Julie?"

"It's just that all the recent events and poking around in a solved case have lead me to some thinking and as I try to connect the dots, I can't help but think perhaps there is more to this than meets the eye."

Zack felt his lungs tighten, his muscles tense, his ire rise. His hands shook. The voice had the same arrogance and evil it had in it the last time he heard it. Time didn't heal that wound.

"I guess you could say that I am a transformer. Now, where is my girlfriend?"

"I'd like to meet with you and talk. When you agree to that, we can discuss that sassy little bitch you call a girlfriend."

"I don't have anything to say to you until I see Julie alive and well."

Warren chuckled. Even his chuckles, his laughs, and his breathing sounded evil. "Is Mr. Whittaker with you? I'd like to see him, too."

"GODDAMNIT, where's Julie? What have you done with her?"

Suddenly Andre snatched the phone from Zack's hand, threw it to the ground and stomped on it.

"What are you doing?" Zack came at Andre furious.

"Relax, man! They were tracing your phone! They probably know where we are!"

"They've got Julie! They've GOT JULIE!" Zack paced, irate and out of control.

Andre grabbed him. "Calm down!"

245

"They've got her. HE'S GOT HER!"

"I KNOW! AND WE'RE GOING TO GET HER BACK!" Andre squeezed Zack's arms. "But first you've got to get a grip."

Zack ripped himself away, he ran his hands over his face, through his hair and then screamed at the top of his lungs before he fell to his knees, collapsed on his butt and crossed his legs in front of him.

"We'll get her back, Zack." Darnell offered.

Zack was silent for a long time. Andre asked him something, but he didn't hear it. Finally, he took a deep breath.

"How long was the phone call?"

"Over a minute."

Zack caught his breath and exhaled a long breath. "Then we have to get out of here." He got to his feet. "Darnell, ride with Andre in the car. Head to LaPorte. We can find a room there."

"What are you gonna do, man?"

"Meet you there. I think there's a hotel right on the highway coming into town. I'll meet you there. Andre, you'll obviously have to get the room."

"Yeah, I know. What are you thinking? You're in control, aren't you?"

Zack walked to the motorcycle, donned the helmet and got on. "Yeah. I'm fine. Don't wait up."

"Damnit Zack, this isn't the time to go ballistic on me!" Andre tried to stop Zack, but the bike fired quickly and then only a trail of dust remained.

* * * * * * * *

"Phone trace ended," the police techie announced.

"What do you mean?"

"I mean it just went dead."

"Turned it off?"

"Probably crushed it. Either way, we can't complete the trace. A few more seconds and we would have had him."

"Well, we at least know what part of the city they're on. Send some cars in that direction. Looking for the sonofabitch should have gotten a little easier."

"Got it. We're on it."

Warren Sapagio left the tech room and went to his office. He looked at the family picture on the wall, reached into a lower drawer and pulled out the bottle of whiskey. One quick drink and then home. The girl will keep until morning.

The porch light went on. He saw his wife in the window. He opened the car door and smiled at her. He always smiled at her. He fell in love with her the moment he first laid eyes on her. Only she was married to a real loser and had a boatload of kids.

Except for the oldest, Davey, he grew to love the rest of her kids. They were good kids. Davey was a mouthy little shit. Always butting heads with his mother, supporting his piece of shit loser father and showing up in places at odd times which prevented him from advancing his relationship with Louise quicker. Little bastard deserved the gun to the head. Warren then wished he would have pulled the trigger. But he would have had to explain to his wife, then lover. And Louise loved her children. Even Davey. Other than that, she was perfect. He walked up the front stairs, and the door opened. Louise Staechel-Sapagio smiled at her husband.

"Hi, babe," he greeted, and they hugged. He kissed her.

"You're late. How was your day?"

"Oh, the usual. Phil sends his best. He invited us to dinner next weekend."

"That was nice." Louise followed Warren into the kitchen where she had a drink- whiskey, and soda- waiting for him. "I'll call Betty and ask if we can bring anything."

Warren drank from the drink and looked at his wife. "How about you and I go upstairs and make love?

CHAPTER 35

Zack suspected the police presence would be evident after Darnell made his ill-advised visit. But it didn't matter. He needed leverage: a bargaining chip. If Julie was still alive and he was betting she was, then to get her back would require more than just asking nicely. Warren wasn't going to acquiesce that easily. But with this: maybe.

He remembered Andre asking him if he were under control. He lied. As he sat in the hedgerow of Viburnums along the driveway, Zack knew he wasn't. But it was Julie. And he could think of no other way.

He heard the hooting of a Great Horned Owl nearby. A light breeze rustled through the early summer green leaves on the trees surrounding the neighborhood. The moon darted between the clouds. Zack recalled reading Ichabod Crane and shivered.

The SUV's lights lit up the street. Zack hunkered lower in the shrubs. The vehicle drove past the driveway. Wrong vehicle. Without a cell phone, thanks to Andre's quick thinking, he was out of touch with everyone. And vice versa.

Time passed slowly. He thought about his plan and realized that Andre probably had a better plan by now, but he wasn't turning back. The ramifications plastered the inside of his head. He covered his face with the black mask. A voice screamed in his head: TURN BACK!

Another vehicle's lights lit up the street. The bright lights were on and the yards brightened by the halogen beams from the SUV. The lights flashed over him as the vehicle turned into the driveway. It stopped in front of the garage as he suspected.

The door opened. A woman got out of the driver's seat, and Zack moved quick. His hand covered her mouth, and he shoved the barrel of his gun into her lower back.

"Don't shout, don't fight back, do as I say, and you'll be just fine."

He dragged her back to the hedgerow, pinned her to the ground and wrapped a handkerchief around her head to keep her from yelling and bound her hands behind her back.

"I mean it, sweetheart, you make a noise, and I'll blow your damn pretty head off."

He flipped her over, and he saw the fear in her eyes, even in the dark. He placed the cold steel of his gun under her chin.

"Listen and listen good; I hate to repeat myself." He heard something like twigs ruffle. He stared towards the noise, expected to see a cop but saw what looked like a raccoon rumble towards the garbage cans in front of the garage doors.

He pressed the gun harder. "We're going for a ride in your vehicle. Don't try anything stupid. You understand?" She stared at him, and he pressed the gun harder to her chin. "I said do you understand? You only have to nod." She nodded twice.

"Good." He lifted her off the ground easily, grabbed the keys from her hand and ran her into the door of the SUV. The door opened, he tossed her inside and shut it before she knew what had happened.

Seconds later the vehicle disappeared from the neighborhood and headed out of town.

* * * * * * * * *

Andre waited beside the window of the hotel Zack specified and waited for the motorcycle to appear. He looked at the clock again: one fifteen in the morning. A silver SUV drove into the parking lot. He thought nothing of it until a man got out of the drivers' side that he recognized.

"Goddamn you, Zack, what the hell did you do!" He ran out of the room.

Darnell opened his eyes but ignored it. He rolled back over and went to sleep.

The side entrance to the hotel opened, and Andre ran to the side of the SUV. "What the hell is this?"

"I need a ride back to town to get my bike."

"You're wearing a mask. What did you do?"

"A: don't say my name and B: I got us some leverage. There's a hostage in the back seat. She's fine now but probably a little shaken. Are you giving me a ride back or not?"

"Jesus!" Andre shook his head and paced. "I found another way. A better way! What you did was just mess things up!"

"Well, now we have options!" They stared at each other. "Now give me a ride back, or I'll walk."

"Well, we can't take you back with a hostage in the backseat. Who the hell is it, anyway?"

Zack scratched his face under the mask. "My sister."

Andre's mouth opened wide.

"Warren likes her best, and he'll do anything for my mom. So now we have a bargaining chip."

* * * * * * * *

Andre didn't care about Zack's beauty sleep and ripped open the heavy shades. The morning sun beamed on Zack's face and in moments his eyes squinted, he raised his bare arm to cover his face and tried to eye the culprit of the deed.

"Get up. We have a dilemma."

Darnell opened the shades even further. "Yeah, man. This is a dilemma."

Zack sat upright and rubbed his eyes. "Where's Becky?"

"I thought it best to lock her in the bathroom."

"Why?"

Andre shook his head. "Put your damn mask on and shut your damn mouth. I'll get her out of the bathroom, and you clean your dumbass self up."

Darnell smiled.

Zack got out of bed, naked and walked towards the bathroom.

"Man, put some damn clothes on."

"Ok." He found the mask and put it on.

Andre shook his head and got Becky out of the bathroom.

Andre sat her down on the chair and took her gag off. "Look, we aren't going to hurt you, I'll make sure of that. But you need not yell or do anything stupid, all right?"

She nodded and then saw Darnell.

"Wait. What is he doing here?"

"He's with us." Andre sat on the edge of the desk in front of her.

"Who was the naked man?"

Andre smiled. "Just the idiot who grabbed you."

"This is the second time I've been kidnapped since you've been released from jail, Darnell. Why?"

"I had nothing to do with it this time."

"Then who was that man?"

"It doesn't matter. What matters is that we return you safely and you don't press charges against me, Darnell or the idiot in the shower right now." Andre flashed his best smile and knew his charm was working on the married, white sister of his partner.

"Why do you have me?"

"My friend decided you could be a useful bargaining chip."

"In what?"

"In solving the murder of your dad," Andre said though he knew that wasn't the reason. He wanted to see her reaction. He read her expression.

"I had nothing to do with it."

"Never said you did. But the man on the bed over there," he pointed at Darnell, "didn't either. And your step-dad is decidedly hell-bent on not allowing the case to be re-opened. Now me personally, I don't care who did it. I heard the story, and maybe he killed himself, I don't know."

"My father would never do that!"

"I didn't mean to imply," Andre apologized. "But I do want my boy over here," he pointed at Darnell, "to be set free of all the wrongful charges. The man in the shower believes that you can help."

"How? I don't know anything. I told you I had nothing to do with it."

Andre cocked his head. "Your step-father may not be the hero this town wants to believe he is."

Becky was silent. She stared into Andre's eyes.

"He kidnapped a person the guy in the shower is very fond of, and I have to admit I'm fond of her myself."

"Why would he do that?"

Andre smiled. "Because he wants Darnell and the man in the shower. And I think if he gets them, they'll both be dead."

Becky looked at Darnell.

"I think that would be wrong and I'm not gonna let that happen," Andre spoke in a kind, gentle voice. Never wavered or showed any emotion. In fact, had it not been the topic, Darnell thought he was telling a story of a family picnic.

"I still don't know how that pertains to me. I don't know who killed my father."

"Becky, the man in the shower kidnapped you to use as trade bait. You're going to see if your step-dad gives a damn about you. If he doesn't, I'd change my mind about that anniversary present you got for them if I were you."

Becky was silent again. "What do I have to do with this? I already told Darnell everything I knew."

Andre heard the shower turn off. "I'm sure you did. Now look, I'm going to blind you, and you're going to be bound. I don't want you moving or struggling or anything. You'll be fine. But for now, just behave, Ok?"

She nodded, and Andre did as he said.

Andre opened the bathroom door. "Don't talk. Just get dressed and do as I say."

"You're not giving the orders here."

"The hell I'm not. The minute you kidnapped her was the minute you put me in charge."

"Bullshit," Zack challenged. "We got her phone. We call Julie's phone; he'll recognize the number and know we have Becky. Then he'll make the trade only in the meantime you'll use your connections and have her line traced so I can go to where she is and bust her out. That's the plan."

He tried to walk past Andre, but Andre put his big hand on Zack's chest and stopped him. The two stared at each other.

"That plan is going to get you and Julie killed, Darnell killed and probably me killed too."

Zack looked exasperated. The lack of sleep and pressure was taking its toll. "Damnit, man! He's got Jules!"

Andre pressed his hand into Zack's chest and moved him backward. "Keep your voice down!" Zack moved, but Andre held him. "Just stop for a second, Zack. Please!"

Zack stopped, took a deep breath and frowned.

"Look, man, something ain't right. I don't know what it is, but I need you to keep it together and work with me. All right? We're a team, right? You and me. We'll figure this shit out and get Jules back, together. I got your back; you got mine. Right?"

Zack let out a deep breath and nodded. "Yeah."

Andre saw the toll in Zack's eyes. He knew Zack would never cry, but if he were capable, tears would fall any second.

"We don't have time to trace no calls, and they'll be tracing us at the same time. They'll be expecting that. They may or may not know that Becky is missing. That isn't good for us. Before we just had the dirty cops looking for us, now we got them all!"

Zack exhaled again, his frown deepened.

"We need to meet. I don't care under what premise, but I don't think we use Becky as bait."

"We need leverage, Dre. We meet anywhere we're all dead. You know that. She's our leverage."

"No, we have to make him believe we have information on him that will ruin his career. We offer to trade."

"We don't have shit. It's all speculation and non-related shit. You understand what shit is, right? That's what we have, shit!"

"Yes, we do! Jules was onto something, or they would have sent her away. But they didn't. We need to know what she knows. So just relax. You aren't thinking straight. Just get dressed, and I'll get us some food. Don't do any talking! Got it?"

Zack nodded. "How do we find out what she knows?"

"We call Michelle. So just chill the hell out, ok? We'll fix this."

Zack nodded. "I'm with you. But get this straight partner: if Jules gets hurt, I'm taking that sonofabitch down."

Andre nodded and smiled. "And I'll be there beside you."

CHAPTER 36

The cell phone rang and startled everyone in the room. Zack donned a baseball cap, pulled way down on his forehead and large black sunglasses to conceal most of his face instead of wearing the wool mask. Andre picked the items up at a nearby Walgreens when he got some food for the foursome.

Becky looked scared yet hopeful. Darnell and Andre watched Zack as he walked to the phone and lifted it.

"I have to take this."

He showed the number on the screen. It was Julie's. Andre shook his head. The ringing stopped but seconds later started again.

"Go outside."

Zack walked outside and answered the phone. He said nothing.

He heard breathing. "Zack, is that you?"

Zack wanted to talk but refrained.

"So now you've added kidnapping to your list of accolades." Warren chuckled. "And what do you plan to do? Tell me you'll make an even exchange?"

Zack thought of Andre's plan. His thoughts scrambled into formation.

"I don't think I can tell you how much this upsets your mother that her oldest daughter has gone missing which means that it really

257

upsets me and you're not going to like it, Zack. Or is this Darnell? Or is it someone else? I have my suspicions. Please talk so I know which one of you to kill first if something happens to Rebecca."

Zack forced a chuckle. "You have a history of killing Staechel family members, so killing me would add to your list too, wouldn't it?"

Warren laughed. "I'm really interested to see where you're going with this."

"Becky is talking. She knows how you killed Frank and how you and Louise conspired to do it for the insurance money. Says she has proof. How's that for where I'm going with this?"

The laugh boomed in mock. "She knows nothing, and you're wrong. Nice play."

"I have the insurance papers. I have proof of the forgery. I have proof the insurance agent was in on it and that you were behind the whole cover-up which sent Darnell wrongly to prison. You give me back Jules, and I don't go to the state's attorney general. That's the best deal you're gonna get, asshole."

"Whoa, whoa, whoa. Why the name calling?"

"I'll call later. You better be ready to turn Julie back to me or else."

"Or else what?" Warren laughed. Zack looked at his watch. He was on too long. He knew it.

"You willing to bet your dirty pig life that this is a bluff, Warren? You dirty sonofabitch. I can't wait to put a bullet in your thick fat skull as you did to Frank."

"I hope you try, you cocky little shit." The laugh had gone.

"Those who try fail, as you did with this sordid life you've created. It's about to come crashing down, Warren Sapagio. Julie for the info, that's the best you'll get."

"Fine," Warren paused. Zack could feel the calculation behind his words. "2 AM, at the zoo, up by the tower. You and Darnell. If you don't show or if you try anything, your precious whore dies. If Becky doesn't show up at her mother's by ten, your whore dies."

"No, that's not the deal."

"NO, IT IS THE DEAL!"

The breathing on the phone was deafening. Zack pulled the phone from his ear.

"You'll do as I say, or the girl dies. You understand? You messed with the wrong man, and you're gonna find out how far I'll go to make you suffer for what you did to my wife and step-daughter."

"Suffer? You don't know the first thing about it. But you're about to." Zack ended the call and tossed the phone as far as he could. It disappeared in a body of water behind the hotel. Andre appeared behind him.

"Dude, you all right?"

Zack turned and looked at Andre. "No. We have to get out of here now, and Julie is going to die."

Andy Gruse
STACKED CASE

CHAPTER 37

They left the hotel within minutes, leaving Becky's SUV behind. Further out of town Zack found a place to park and got off his motorcycle. "We'll be fine here for a while."

"Sure, as long as they don't call the county and state cops to find the girl you kidnapped!"

"Now what?" Darnell had to ask the obvious, and Zack wondered himself.

Andre dialed a number on his phone. "First, you two are going to stay the hell out of sight. I don't care what you do with her. Let her go for all I care. But you two aren't doing anything stupid!"

"Yeah, you hear that, Zack?"

Zack shook his head at Darnell.

"Then what? What are you gonna do?"

Andre looked at Darnell. "I'm going to the zoo. I need to see what the environment is all about. If we show up their blind, we're dead." Andre walked to Zack's motorcycle and grabbed the helmet.

"Whoa, you aren't taking my bike."

"You two walking around with a hooded woman? Not suspicious at all."

"We're gonna need help, Andre," Zack said.

"We're gonna need a miracle."

"Look, you take the car. Take the girl. I know what you're planning, but I think I can get us an ally." Zack knew it was a battle to get Andre to believe what he said.

"Oh yeah? Who is that?"

"The cucarachas."

Andre laughed. "The Mexican gang?"

"If we're stirring the pot, then you can count on Warren and his dirty band of brothers tying up loose ends. Even gang members talk. Warren isn't stupid. He's setting them up, too."

Andre nodded. "You're right. What makes you think they won't just kill you and Darnell?"

Zack shrugged. "I don't know. But it's worth finding out, isn't it?"

Andre shook his head. "Dude, sometimes I don't know if you're brilliant or the stupidest sumbitch alive."

Zack smiled. "We'll meet you behind the city golf course at dark. Stay off the main roads. Come on, Darnell."

"Why am I going with you?"

Zack smiled. "Because you like me. Now put on the helmet and hold on."

* * * * * * *

Zack looked at his watch. A car turned the corner up the street. It was a police cruiser. Another turned behind it. "What the hell is this?"

Darnell saw. "Five-O making themselves seen." He heard the quick sound of a siren from behind them. He turned and saw another

262

cruiser approach from the other end of the block. "Don't move, man. We're surrounded."

Zack watched the two cruisers, each with two men, creep down the street, their eyes searching. They didn't know what for. At the intersection, an unmarked car crept through. The officers acknowledged each other with a head nod.

The other cruiser slowed to nearly a stop in front of a decrepit, abandoned home. It pulled away.

"What the hell are they looking for?"

"Things aren't working like they're supposed to." Zack guessed. They hid inside a stand of overgrown Glossy Abelia shrubs which were nearly twelve feet high and almost as round. They blossomed in white and pink flowers that made the perfect cover. He didn't know what to expect, but he knew they weren't looking for him and Darnell. They were making a sweep. They were clearing the place.

"They're all over this neighborhood."

"They're making sure no one is around," Zack said.

"Why?" They were silent. Ten minutes later the El Dorado they saw a few days earlier with the gang details, the low-tires, and shiny rims, slid next to the curve and stopped.

"That's why."

"We got them behind us, too."

Zack saw another gang banger vehicle behind them along the street. It was filled with bangers, and there was another car behind it. "Looks like they are planning something."

"Yeah, planning on Chief Pig to not screw with their leader."

They saw the black Escalade two blocks away approaching from the east. The truck stopped in front of the gang-bangers car just like before. Only this time, a man got out of the passenger door.

"Who do we have here?" Zack immediately recalled that last time no one got out of the Escalade. The gang member went to it. This was different.

"Probably one of the Chief Pig's yes-men."

Zack raised the binoculars to his eyes. The man looked in his mid-thirties, wore regular jeans and a white button shirt. He wore leather loafers. He wasn't wearing a gun that Zack could see.

"Fancy shirt. One of Warren's play pals?"

"Let me see." Zack gave Darnell the binoculars. "Dude is cut. Looks like he works out. Probably belongs to the gym. But he ain't no cop."

Zack took away the binoculars and looked at the man as he talked to the driver of the gang-bangers car. "What makes you say that?"

"Look at him, man. He's afraid to get his hands dirty. He dresses too nice to be a cop. Look at those jeans. Probably cost eighty bucks, and that shirt is as pressed as they come. Probably custom. And his shoes? Those things are too nice to be cop shoes. Look at his hair and shit? All slicked back. Dude is probably some cracker lawyer."

Zack nodded. He sized up the man the same way. Darnell was smart. Pegged him. "So, who is that guy and why is he talking with the gang-bangers?"

"If he's a lawyer, he's probably telling them their best move after they finish doing whatever they are getting paid to do."

Zack nodded again. Could that be it?

"And the show of force before the gangbangers got here tells me Warren has a force behind him. That's not encouraging."

"What about this is?" He handed Darnell the binoculars. "What do you see?"

"Another payout." Darnell lowered the eyepiece and looked at Zack. "For what?"

"I'm guessing two hits." He stared at Darnell. "Us."

"Now what?"

"We have to sit tight and hope no one sees us. Then we get the hell out of here and go talk to their leader."

A few moments later the Escalade and the head gang-banger car left. The other gang members left the neighborhood. The police cruisers appeared out of nowhere and swept the neighborhood again. Zack and Darnell waited an hour after that.

Andy Gruse
STACKED CASE

CHAPTER 38

Zack drove the bike down the streets slowly. He and Darnell looked for any sign of life. It wasn't much of a plan, but it was the only thing Zack could think of. Then, they saw the car. The El Dorado. Zack stopped.

"This is the best you can do?"

"We need help. Warren is going to have us outnumbered at least four to one. What can this hurt?" Zack shrugged as he looked down the street.

"I'll tell you what it can hurt: they can kill us!"

"Then the problem is solved. Leave your gun here."

"What? Are you kidding?" Darnell clutched it like it was his only possession in the world.

"They're only going to take it. And, they might take it as a direct insult and threat."

Darnell shook his head. "Your step-dad had his gun!"

Zack looked at him. "Leave it."

Darnell did as Zack suggested. "Good idea. You're full of them, man."

It was nearing three in the afternoon. Zack wondered if the gang had any plans of further pillaging and plundering the depressed largely abandoned area that day.

"Just let me do the talking, alright, Darnell?"

"What? Why?"

Zack looked at him as the two men walked down the middle of the street. From the corner of his eyes, Zack knew they were being watched. He counted at least twelve men, probably was double that between him and the leader of the gang. All were well armed and ready to shoot. Part of him was surprised he hadn't been shot already.

"Just keep your mouth shut. If you bust out your ghetto lingo, I doubt they'll listen."

Darnell was close to Zack and talked low. "Like they're going to listen to you? We're both dead. You know that, don't you?"

"Yep."

* * * * * * * *

Andre walked through the zoo as if interested in the animals and displays. He watched each attentively. He had paid a few dollars to buy a handful of food to feed some goats and a map overview of the zoo. Then as he walked past the lion cage, he thought how it would be fun to feed the lions with the goats.

He saw the tower and stopped in the middle of a walkway that opened to form almost a patio. There were cages to his right and a fence to left that guarded against people falling over into a moat. Beside it was the tiger cage where one tiger paced around his "natural surrounding" cage as if looking for a way to get out and get at those same goats Andre offered to the lions. Or perhaps the tiger wanted to eat one of the people.

Either way, it seemed dreadful for the tiger to spend his existence staring through glass and chain link fence.

But as he looked at the thick trees on the hillsides leading up to the closed tower with several entries and exit points from the patio, he knew this had to be the meeting place. He moved to a bench, with his soda can and hot dog, and slowly ate his food.

He watched the small groups of people walking past, gawking at the monkeys, tigers, elephants, giraffes, lions, and bears. And no one paid attention to him. He wished he had some of the surveillance equipment but realized that it wouldn't work. Too much background noise, even in the middle of the night; especially in the middle of the night, the sound equipment would not work. But he still had to know the ins and outs.

He checked his watch. He had to get up those paths. If he was right about the meeting spot, the patio had to be covered from every angle and so did the escape route he determined Zack, Darnell, and Julie would need to survive. Another bite of hot dog. More people walked past. He looked at his watch and knew time was running out.

* * * * * * * *

"Stop right there, amigo!"

Zack and Darnell stopped. Three Mexican men approached from each side. Zack saw the weapons: guns and knives. They were prepared. The accents were harsh but whoever yelled at them spoke English enough to be understood.

"What do you want here? Your kind is not wanted."

A member of the gang went behind them and frisked each Zack and Darnell. Zack saw the one shake his head to the leader in front of them. It was not the leader, just a higher up in the gang. You had to get through this one to get to the big boss.

"Want do you want?"

"We need to see your boss."

"My boss doesn't want to see you or your black friend."

"We're not here to cause you trouble," Darnell spoke, but he was hit immediately.

"I didn't say you could talk, man!" The second-in-command (SIC) pointed a finger at Darnell. "What are you doing with this gringo, anyway?"

Darnell stared at him.

"I asked you a question."

"If I'm going to hang out with dogs, I prefer them not to smell."

The SIC smiled first then whipped out his switchblade and clicked it open. "You won't be so tough after I cut your tongue out, muchacho."

"You aren't my friend, hombre," Darnell said. "I've never held with high esteem gang-bangers."

"You don't like Mexicans?"

"I don't like gang-bangers."

"How about if I just kill you both right now?"

"LOOK," Zack yelled, "this isn't about you or us. This is about your gang about to get screwed by your pal in the police force. Take us to your boss, and I can explain all of this."

The SIC stared between Zack and Darnell.

270

"If he doesn't like what we have to say, you can kill us both. Just give us five minutes with your boss." Zack shrugged like it was the easiest solution.

A man yelled something in Spanish from down the street. The SIC turned, nodded and stared again at Zack. "You I trust. Your friend, I do not." He eyed them both and nodded. "Come."

* * * * * * * *

Andre returned to the car, started it and looked at his passenger. "I'm surprised you didn't run away."

Becky shrugged. "I'd like to see how this all ends. I have an idea of how it will. You should probably leave town now."

"Why is that?"

She looked at him as he drove out of the parking lot, down Lakeshore Drive and turned at Stop 2 to head back to the area behind the tower.

"We just want the truth, Becky. We aren't here to hurt you."

"Darnell didn't hurt me, and besides the naked guy being a little rough, none of you have hurt me. I just don't know why you're holding me."

Andre thought about how stupid Zack was and wanted to hit him. "My friend thinks you know more about the day your father was murdered than you're telling us."

Becky crossed her arms. "My step-father will have all three of you arrested for kidnapping me. You understand that, don't you?"

"What happened that day? Tell me what you know."

"I already told Darnell."

"I don't like Darnell. I won't ask him what you said. Tell me. I like listening to your voice."

"I've told you twice already too; I had nothing to do with it."

CHAPTER 39

The soldiers in the gang guided Zack and Darnell down the street into the front yard of a broken-down home that still had electricity and running water. Zack could see that all the houses surrounding this one were occupied by families of Hispanics. Young kids played in the grass-less front yards; a few dogs were chained to posts or trees and laid on the ground careless of life around them.

Old cars parked on the street and the lawns, littered the block, but Zack noticed that the cars specified for the gang members were clean, parked on the street and had a clear path to exit. Nothing went near them.

The people were not old. He didn't see any old Hispanics. A few young "chicas" hovered around the gangbangers, eager to impress their loyalty, eager to use their bodacious bodies to find security inside the gang and the wealth it offered if even it was only temporary.

They all paid close attention to Zack and Darnell as they were guided to the boss. Zack knew guided wasn't the right word. Forced was the right word. It's what he asked for, and that was all he was going to get. Getting out was not a consideration of the gang.

The boss, a muscled, oily, bald Hispanic, waved his hand and the woman beside him scattered. She grabbed two kids off the lawn and disappeared into the house.

Zack saw the tattoos up and down the boss's arms and on his bare chest. The tattoos signified accomplishments, achievements, even killings. No one else had as many as the man sitting on the rotting wooden steps of the house in front of them. And someone would have to kill this man to claim the top spot.

Zack figured the average lifespan of a person in this gang to be maybe twenty-nine before they were incarcerated or killed, no different than life in the projects. The typical life for a male minority in that town was that. With no jobs, no education and no way off the streets, what other alternative was there? The life of a gang-banger didn't have a happy ending.

Zack was pushed. Zack normally would have dropped the man already. None of the gangbangers were bigger than he was; in fact, he was taller and as muscled as all of them as was Darnell. The boss in front of them had well-defined arms and chest, but strength didn't signify one could fight. Zack wasn't here to fight though. That was a losing proposition. That would mean certain death and being pitched into Trail Creek, the river that went through the town that bordered the Triangle.

"What right do you have to set foot in my territory?"

The boss spoke, and he spoke nearly accent-free. A lifer in the states, probably Chicago, his knowledge of the English language had given him a head start in the gang.

"We have a mutual problem."

"What?"

"The Chief of Police is determined to kill the two of us," Zack motioned to Darnell and him, "and most likely pin it on you." Zack didn't think it would be worthwhile not to tell him what was going on. Most gangbangers had little patience.

The boss laughed. "Did you hear that Pablo? The Chief of Police is blaming me for something." All the gangbangers laughed.

"Kill them now."

Zack heard the cocking of a gun. "I wouldn't do that if I were you."

"You think you can tell me what to do?" He stood and walked close to Zack.

"I wouldn't think of it, but you should listen to what I have to say before you kill us."

"What? Who the hell are you?" He looked at the SIC, second in charge. "Carlos, who the hell is this perro?"

Carlos shrugged.

"Look, man, the chief is dirty, and he's planning on killing us and then blaming you. Then he'll either kill you or arrest all of you."

The leader ignored Darnell and stared straight into Zack's eyes. He knew Zack was the leader and he was determined to intimidate Zack.

"The pigs are looking for you and this perro, and you come here? To my home? Where my family is? I should kill you just for that."

"They haven't touched you yet." Zack smiled. "What is your name anyway?"

"Diablo."

"Devil? That's your name." Just then, the cute woman he flicked away earlier stuck her head out the door.

"Alejandro, es tiempo de venir adentro para cena. Venga ahora antes que se ponga frio."

"Ok, leave me alone, woman. I'll be inside when I'm ready."

"Ok, Alejandro," Zack said. "Look, the Chief of Police is planning on bulldozing this whole area to put up condos, hotels, casinos, strip malls and in the process run you and your family out of town. If need be, they'll come in with the SWAT team and shoot to kill. Do you want that?"

Alejandro stared at Zack. "Why do you come to me? Why would a white man, a gringo dog like you, tell me this?"

Zack took a deep breath. He hated being called names. "Because unlike you I don't judge a person by the color of his skin. Nor do I give a shit about your relationship with the police in this city. But I do care about my girlfriend, who he is holding hostage and I don't like people who use other people, and that's exactly what Warren is doing to you and your gang."

"You don't know shit."

"I know he's paid you at least twice in the last week. We watched you meet him personally a few days ago and again today. I know he's using this gang to create enough trouble to get the city council to vote the entire neighborhood get razed. Abandoned. Then they'll treat you like dirt. Like a common stray dog."

Calling Alejandro a dog was not smart. Zack knew it. Darnell knew it. The only thing worse would be to talk bad about his mother or to use the f-word in any negative fashion. Zack kept his stomach tense, ready for a quick punch. If he did get punched and buckled, he'd never get up.

"They have your girlfriend?" Alejandro smiled. "And you want me to help get her back?"

276

That's the gist of it, Einstein! "Look, Alejandro, I have to meet him tonight at 2 AM at the zoo hill by the tower. He's going to kill Darnell and me."

Darnell couldn't keep quiet any longer. "And I bet that payment he gave to you this morning is to get your gang to destroy the church and finish off the minister there, right?"

"What do you care about that old church and the old man who runs it?"

"That's my uncle." Darnell stared at Alejandro. Zack could see the anger and hate.

Alejandro scoffed. "Are you here for revenge?"

"If my uncle ends up dead, yes."

They stared at each other and Zack felt the proposition slipping away.

"I am sorry, then, because your uncle is already dead. Only we can't take credit for that."

"What?"

"He was beaten and died two days ago. Don't you read the newspaper? We're already blamed, but look, there are no cops here to arrest us!" Diablo laughed as did his men.

Darnell rushed at Alejandro but was hit in the back of the neck and hit the ground. Two guns suddenly were pressed firmly against Darnell's head while two men held him.

"Alejandro," Zack barked, "look at me! You go through with that and Sapagio will issue an order to remove by force the minute the city passes the ordinance! He's going to cover his ass, and the only way to keep you quiet is to kill you."

"Don't talk to me like I don't know nothing, white man!" Alejandro shook his head. "It's already done, man. Don't you read either? The church was burnt down late this morning. It's gone, man. You're too late." Alejandro paused. "Now kill them!"

"STOP!" Zack yelled. "STOP IT!" Everyone halted while Darnell held the back of his neck with one hand. He was on his knees. Darnell started to talk, but Zack punched his mouth. "Just shut up!"

"Man, they killed my uncle! They freaking killed him!"

"We didn't kill no one, you dirty dog," Alejandro spit at Darnell.

"Don't lie to me. I know goddamn well you did it!"

"WE DID NOTHING, MAN!" Alejandro yelled and kicked Darnell in the stomach.

Zack waited his turn. It was over. Darnell incited Alejandro, and it was soon to be over.

"How do we know you didn't do it, huh? How do we know you aren't setting us up?"

"Look, Diablo," Zack started carefully. "The police are about to start a war with you. Whether you did it or not, they are going to blame you. Help me get back my girlfriend tonight, and you and Darnell can work out your differences later, all right?"

Alejandro stared at him; anger boiled on his face. His soldiers pointed their weapons at Zack and Darnell. Something in Zack's look got Darnell to quit talking.

"Do you have a cell phone?"

"Yeah, but I didn't bring it with me."

"Why not?"

"Because after I walk out of here, I'm planning on using it again and I figured you would steal it if I brought it with."

Alejandro smiled. "What is your number?"

"Why? You going to text me?"

"I might kill you. I have to decide. In case I do, I want to know how to get in touch with you, so you can tell me where you are."

Zack liked the sarcasm. He told him the number of Andre's secondary phone since Zack threw the primary into a lake.

"You two will walk out of here and never set foot in my neighborhood again, do you understand? If you do, I will kill you both."

"I'm not coming back to this shithole," Darnell mumbled.

"What?"

"He said," Zack interrupted, "that neither of us will come back."

Alejandro stared at Darnell who stared right back.

"I'm not killing you now because I don't want my babies to see such violence."

"That's commendable of you, Alejandro."

Zack grabbed Darnell's arm, and the two slowly walked backward.

"Go on! Get out of here!"

Andy Gruse
STACKED CASE

CHAPTER **40**

"You knew, didn't you?"

Zack nodded.

"Why didn't you tell me?"

Zack got on the bike. "Because I didn't know how to tell you."

"When did you find out?"

"Late this morning. Andre and I called Michelle. She told me."

"What else did she tell you?"

"Enough to know that we are in deep shit and we need to stick together. I'm sorry about your uncle, and I'm sorry about the church. It was all part of Warren's plan."

Darnell weighed the answer and shook his head.

"We part ways as soon as we're out of here, you got it?"

Zack shook his head. "Why? Because I glossed over the burning of the church to save Julie?"

"That's exactly why! Those bastards killed my uncle and burned down the only thing my family ever had, or did that was worth something, and you don't care?"

"I do care!" Zack yelled. "But us getting killed isn't going to solve anything."

"It's solved something for you. You at least have somewhere to go and someone to go back to."

Zack had to think about that. *Do I really?* "I don't think the gang-bangers did it. That's not their style, so the only justice is bringing down the piece of shit that is responsible."

"You believe that shit?" Darnell yelled.

"Why would they give a shit about an old broken-down church and the minister there? Huh? They wouldn't. They are all God-fearing. Didn't you see the crosses? They wouldn't do shit to that church or your uncle. There's no profit in it."

"Your step-dad paid them."

Zack shook his head and took a deep breath. "I don't think so. As much as you want to hate them, I still think they have boundaries, and that's one of them."

"Like I said, do you believe that shit?"

"I'm trying to believe anything I can to help keep me going. I got nothing left either, Darnell. If this doesn't work out for me, if we're not dead I'll be right next to you in prison."

"Freaking cracker like you wouldn't last five minutes in the cell."

"Whatever, you racist prick."

Darnell looked at Zack. He stared at him as if he wanted to punch him again. Zack stared back. Then Darnell smiled and shook his head. "I owe you a punch, you asshole."

"If you would have said one more word we'd be dead right now. I couldn't let that happen."

Zack heard a sniffle. Darnell was hiding tears. "This isn't over, man." He got on the back of the motorcycle.

"Well, I'd have to say that other than for the nasty contusions you're going to have on your neck that that went well."

"I'd like five minutes alone with that guy."

Zack drove away. "Never happen. That guy is never without many bodyguards."

"Damn coward, if you ask me. His ho was hot though, for a Latino."

"Remind me, if we survive this, to get you some pussy that isn't attached. You're likely to get yourself killed if you start messing around with another man's woman."

Darnell offered a little smile. "What makes you think I'm gonna stay with your ass after this is all over?"

"Ha!" Zack laughed. "You're starting to like me. Why wouldn't you want to hang around me?"

"Yeah, right."

Zack's mind, though, went immediately to Julie. He remembered the zoo, though he hadn't been there in a long time, and knew there was no way he could do any reconnoitering of the area before the meeting. Warren set it up for a reason. That told Zack that Warren was familiar with the area, used it before and access was probably easier than it should have been.

As Zack drove out of town, towards LaPorte and away from the city cop's jurisdiction, he played all the scenarios in his mind. He knew Darnell was talking but could not hear him. He was focused elsewhere. On Julie. That's all that mattered to him.

He found a pizza place in LaPorte and stopped in the parking lot.

"What are you doing, man? You're hungry?"

Zack stopped the bike and looked at Darnell. "All we can do is wait. And since I'm figuring it to be the last meal we get for the rest of our lives, we might as well eat something."

"Shouldn't we be planning or something?"

"Planning what? We don't have a layout, we won't get there before they do, and we'll be horribly outnumbered." Zack read the menu for the pizza though he knew what he wanted.

"So, we go in and die?"

"Pretty much."

"What about Andre?"

"What about him? He'll be safe."

"What?" Darnell's voice hit an octave higher than anything he ever had done before due to incredulity.

"He's not dumb, and he won't be with us. We'll see him pretty soon. We'll take him some pizza. He'll enjoy it."

"Man, you're out of your mind."

* * * * * * *

Andre looked at his watch and wondered if his boy was dead. A grown over field with dirt bike trails had a nice parking lot, and Andre waited there. Becky knew exactly where the masked naked man had meant.

"Now what?"

"We wait."

"For how long?"

"Until dark."

284

"Then what?"

Andre shrugged.

"Who is that man I saw naked?"

"Why? Think he had a nice body?"

She rolled her eyes. "You men are all the same. Think all you have to do is get naked and any woman will throw herself all over you."

Andre chuckled. "Never failed me yet."

"Who is he and why wouldn't you let him talk around me?"

"He's no one you need to concern yourself with. End of discussion."

Andy Gruse
STACKED CASE

CHAPTER 41

The headlight of the motorcycle appeared from the north. Andre felt better. "Here they come."

Becky nodded. "I know. That means tie me up and blindfold me."

"Security measures, that's all."

The motorcycle turned into the parking lot after Andre had her bound and blinded.

"You're alive. How did it go?"

Zack shrugged as he got off the bike and walked away from the motionless Becky. Once out of earshot, he shrugged again. "They didn't kill us. That's about it."

"Great. Now what?"

"You got the zoo figured out?"

"Yeah, look at this." He pulled out the map of the zoo and unfolded it.

Zack laughed immediately. "What is this? This is a children's map with crayon all over it!"

Andre chuckled and then straightened up. "It was all they had, now look it here," he said as he pointed to the red crayon circle he made on the map. "You have to make sure this is where the meeting is. It's the only place there I can get a clean shot and a clean getaway. And it has the most exit points for you. No matter what, don't stray from this path here," he pointed again. "That's your best way out. My guess is, if and when the shit hits the fan he'll have backup swarm that place but not from back here. So, don't even think about any other way out."

Zack nodded. "So, stay between the birdcage, the monkey nest, and the tiger pit?"

Andre shook his head. "Stay away from the cougar cage. They like to escape and eat people." The smiles left their faces. "You ready for this, man? You gonna be ok?"

"Have my back. If I need help, you'll know. What time are you splitting?"

"Figure I'm gonna have to get there between ten and eleven. You know he'll have it staked before that." Andre looked around.

Zack nodded and looked into his partner's eyes. "I owe you."

"Shut up and don't get mushy on me. I smell pizza. Where is it?"

Just then, Andre's cell phone rang. "I'll take that. It's for me."

"Is this the perro?"

"I'd appreciate it if you wouldn't call me a dog. By the way, Alejandro, how was your dinner? Did you get inside before it got cold?" Zack loved it when Spanish speaking people assumed he couldn't speak Spanish.

"Muy Bueno, muchacho."

"Good. I'm glad. Why are you calling me?"

"I got a phone call tonight. Very interesting one."

Zack hated having to pry for information. "Did the INS call and issue you a new green card?"

"You a very funny gringo."

"What do you want?"

Alejandro laughed. "Our mutual friend has offered me a great deal of money to complete a job for him. Three jobs actually."

"His pool need cleaning?"

"Ahh, amigo, you should be nice to me."

"Then get to the point, Alejandro. I don't have all night."

"No, you don't, my friend. It seems you have less time than you probably expect."

Zack exhaled and shook his head. "No, I fully expect to be dead by two tomorrow morning. Do you know of other plans?"

"No," he chuckled. "That sounds about right. You, your friend and your girlfriend are the three jobs he's going to pay for me."

Zack wasn't sure if he should be happy or further discouraged. "Ok. That's nice. How much did he offer?"

"What?"

"How much are our lives worth to that piece of shit?"   "Fifty grand."

"That's it?" Zack raised his voice. "That's all we're worth? And you accepted? Jesus Christ. Didn't the going rate for contracted murder used to be much higher?"

"Calm down, amigo. Fifty apiece."

"Who said you couldn't put a price on a life?"

"If what you told me is right, I won't kill you, your friend or your girlfriend."

"I feel relieved." Zack snorted.

"Your sarcasm is refreshing."

"Get on with it, Diablo."

"There's a rear entrance to the zoo. Don't go in over the bridge or the lakeshore. They will spot you and probably cut you down. Cut through the old part of town, use the bridge by the burnt down church. Three blocks past the bridge turn left and then keep heading north. The tower has a single light atop it. Look for that. You'll have to park a block away and then walk. Stay in the shadows. Juan Carlos will be waiting on the bridge. You pick him up. He will show you the way. But he will not help you, and if the cops find you, he's helping them, do you understand?"

Zack scratched his head. "This doesn't exactly sound like a great idea. I mean, you were paid to have me killed."

"Paid well. But I can have you killed anytime. If you're right, then you'll be solving a problem for me, and perhaps I'll show mercy."

"You're all heart, amigo."

"Be at the bridge at midnight. If I learn I can trust you, you are in a good position."

"That's good to know. Anything else?"

"Your girl is still alive. They haven't hurt her. But she will be the first to die." The line disconnected.

Andre heard most of it. He looked at Zack. "What do you think?"

"It's either a trap and we're gonna die, or it's on the up and up and we're gonna die."

Andre snorted this time. "We've been in worse positions. I'll be on the lookout. If I think it's a trap, I'll eliminate the threat."

Darnell had crept behind them and heard most of the conversation. "How are you gonna do that? They'll see you long before you see them."

Andre smiled. He looked at his watch. "It will be plenty dark soon. I'll be leaving shortly. Listen Darnell just do as Zack says, all right?"

"Because white men have done me right all my life?"

Andre stared at him. The look told Darnell what he was thinking.

"You think I'm a racist, don't you?"

"Yep." Andre didn't hesitate. Even Zack was surprised by the quickness of the answer.

Darnell exhaled a long thoughtful, almost sorrowful breath. "Every white man in my life has discriminated against me. The police, the shitty lawyer, the judge, the jury, everyone. The world hasn't changed."

Andre shrugged. "Not much it hasn't. So what?"

"Yeah, well, he's the first goddamn white man to treat me like I'm not just another uneducated nigger. Or a drug-addicted nigger who fathers kids and leaves the mother and belongs in a gang and all that shit." He looked at Zack. "So maybe if one white man can treat me like I'm equal, then maybe I can treat that white man not as a white man, but as a man."

"That's the first thing you've said that's made sense since I got you out of jail." In the dark, he saw Darnell's hand extend. Zack grabbed it, and the two men shook.

"That's the first thing you've said that didn't want to make me put you back in jail," Andre said, and he shook Darnell's hand.

"If you want to trust those gangbangers, fine with me. I'll die alongside you. I mean, you fed me these last few days so it's the least I can do."

"The least," Zack smiled. "I don't feel like dying tonight though."

CHAPTER 42

"That's got to be Juan Carlos." Darnell pulled back the slide of the Glock. "If I as much even think he's pulling some shit, I'm shooting his ass."

Zack drove the car down the hill toward the bridge over Trail Creek. "Fine with me. Just make sure he doesn't cap me first, all right?"

He slowed the car over the bridge and stopped when the figure walked from the edge into the road. Zack could see Darnell's gun at the ready.

"This is crazy man."

"You watch the other side; I'll watch this dude. Perfect place for an ambush."

Zack kept his hand near his gun as he stopped the car. The man came closer and tapped on the window. Zack rolled it down.

"Amigos." It was Juan Carlos. Zack recognized him. He checked the car. "Put the gun away, man, my orders are specific."

"Get in."

He opened the rear door and slid into the backseat. Darnell kept an eye on him.

"Turn left at the next sign."

Juan Carlos watched the street as it passed by. He was silent until he gave a direction. Four minutes and three direction orders were given. Zack's watch illuminated. 12:10 AM.

"Stop here."

Zack did.

"I'm out. Drive ahead another block. Park and walk the rest of the way. You'll have to hop a fence. You'll see a trail that will take you to the back of the zoo. At the end of the trail, there will be another fence. Follow it to the north until you reach a gate. The combination is 32-14-7. Leave it unlocked but shut the gate. You'll be on a dirt path. Follow that path west. That will take you past the tower and up the hill. On the other side will be the animals. The path will turn into cement. Stay on the path. You will walk down the hill, and the path will become very wide where several paths come together. Stop there and wait."

Zack looked at Darnell as Juan Carlos started to exit the car.

"Wait for what? Our execution?"

"Stay in the shadows until you see the men you want. Then be careful."

"And if we get the chance to get out, let me guess, that same path is where you and your boys will be waiting for us?"

Juan Carlos closed the door and tapped on the driver's side window again. He leaned over after Zack rolled it down. "If we wanted you dead, you would be dead. Once outside the fence, don't come back this way. We'll move the car east of here, towards Stop 2, out of the city. It will be parked near the highway. But you'll have to get there on foot. It's the only safe way. The police will find you parked here if the car is left behind. Good luck, amigos."

Just like that, Juan Carlos turned and disappeared into the dark.

"This isn't good man. This has a bad feel to it. A really bad feel!"

Zack turned off the car, put the keys on the seat and got out. "Well if it gets stolen I'll let you explain it to Andre."

They looked around, walked to the sidewalk and headed towards the fence at the end of the dead-end street.

* * * * * * * *

Andre stopped the motorcycle. Becky got off the back of it and took off the helmet. She handed it to Andre.

"Just like that, I'm free to go?"

"As long as you promise not to press charges if this goes bad for us."

"What's going to happen?"

"You're going to go to your mother's house and have her call Warren. You're going to tell her you're fine and that you know nothing. There were only two men, but you only saw Darnell. You never saw me, you understand?"

"Why would I help you? You're going to harm my step-father, aren't you?"

"I'm hoping he's a reasonable man and it never gets to that. But so far Warren has been anything but reasonable. He's hiding something and probably responsible for a lot of bad things. You'd be wise to distance yourself from him as quickly as possible."

"Why won't you tell me who the naked man was?"

Andre put the helmet on and flipped up the visor. "Same reason Warren won't tell you the truth."

He revved the bike, let out the clutch and peeled off. Becky watched him disappear and then ran to the nearest phone.

* * * * * * * *

The fence rattled, but the two hopped it easily. Not much of a deterrent, Zack thought. It was dark. Clouds blocked out the stars and the moon. Messed up weather. The only thing that could make this better would be rain and storms. As if on cue, Zack noticed the wind increase.

"Can you smell that?"

"What?" Darnell sniffed.

"Wind is coming off the lake. A front is coming in. What do you think is going to happen?"

"If it involves me getting shot, I don't want to know."

Zack motioned, and the two started through the long grass and reeds and found the path. They headed towards the tower. "It's going to rain. Probably soon."

Along the shores of Lake Michigan in Indiana, what civilization and industry haven't destroyed remained live, moving dunes. Covered in tall grasses, trees that would slowly get buried by sand and either would die or fall over the dunes went deep inland where allowed. Though they were over a half mile from the lake, this area had been untouched because of the zoo, and the city owned the property.

They were trespassing, but the area they were at now was a huge spot for teenage lovers to sneak into. Getting to the tower to "make it" was considered an accomplishment to the teenagers in the city.

The dirt trail was sand as they neared the hill leading to the tower. The tower was nothing more than a miniature lighthouse, but it did have a beacon at the top, and for many years it flashed. But budgetary constraints forced the city to lock the doors and put up the fence around it.

Years later, a foundation formed, and money was raised to 'rehabilitate' the tower. It was repainted, the stairs inside leading to the top repaired and the light bulb replaced. After two years of vandalism and the constant police presence needed to prevent the tower from becoming nothing more than a beer and marijuana enjoyment place for teenagers, and later an area for local gangs to fight and cover the walls with graffiti, it was closed again.

The foundation still cared for it, but the area was closed. The street was blocked and unkempt and now was impassable. The doors were padlocked, and the police still made random sweeps of the area, but automatic arrest was the result of anyone caught there.

The wind whipped through the willow and poplars amongst the sucker growth on the hill leading up to the tower. It smelled like rain. Zack and Darnell reached the other fence.

"Damn, man. Why don't we just hop this damn fence and forget that gate?"

At first, it was a good idea to Zack. But then he thought of Julie. She was more than able to hop a fence, even with a little barbed wire atop of it. But what if she or one of them were injured? What if they were chased? Fences were obstacles. Obstacles were something they didn't need.

"No, we have to find that gate. He told us that for a reason."

"Yeah, he told us that so we could walk into an ambush!"

"Maybe," Zack conceded. "Or maybe they know more than we do."

"Of course, they do! They know exactly where we are getting killed!"

The two followed the fence for two hundred yards around the hill on uneven terrain before they found the locked gate.

"It's already unlocked."

"Check the combination." Zack looked behind them and all around despite the darkness of the night and inability to see anything.

"What? Why? How many damn gates do you think they have on this fence? We go any further, and we'll be in Michigan."

"Quit whining and check the damn combination." Zack took off his jacket, removed his shoulder holster, took his Sig out of the holder and slid it behind his back in his beltline. The extra clip held in the holster went into his underwear as he put on the jacket.

Darnell did what he was told. He locked it, used the combination and unlocked it.

"What does this mean?"

"How the hell do I know?"

Darnell scoffed. "Well, you got the answer for everything else."

"It obviously means that someone beat us to it. Why they left it unlocked is beyond me."

"I'll tell you why because after they shoot us, they're running!"

Zack tossed the shoulder holster in the grass beside the gate.

"Why are you leaving that there?"

"If they frisk us, they'll notice the gun. Most amateurs only frisk the sides, never the front or back. And I like this gun."

"We coming back for that?"

"Yes, we sure as hell are. Cost me eight hundred bucks." Zack readjusted the clip.

"You think they'll notice anything else?"

"I hope not. They're trained to shoot the heart. Keep your fingers crossed."

They opened the gate. The wind blew harder, the gate creaked. The two bent over, beneath the tops of the five-foot-tall grasses. Zack heard thunder rumbling in the distance.

They continued on the path. It wound and bent, always going up and then straightened, passed the tower and headed down. The trees got taller; any light from the city lights reflecting off the low cloud cover was lost in the canopy of the trees. The wind gusts steadied. There was definitely a storm coming, and they couldn't see in front of them more than a couple of feet.

"Just be quiet and remember if Warren talks to us to not use my name or your name or Julie's name. You got it?"

"Yeah, I got it."

"And remember, if we get the chance on the way out of here, just freaking run."

"Yeah, I got it." Darnell sounded a little discouraged. "I'm not an idiot."

They entered the trees along the paths. They were thick with mature hardwoods, and saplings covered the forest floor. The zoo staff did not do much to maintain the premises outside the flower plantings and what was around and inside the cages.

Moments later they got back on the path took a few steps and stopped. They were there. They were waiting. The question was who was they? Warren and his dirty brigade or Alejandro and his soldiers? He looked at his watch. It was almost two o'clock.

He stepped forward, passed the end of the protection by the trees. A gust of wind whipped by him and the stench of animal manure blew past. They were at the zoo. Julie was there. Somewhere. He knew it.

He stepped again. Darnell followed him and moved to his right. He stepped further away from Zack. They both stepped again and were six feet into the path that widened out to a seating area, like a patio. There was a cage to the left, on the side of the hill. Whatever inhabited that was sleeping or inside. Another animal enclosure was directly in front of them on the other side of the patio, and another to the left was lower on the hill and protected by a tall fence. Snorts, soft growls, an occasional scream from a monkey or bird and a hoot of an owl along with the wind and the approaching storm filled the air.

Zack knew he was being watched. He turned and could see the top of the tower. He looked at his watch. The journey had taken them longer than expected. It was time to wait.

CHAPTER 43

The hair stood on the back of Zack's neck. He heard footsteps behind and to the side of him from paths alongside the one he and Darnell came.

"That's far enough," the two heard. The voice was ahead of them.

"I wish I could say welcome back, Davey."

Zack had nightmares with that voice in it ever since the .38 was pressed against his forehead so many years before. Zack knew it was just time before Warren would figure out his identity. It was a risk he knew was stupid. If this didn't end right, Zack was about to ruin the lives of everyone he cared about. But he wanted Warren to know he wasn't that scared little teenager anymore. He wasn't afraid of Warren at all. "I bet you do."

Warren laughed, but Zack could not see him. He didn't want to turn around to see the men behind him, but he knew there were at least four.

"Where is she?" Zack's eyes adjusted as much as they were going to in the dark. He still couldn't see anything.

"Calm down, stepson, let's get reacquainted."

"I'm not your stepson, and I want to see her now."

"Or what?" Warren laughed again.

301

"You really think I came here without a backup plan? You think I was dumb enough to walk right into your trap without some insurance?"

"Yeah, I do."

"That makes you the dumb one, Warren."

Warren ignored the comment. A large outline of a figure appeared in the dark but stopped before coming into the opening. Distant amber lights down the paths gave a faint enough glow, but just not enough. *Where the hell is Julie?*

"So where have you been all these years? We figured you for dead."

"Sorry to disappoint. Where is she?"

"In due time. I want to talk to you. Find out what you've been up to. All that fun stuff a step-dad is supposed to give a shit about."

"Show me her right now."

"You don't get it, do you? You have no bargaining chip. You lost. Now answer my questions. Search him."

Before either Zack or Darnell could react, two hands were on both of them. Darnell was shocked when they frisked him exactly like Zack said they would. They missed his gun, which was in his beltline in front of him. They only touched the sides.

The man frisking Zack came close up his leg.

"Hey, watch it, pervert. That's my dick."

"They're clean."

Warren stepped closer to Zack. "You know, I had no idea who I was dealing with until you made the comment on the phone about killing Staechel family members and adding to the list. I knew right then it was you who came back. Why?"

Zack wasn't sure if time was an ally or not here, but he decided to indulge Warren. "To save the life of an innocent man, you know, the man you wrongfully imprisoned."

"Innocent my ass!"

"You know damn well I didn't do it!" Darnell snapped. "You framed me, and your dirty cops planted those drugs on me! You kill my uncle too?"

"Shut up, Whittaker." Warren raised his gun. "I'm not talking to you."

In the dim light from the amber bulbs around the zoo, Darnell saw Zack shake his head at Darnell. He was saying be quiet. Darnell relented.

"You shouldn't have come back, Davey," Warren lowered his gun and looked back at Zack.

"How did you do it? How did you get away with murder?"

Warren laughed. "You know, your mother was worried about you at first. She asked me to search for you, so I did. I just wanted her happy and knowing you were either dead or alive would have made her happy. But just disappearing like that was downright cowardly and cruel to your mother."

"You pointed that .38 at my head. My only other choice was dying. So, tell me, was it the same .38 you used on my dad's head?"

Warren laughed again. "You think because you're going to die that somehow you'll get me to confess? This isn't the movies, boy. You messed up. Tell me where you've been. Baltimore is it? How did you start a new life there?"

"Was my mother in on it, too? You two were having an affair. Surprised I didn't realize it as often as I saw you around her. How long were you having the affair before you two plotted to kill him?"

"Darnell Whittaker killed your old man. The evidence proved it."

"You mean the lack of evidence in the police file that was doctored for the trial? Yeah, Warren, I saw it. We have a copy. Got it off your computer." Zack laughed. "You dumbass. Why the hell would you store it on your hard drive? Anyway, you gave his lawyer the doctored one, but we have the real one. All that evidence was planted. Did you have help?"

Warren hesitated. Zack sensed it. "You're a convincing liar, but there is no such thing."

"I suppose you can't admit that the case that launched your career was a fraud in front of your band of blind followers, can you?" Zack bated him, but Warren wasn't biting.

Warren laughed and changed the direction. "You have a pretty good personnel file. I was amazed when I saw it. Is that all real, or did you have that faked like your identity?"

"It's real. Now, where is Julie? I held up my end of the bargain, now hold up yours."

"I want to know what I'm bargaining for. You claim you have a fake police file that what? Does it prove my guilt?"

"It proves Darnell didn't do it. There were no footprints to his house; there were no bloody shoe prints, there was nothing. That was all staged. But right now, Warren, I don't give a shit about that. I just want my girlfriend back. You give me the girl and let us out of here. When I feel we're safe, I'll turn it all over to you."

"And then what, Davey?"

"That isn't my name. And then you leave us the hell alone and forget we were ever here. The charges get dropped on Darnell, and if you want to continue your dirty, illegal ways, I don't give a Goddamn, but it ends for us tonight."

Darnell looked at Zack, taken aback that his name was mentioned. He mumbled to himself, "we said no names."

Warren laughed. "You certainly have more guts than you did the last time I saw you."

"I've faced down bigger men than you with bigger guns since then, Warren. Did you tell my mother that you threatened to kill me if I didn't shut my mouth and leave town? When she was supposedly so worried about me, did you explain to her that I had to be shut up or you two would end up in jail for murdering my dad? Did you ever tell her that?"

Warren silenced and stared at Zack.

"Now give me my girlfriend you lying sonofabitch."

Even in the dark, Zack could tell Warren was angry. He motioned with his left arm and two men holding Julie dragged her out of the darkness, so Zack could see her.

They held her arms behind her back; one man covered her mouth while his other arm was around her neck. They held a gun to her side. A small flash of lightning showed Zack that she was Ok. Her eyes were on him. She begged him with her eyes to get out of there. He saw it clearly. He felt like crying but hid it.

"Let her go."

"No. We're going to talk more."

"I don't have time."

Warren raised his gun. "Yes, you do." He laughed. "This girlfriend of yours is a feisty one. I'm guessing she bosses you around, doesn't she?" Two men appeared at Warren's left. "I remember the look in your eyes when I held that gun to your head. I swear you were going to piss your pants." Warren laughed as did his men.

"Ok, Warren. You want to talk, tell me what really happened. Tell me how you killed Frank Staechel."

Warren lowered his gun. "Your mother and I were having an affair for a couple of years. Started before your old man lost his job at the mill. Fine woman, she is. Too damn good for Frank. It was never about the two-million-dollar life insurance policy, though that made life nice." He added a laugh.

"The insurance policy you forged when you started plotting the death of Frank? That's a nice nest egg you and Louise would get. How much did you have to pay off the insurance agent? How many other people did you have to pay off?"

Warren ignored his comments. "But he wouldn't give her a divorce. All he needed was a little time, and he was going to show her he could provide for her. He said it with such passion, too. I think your mother would have stayed with him."

"But you killed him."

Warren hesitated. "I was never sure if she loved Frank, or she just stayed because of her children. She still has a giant footlocker in the basement of my house with all his worthless shit. Your brothers and sisters don't want it. Why don't you stop by the house and I'll give it to you?"

Zack chuckled. "Somehow I don't think that is going to happen."

"I'm sure the family reunion would be fun."

"Right up to the point where you frame me for my dad's murder and destroy the lives of everyone around me? Not gonna happen, Warren. Release Julie, I give you my shit on you, I disappear, and you never mention my name again."

"Or what?"

"Or I expose you for the fraudulent crook you and your band of idiots are, and you lose everything, including my mother and end up being sodomized in prison by the people I'm sure you wrongly stuck in there. That's or what."

Warren laughed. "I should kill you know." There was silence. "But I won't because you're bluffing. What else do you think you have?"

"Did you have the reporter that was asking questions killed, too? Is that how it all started? First my dad, then you had to clean it all up?"

"The reporter?" Warren laughed. "You did your research."

"You had Darnell's lawyer killed, too. Was it the same drug?"

"Science can be both our friend and our enemy."

"Yeah, especially when your partner at the time of the murder you committed is now running the state forensics lab, so it makes it easier to lose a tissue and blood sample from the deceased lawyer, doesn't it?"

"The United States Postal System makes mistakes. Sometimes they misplace packages."

"Then you had your men beat up Reverend Whittaker, hoped you could pin it on someone until Julie showed up, luckily for you he died at the hospital or did your men sneak in and finish him off there?"

"He was an old, pitiful man holding up progress."

"And then you had the church burned down. All you have to do is get rid of Darnell, and the city can claim the land and no more obstacles to your Ventures Unlimited scheme. Is this your last payoff before retirement or just another one? And do you plan on stealing the money like in Vegas and Atlantic City or actually plan to redevelop that part of town?" Zack's conversation with Michelle filled him in with some details. Warren tensed, Zack saw it even as the wind blew harder, rumbles of thunder increased, and the light flickered as the branches on the trees swayed in front of the lights.

"I don't know anything about whatever this Ventures Unlimited you mention is."

Zack laughed a mocking laugh. "Come on, Warren. It took some digging, but the paperwork is there. You may be silent, but you're the force behind it. How much did you pocket after you bilked Atlantic City out of millions for a development that never happened? How much from Vegas? I couldn't see the amount in your offshore accounts, but it has to be huge by now. And now you are about to have the part of town you call the Triangle condemned and razed so Ventures Unlimited can come in, get a bunch of government money, doze some stuff and run off with the rest of the money? Is that the plan, Warren? It certainly has been the MO everywhere else."

"Davey, you're so stupid, you know that?" Warren laughed. "I don't know where you think you got any of the information, but I know none of it was obtained legally."

"Let Julie go, let us get out of here, and I don't care if you doze the whole damn town. You can keep your dirty little guild running strong, but it's over for Darnell, myself, Julie and anyone else you think is connected to me tonight."

Warren laughed even louder. "Boy, you sure do have a set of balls on you! Goddamn, your mother and sister used to laugh about how naïve you are!"

"Who killed Frank Staechel?"

"Some secrets will never be learned, Davey. It's a mystery."

"You know who killed Frank Staechel, you covered up the evidence, planted enough evidence to convict Darnell and paid off the lawyers so they'd all be quiet. Then you and Louise started a new life with the insurance money that you collected off the fake policy you forged. And you paid off the insurance agent too. And this is how you got your start and became the dirtiest police chief in this city's history." Zack wished someone was recording all of the conversation but knew it wasn't. The storm blew closer.

Warren stepped forward and the gun raised at Zack. "This city needed me and my men. It's clean now. It's safe now. People know their place, and how things work, and nothing goes on without us knowing about it."

"And that includes sending an innocent man to prison?" Darnell stepped forward. Warren pointed his gun at him.

"Easy nigger."

"Why Darnell? Why did you frame him?" Zack grabbed Darnell's arm.

"After you showed up because you're so goddamn irresponsible, we had to re-think our plan. Suicide wouldn't work. The funny thing was that your mom said that. We wouldn't get the money if Frank killed himself. So, I had to stage it to look like a burglary and a homicide. The only thing was that I had to find a scapegoat to close the case or someone might ask the wrong questions and find us out. I couldn't let that happen."

"You sonofabitch." Darnell snapped.

"Darnell had no alibi, he's black, and a white man was killed. Slam dunk case."

"That was seventeen years of my life!"

"What kind of a life would you have had? Probably ended up in a gang, on drugs, dead by twenty-nine or earlier like your piece of shit brother. On welfare, making babies and not supporting them. A drain on society! I did you a favor. You should be lucky you weren't given the death penalty. We asked for it, but they said you were too young."

Darnell moved, but Zack stopped him when Warren raised his gun higher.

"What do you think you're gonna do," Warren paused, "nigger?"

"You racist mother..." Before Darnell finished the sentence, the gun fired. The bullet drove Darnell off his feet, and he landed in the shrubs behind them. Zack looked but only saw Darnell's motionless feet. The rest of him was hidden by the pitch-black night.

"Now just calm down, Davey. Don't make me shoot you. I really don't want to have to tell your mother you're dead because I shot you."

Zack remembered what he was doing. He thought of Andre. Julie looked terrified. "And when I figured out it was wrong, that's when you turned on me." Zack wanted everyone to hear it, especially Julie. Validation.

"Yeah, that's right. You were the only one who could have said anything to put the story into question. Well, and that damn reporter. And you played along perfectly without knowing it." Warren laughed. It reminded Zack of the Joker's laugh in the Batman movie. "You acted so tough and defiant. Your mother knew you would run. We would never have guessed you would go east. We figured you'd head to California. Maybe try to find your uncle and cousins out there. We figured you'd never come back. You had nothing. No proof. Just the word of a scared, cowardly, grieving seventeen-year-old whose friend killed his dad. No one would have believed you. Honestly, the over/under on your death was six months. Your sister will win the pool once I tell her."

Zack stared at Warren disgusted, enraged and tired. "No one will believe that I'm alive because you are going to let her go and we'll be on our way."

"No, you won't."

Zack took a deep breath. "Warren, you're a coward of a man, hiding behind a badge and a gun. You can't see past the color of a person's skin because why? I'll tell you why. Because you're a small, ignorant man. You make me sick. You ruined a man's life to make a career for yourself. You helped kill a man; you KILLED MY FATHER, for what? So, you could win my mom? You're a pig. A goddamn pig! You aren't worth shit! Do you know that?"

Warren raised his gun.

"Go ahead and shoot me! Your life is over, you piece of shit!"

Warren cocked the gun, but they heard a whistle, and he stopped.

"I wouldn't do that if I were you, hombre." Alejandro appeared from the path behind Zack surrounded by several of his soldiers. "You offered me a payment to do that. I wouldn't be happy if I came all the way here to find you did my job for me."

Warren lowered his gun. "You're supposed to wait and get them on the way out."

Alejandro laughed. "I don't think so, amigo. I started thinking that maybe I should come earlier to get my money. I think this place will be surrounded by police. That would not work well in your plan for me. Where is my money?"

"I'm good for it. You know that."

Zack stepped backward very little. He had to see if Darnell was still alive. The four men around them moved to the side. Lightning flashed, and Zack saw metal everywhere. If a shootout started, he was not in a good spot. And Julie was still helpless.

"You said it would be here with you. I would like my money now, Chief of Police, por favor."

Warren nodded. A man appeared from the dark with a briefcase. He put it on the ground and slid it to the center of the patio. Alejandro motioned, and Pablo walked from behind him, grabbed the case without ever taking his eyes off the dirty cops and walked back to Alejandro. They opened it. Alejandro fingered through the stacks of cash.

"Muchos gracias. It is all here. Now I have some questions for you, senor."

"You have your money. Now let me finish my deal and then you finish your end of the bargain."

Alejandro chuckled. "I think I want more money."

"What? We agreed. Forget it."

"I don't see it that way, amigo. You see, someone pointed out to me that fifty-grand is not very much for a contract killing. It should be much higher. Especially for three killings when they have a secret on you." Alejandro looked at Zack. "What do you think it should be?"

"I'd say a minimum hundred a piece." Zack offered his opinion.

Warren laughed. "These three aren't worth half of what I gave you, and I already killed one!"

"That may be true, senor. But if what they say is true, I will need a lot of money to get out of here safely. I have a big family, amigo. So, tell me, Mr. Chief of Police. Is what they say true? Are you going to turn on me as soon as they are dead?"

"I don't know what you're talking about."

"I think you do, perro. Now tell me the truth, por favor."

Andy Gruse
STACKED CASE

CHAPTER 44

Zack surveyed the area. He had calculated the risks and rewards of every action he could think of. The one thing he couldn't do though was risk Julie's life. She seemed calm when he looked at her. Her eyes were on him. Zack could see her stare. She didn't blink. The man holding her seemed to relax his grip. He took his hand off her mouth, but she didn't make a sound.

She moved her lips. She was mouthing "I'm sorry" to him. He didn't want to see that. It made him feel worse. He wanted to react and charge but couldn't. He had to stay in control despite his heart pounding and racing.

"Who did the church, Mr. Police Officer? It wasn't us."

Warren smiled. "Yes, it was. Your gang did the church. That's what we agreed upon."

"It burned down yesterday. Are you trying to put that on us?"

"A deal is a deal."

"And you killed the minister and are blaming that on us?"

"You got paid well, Diablo."

"NO! I don't think so! We are not in business with you so that you can set us up and make us run from the neighborhood you let us have. That is our home. It is safe over there because of us. Your police never enter the neighborhood unless you need us to do something for you. And now you are going to take it from us, so you can make a casino and a hotel? I don't think so, man."

"Look, Diablo, you knew all along there was a plan, and as long as you've were paid well, you went along with it. Why the change? Because those two told you some lies?"

"Lies?" Alejandro looked at Zack. "Did you tell me lies amigo?"

Zack answered. "No."

"He says that they are. Why should I believe you?"

"What do I gain by lying?"

"Maybe your life, hombre."

Zack chuckled. "You really think he is planning on me being alive after tonight? He's paying you to kill me. I gain nothing. But don't trust me." Zack pointed at Julie. "She investigates for a living. She has no reason to lie to you."

"Maybe to keep herself alive."

"Her and I are a package deal. So, considering the circumstances here, staying alive doesn't seem like a viable option."

"No, it doesn't." Alejandro looked at Julie. "Is he lying to me? Should I kill him?"

"No, he's not lying, and no, you shouldn't kill him."

"SHUT HER UP!" Warren yelled. "We have a deal; you got your money, now let me do my job, and you do yours!"

"Did you burn the church and kill the minister?"

"YES! WE BURNED DOWN THE GODDAMN CHURCH AND KILLED THE OLD MAN! NOW LET ME DO MY JOB, AND YOU DO WHAT I PAID YOU FOR!"

The two men yelled back and forth. Zack saw Warren's gun rise. Alejandro's men all raised their guns.

Zack slowly moved his hand to behind his back.

"You aren't my fight, Diablo. He is! That coward loser right there!" Warren pointed his handgun at Zack.

"Coward? I'm not surrounded by thugs that do my dirty work. You're the coward, Warren. If Louise could see you now, she'd know that you were never even half the man Frank Staechel was!"

"Sorry, Diablo. I'm killing him myself."

Julie bit the hand of the man holding her, slammed her head back, broke the man's nose and kicked his shins. The man yelped, let her go and Julie dodged for the black brush beside the path.

"GET HER!"

Zack grabbed his gun and swung it in front of him. Warren fired his gun twice. Zack saw both flashes from Warren's gun. Julie screamed. Gunfire erupted from every direction. Thunder cracked as the men dodged for cover. One of Diablo's men hit the ground as did one of Warren's.

The slugs slammed into his chest, and Zack hit the ground on his back with a thud. A man chased Julie but was met by a .50 caliber shell. Another whir screamed through the air, and the other man near Julie died via gunshot.

The gunfire continued. Julie heard someone yell to get her. She ran but not before peaking one last time at Zack. He was motionless on the ground. She heard Warren yell that there was a sniper. She didn't wait. She disappeared into the darkness, and then it was silent. She didn't realize it, but all of Diablo's men vanished as soon as the gunfire started.

317

Andy Gruse
STACKED CASE

CHAPTER **45**

Zack felt a hand grab his shoulder as the pain in his chest kept him from breathing. He felt a tug, his eyes opened, and he realized that he was alive and that it was silent. He moved, then two hands grabbed him, and he got off his back.

Zack stumbled into a hedgerow and fell behind a tree in the darkness as three gunshots fired, ricocheted and echoed. Then it was silent.

Darnell poked at Zack's chest. "You alright, man?"

Zack struggled to breathe. Darnell shook him and asked again.

"No," Zack choked. "I'm not alright! I got shot!"

"So did I."

"You all right?"

"Yeah, I'm fine. He almost missed me. I felt it brush past the vest and knew it would be better if I acted like it was a direct hit and played dead. Remind me to thank that partner of yours for sending the vests."

"You didn't even get shot?"

"Not really. You?"

Zack grimaced. "I GOT SHOT TWICE!"

"Shut up man; they'll hear us, and you were wearing a vest!"

"I don't care. It still hurts." Zack fumbled with his clothes. "Get this damn thing off me."

"Dude, you're going to need it again."

"I can feel the bullets against my chest, get it off!"

The crack and pop of semi-automatic gunfire filled the night air again as bullets hit the trees and shrubs around the two. They ducked to the ground and scurried away. They found another quiet refuge in the dark about thirty feet away and leaned against the trunk of a giant White Oak tree. Zack finally ripped the vest from his body, but now only wore a tee shirt.

"Now what?"

"I'm going for Julie. I have to find her." Zack looked around. The wind whipped through the trees faster, lightning flashed, and thunder cracked. Another flash of lightning lit up the area. He saw two men, guns in front of them, approaching. All four men fired as Darnell and Zack dodged again. Zack fired several rounds and saw both men drop to the ground. He didn't know if they were dead, but he wasn't going to ask them.

"I'm going for that damn pig. I got a score to settle," Darnell said.

Zack grabbed his arm. "Hey, be careful, man. Don't do anything stupid, you hear me?"

"You're the stupid one for removing your vest!"

"Touché."

The two men stared at each other and then flashed small smiles. "I'll meet you at the gate in ten minutes. Grab the gear."

"Just make sure your woman is with you."

"If I'm not back, you get out of here. You know where the car is going to be, head in that direction."

Darnell disappeared into the darkness.

The soreness was real. He was going to bruise; in fact, two deep bruises. Every contraction and expansion of his lungs hurt. Each beat of his heart pained him. Moving hurt. His left shoulder was going to be sore, and it already was. The low rumble from the sky erupted into a full-blown blast that rattled the ground beneath his feet. A second later, the rain came down. It came down hard and fast, and if the darkness wasn't blinding enough, the rain was.

Lightning ripped across the sky. Another loud crack and boom deafened the ears. Zack ducked. He saw a shadow dodge across a path. He pointed but did not fire. Zack wasn't sure who was who in the rain and darkness.

He moved through the trees until he reached the path and hopped over the short fence. Where was Julie? And were they waiting for him? Only one way to find out. He knew which direction he had to go and ran down the path, across the patio and jumped into the same bushes Julie had hidden as bullets fired again.

The thorns of the rose bushes tore into him and ripped his shirt. He cursed and fought his way through them. He saw a man raise and point. Zack pointed to fire, his gun clicked, he was empty. The man smiled and pointed, but suddenly a burst of blood and skull exploded from his head and covered the patio as the lifeless body collapsed to the ground.

"Thank you, Andre," Zack whispered. He dug the spare clip from his shorts and reloaded his gun. He took a deep breath. His pulse raced, his heart pounded, the pain was pushed away by the surge of adrenaline. He had been in combat before. Pinned before. But this was different: Julie was out there. He struggled to control his emotions and knew he had to find her.

The rain intensified. Thunder and lightning boomed and streaked across the sky.

It was silent outside the storm. Then he heard Warren.

"Call him!"

It came from his left, down the hill. He looked around. He ran straight and turned to the right. He passed in front of a large cage, in the dark he couldn't tell what animals there were, but the storm chased them all inside their enclosures. The path circled the enclosure. He followed it.

A gun fired. Sparks flew off the cage behind him. He could feel bits of hot metal landing on his skin. He heard screaming from what must have been monkeys. He ran and fired in that direction.

More gunshot rang out. But it stopped. Zack saw Darnell pointing the gun and disappear into the darkness.

Zack thought he heard a muffled sound. Someone was right around the corner. He sneaked forward and saw Julie held by Warren who had a gun to her head.

"Call for him! DO IT!"

CHAPTER 46

Warren didn't see Zack. His back was to Zack. The gun held loosely to her head. Darnell came from the opposite direction. Zack's mind raced. Water poured off his face and half blinded his eyes. A flash of lightning caused Warren to duck.

"Call him now, or you'll be dead right here bitch!"

"Screw you."

That damn spunk of hers is going to get her killed! Damn it, Julie! Zack moved across the path, hid behind a large planter and light fixture and crept along the fence behind him. *Come on lightning. Crack for me!*

Lightning flashed, brightened the area and disappeared. Zack readied. The thunder boomed atop of them, and another flash of lightning cracked, hit a tree and exploded part of the tree.

Warren ducked, and Zack leaped from the darkness. He knocked the gun away from Julie as Warren's hand squeezed the trigger, the bullet flying harmlessly away. The two crashed to the ground.

"ZACK!"

Zack rolled to his feet and yelled at Julie. "Get out of here! Go now! Darnell, out the back."

Warren tackled Zack, and they smashed to the ground. The rough brick surface tore through Zack's shirt. They rolled. Zack felt Warren's hand grab his face. Zack slammed his elbow into Warren's gut, grabbed his wrist and bent back his hand. Warren let go, and Zack rolled away. He got to his feet.

Warren got up. "So now what, hotshot? You going to kill me, the Chief of Police?" He laughed with balled fists. He swung at Zack.

Zack ducked and punched Warren in the stomach and the side of the head. The big man wouldn't go down.

Warren slapped his arm backward, Zack couldn't see it in the dark, and the fist hit the bottom of Zack's jaw. He fell backward, and Warren came at him.

"I'm going to finally finish what I should have done all those years ago."

"Not likely."

Fists clenched, rage in his eyes, spit flying from his lips, Warren hunched over. He punched Zack in the stomach, then the chest and the side of his face. Zack hit the ground. Warren stood over Zack. Zack moved, but Warren kicked Zack in the chest. Zack couldn't breathe. He clutched his chest, curled on the ground and gasped for breath. Warren looked around and rested his hands on his hips.

"You're supposed to be dead." Warren's voice was barely audible to Zack over the rain and wind.

Zack struggled to regain his breath; he was sure his heart had stopped.

"You left town like the coward you are which was the right decision. Your mother didn't want me to kill you, just for you to keep your damn mouth shut. We realized you had to go. You were always too naïve, too righteous, too Goddamn doo-goody for me. I knew you couldn't be trusted."

Zack felt his life slipping away. Warren turned and kicked him in the chest again. As much as it hurt, as much as Zack was sure his sternum was cracked, he felt life again. He coughed but still could barely move.

"But you left, right on cue. And poor Darnell, your little nigger friend was left holding the blame. See, if you hadn't come home, none of that would have happened. If you weren't so Goddamn irresponsible, Darnell would never have served time."

Zack bid his time and waited for the right moment to strike and hoped Warren wouldn't kick him again.

"After you disappeared your poor mother worried sick about you. That much was true despite her knowing you had to go. Where you went, how you were surviving and all that crap. We expected you to be found dead in a ditch. As worthless as you were, there was no way you were going to survive on the streets. Then, the lawyer was going to re-open the case, you were going to be blamed as a person of interest, the nigger exonerated, and no one is serving time. So, you ruined his life twice, Davey."

Zack coughed. "So, you did it for the money?"

"Maybe he killed himself. Did you ever think of that?"

"He wouldn't do that! He loved us; he would never have done that!"

"He was a big a piece of shit as you are! A bigger coward! He couldn't take care of his wife, his family or anything! He deserved to die!"

"No, he didn't. He was as innocent as Darnell."

"You're still so naïve. Do you think your father would have amounted to anything other than a burnt out drunk? Darnell had no life in front of him. Do you remember what it was like back then? There were no jobs. Drugs and crime were controlling everything this side of town. You were living on the edge of it. I met your mother after your bike was stolen. Your third bike was stolen! Remember that? So goddamned irresponsible. You never leave it outside, not where you lived! So really, Davey, you are the reason I met your mother, the reason we fell in love, the reason your dad is dead, and the reason Darnell ended up in prison and why you both are going to die tonight."

"Sorry to disappoint you, asshole, but I'm not dying tonight."

Zack lunged for Warren who quickly knocked Zack in the side of the head. Zack sprawled on the concrete. The rain beat harder. Zack thought he heard sirens, but it could have just been ringing in his head.

"Yes, you are."

Warren reached for Zack, but Zack kicked his knee. Warren stumbled, and Zack kicked Warren's face. Warren fell backward but still on his feet. He watched Zack struggle to get off the ground. Warren reached for his sock.

His backup piece! SHIT! Warren grabbed it, and Zack charged. He lowered his shoulder, slammed into Warren's chest. The backup piece fired. Zack felt the searing heat in his calf.

Zack yelled and charged. They slammed into the short fence. With every bit of energy, he had left he lifted and threw Warren over the fence. Warren disappeared into the night and dropped into the animal enclosure below.

Zack fell to the ground, out of breath. The rain covered him. He heard Darnell's voice. "Come on, man!"

He got to his feet and heard the cops. The pain in his leg buckled him; he fell again and grabbed it. He got lucky, no bone, but it hurt. He heard sirens and was sure the sound was sirens from more police.

"Oh good, the police are here," he deadpanned to no one. He heard animals stirring. He limped across the patio. The briefcase was still there. He picked it up and headed up the path and saw Alejandro. Zack stopped.

"Uh-oh."

Alejandro stared at Zack, nodded and lifted a hand. There was no gun. He gave a simple thumb's up sign, turned and disappeared into the darkness. Zack made his way up a different path and out of the zoo.

He reached the fence. The gate was locked. "Seriously?" He struggled over it and hit the ground hard. The shoulder holster was gone. Zack limped down the path, through the tall grasses, and down the hill. The trail was slippery, and Zack hit the ground and slid. He got to his feet only to stumble on a clump of grass and fall head first onto the trail and slide down even further.

Finally, he reached the bottom, grabbed the briefcase and tossed it over the second fence. He grabbed it, tried to climb it but faltered. He hit the ground once. His second try was successful. He hit the other side of the fence on his back. The air escaped his lungs again.

"Zack! Over here!" He heard Julie's voice coming from between two houses in the dark. He got off the ground; his breath labored; Julie raced from the darkness and leaped on him. Arms around his neck, legs around his waist, they hit the road like a sack of cement.

327

"Oh my God! Are you all right? Did you get shot? Oh, Zack, I'm so sorry. Please, say something!"

"Get off me!" He coughed and pushed her off.

"What? Are you hurt?"

He coughed again, rolled to his side and didn't know what part that hurt to hold.

They heard more sirens in the distance.

Darnell appeared. "Come on, man. Get your ass off the ground. We got to go, and we got to go now! They know we went out the back and they're looking for us."

Darnell grabbed Zack's arm and helped pull him off the street.

"Where's your boy, Dre?"

"I don't know." Zack coughed, pain overtaking his senses. "Take this." He shoved the briefcase into Darnell's hand. "Just run."

"Come on, man. Just push it! Come on; we got to go!"

"Zack, please!" Julie tugged his arm. "We have to get out of here."

They saw the same bridge ahead of them that they had met Juan Carlos. "Zack, we're going the wrong way. The gang dude told us not to come back this way."

Zack saw flashing lights from the other side of the river. "Shit, more police."

"But we aren't the guilty ones." Julie recognized his sarcasm. "Maybe those are the good cops?"

"Yeah, well, guess what? Once we're dead, they'll change the questions to get the answers they wanted all along. We shot cops up there."

"But they were bad cops!" Julie said.

"If they're all bad, are they really bad?"

"Zack, we need help!"

They approached the bridge. A park was on their left, businesses on their right.

The flashing lights of the police cruisers turned onto the road. The rain poured and covered the streets.

"Now what?"

"RUN!"

Andy Gruse
STACKED CASE

CHAPTER 47

Zack pulled Julie into Trail Creek when he jumped. They immediately felt the pull of the current. Darnell wasn't as fast. He darted into the park with the case. The cruisers saw the two had jumped into the creek, but they didn't see Darnell.

Darnell raced across the park, hit the tree line and looked but the two cop cars had stopped: one on the bridge and the other just past it. They called for backup. Darnell knew from the stories in prison that when a cop was shot, every cop would respond. If a brother were shot in a domestic dispute, only the nearest on-duty cops would respond. He knew the county, and state Five-O's would be in the city shortly. Even if they could get to that car, it was doubtful they could get anywhere.

But it was their only chance. If they spotted him, a black fugitive on the run, they would definitely shoot him first. He wondered what happened to Andre. Finding that car was his only chance to get out of there alive.

Darnell watched for a few more seconds. He heard more sirens approach and then turned and ran along the creek. He'd have to find a place to cross later. Now, he had to get out of that area.

* * * * * * * *

Zack kept one hand on Julie's arm as the creek pulled them towards the lake. The black of the night and the storm worked to their advantage. But in minutes, Zack knew there would no place to hide, and the stormy lake would not provide them safety.

"Come on, we have to swim across," he said to Julie, and the two kicked to swim across though Zack only had use of one fully functioning leg.

The creek bent, and the current pushed the two into the bend, but there was no shore. It was all man-made structure to keep the banks secure for the boating slips and the businesses alongside the creek.

"How are we going to get out of here?"

"I don't know," Zack responded. "Stay with me."

The water lapped off his face, his leg tired. The other leg cramped and refused to cooperate with his wishes. His chest hurt and tightened, and the struggle to move his arms exhausted him.

"You're not going to lose me, baby. Trust me."

"Grab the wall."

The metal wall rose three feet higher than the water level. Zack could no longer see the bridge around the bend in the creek. He couldn't see the sirens or hear the commotion. Nor did he know that almost the entire city police force was converging on the area.

"I can't reach it," Julie moaned. "It's too high."

"Bullshit." Zack moved behind her. "Now jump."

She kicked with her legs and reached high. Zack lifted her. She reached it and pulled herself out of the water. The forces and weight of the water fought against her.

Zack struggled but with all his strength grabbed her legs and tossed her out of the water. She climbed over the wall and rested on the grassy bank. "Zack, come on."

She crawled to her stomach and looked over the wall. "Zack! Zack!"

He was gone. She got to her feet and ran alongside the wall. She saw nothing. She thought of diving back into the water. She moved further down. "Zack!"

She heard a splash, and he appeared. "Shut up!"

He struggled to stay afloat.

"Baby, grab my hand! Come on, please!"

She reached, and he grabbed it, but he knew he couldn't get out of that water with just her help. The water rose and the current quickened. "Get out of here, Jules. Now."

"No, I can't leave you! Come on; we can get you out."

"NO!" He snapped, and his head went under. He emerged and coughed. "Go! Get out of here. I'll find you."

"NO! ZACHARY! NO!"

He slipped under one last time, and he was gone. But she wasn't going to lose him that way. She jumped in after him.

* * * * * * * *

Slipping across the roads, down alleys, between houses and staying out of sight was easier than he hoped. He saw cop cars race down streets, lights flash, and sometimes the sirens bellowed, but they didn't see him. He entered the triangle and knew where he was but didn't know how to get to that car. He assumed Andre had gotten out of there on the motorcycle. He didn't know what happened to Zack and Julie, but he figured Zack would keep his woman safe and even though he had been shot at least three times that he saw, he wasn't about to quit or get caught. Darnell just needed to get out of town.

The block where the Church had been burned down was still barricaded and closed. He crossed the barricades and walked down the block. A cop car raced through the intersection. Its spotlight made a haphazard search of the street. He ducked behind the porch of an abandoned house and waited and realized the irony of being black was helping him hide. He waited and then moved down the street again. He was calmer than he should have been, he thought, but again realized what he had already been through was worse than anything about to happen. Even if they killed him. The rain had stopped to nothing more than a light rain now, the thunder and lightning in the distance. Or was more coming? He had to get out of there. Where the hell was Andre?

Then he ran. He didn't want to get caught, fear won over his emotions, and he ran as fast as he could. It felt like his lungs were going to explode. He couldn't keep going, but he couldn't stop. Suddenly a car skidded to a halt beside him. The door opened. He recognized the voice.

"Dude! Get in the car!" He recognized Andre's face and smiled. "Dude quit your damn smiling and get in the damn car!"

Darnell jumped into the car and threw the money-filled briefcase in the backseat. The door slammed, and the car raced away.

"Where the hell is Zack?"

Darnell shook his head. "I don't know. Julie is with him. The cops came down the road. I went to one side, and they went to the other.

I think they jumped into the river. I'm not sure. He yelled run, and I ran!"

"Jules is with him, you sure?

"I think so." Darnell fought for breath.

"DUCK!"

A cop car turned the corner and raced past.

"We got to get out of here." Andre looked both ways on the street.

"Where to?"

Andre accelerated. "I don't know. But we need to get out of this town before it's shut down."

"But what about Zack?"

Andre knew this could happen. So, did Zack. Never wanted to leave a man behind, but for the good of the whole, sometimes a part had to be sacrificed. "He'll be ok. He's got Julie with him. That makes him stronger. He knows my cell number. He'll call when he's safe."

They were silent the rest of the way. Andre drove with no headlights, aware of everything. He stayed on the back roads and got out of town without hitting a highway. It was the most difficult thing he ever had to do: he didn't want to leave Zack and Julie behind.

Andy Gruse
STACKED CASE

CHAPTER 48

Zack didn't know how far the river pushed him towards the lake. He was disoriented due to the cold, the exhaustion, the beating he took and now another storm.

He swam with the current, fighting to keep close to the shore as long as he could. He went under a couple of bridges. Then the current pushed him right into a docked boat. He fought to the back, grabbed the ladder, wrapped his arm around it and finally took a breath. He closed his eyes and prayed Julie didn't get caught.

The rain lightened but he saw more lightning and heard more thunder and knew more was on the way. He heard some splashing, and he thought his name. He heard it again.

"Zack! Where are you?"

Light from the condos lining the river before it entered the harbor and the lake gave enough light on the water for Zack to see the person coming at him. She was a little further out though and moving fast, but he stretched and reached as the river current washed her past him.

He caught her and held tight. She readjusted her direction and suddenly was holding him tighter than she had ever held him before. His one hand hung onto the ladder, and he felt it slipping. He tried to clutch it, but they fell away from the boat.

"Hang on; we're going for a ride if we don't hit that next boat." They fought towards the shore. It was a battle, but the river current pushed them into the boat again, and Zack grabbed the ladder with one hand and Julie with the other. She got to the ladder and pulled herself out of the water, then helped him up.

He fell to the floor, and she fell atop of him. He wanted to yell at her but couldn't. He would have done the same thing for her. The light rain stopped, and he kissed her. She kissed him back.

"Oh Zack, I'm sorry."

"So am I."

The light rain stopped briefly, but the rumble and light show in the sky returned, and the downpour prevented a respite. They crawled closer to the cabin, were out of the rain and held each other. They didn't know if it was safe to be on the boat, but it was safer than being in the lake or on the streets. They couldn't stay. But they could look inside the cabin. See what they got. Maybe a band-aid. After he rested. He needed rest.

He shut his eyes despite being soaked and slightly chilled. She clung tight to him with her arm draped across his chest. "I never thought in a million years we'd be spending a night on a boat this way."

"Sorry," he replied. "It's been a long day, baby. I need some rest."

Zack rested for only a few minutes when the thunder rumbled again, and the clouds opened up again, and even under the canopy on the boat, they couldn't escape getting wet. He struggled to his knees, and they moved closer to the front of the boat, deeper under the canopy and more sheltered from the wind that rocked the boat.

"I should be mad at you; you know that, right?"

She raised her head and lightly kissed his lips. "I know. I should be mad at you, too."

"I'm sorry. I wanted to tell you the truth for a while now about my past. I really did. I was just afraid."

"I know."

"I wanted to tell you right after we started dating and I fell so madly in love with you. I just thought you would leave me."

"I almost did this week."

He was silent. He flexed his arm to bring her closer. "I'm glad you didn't."

"You have an interesting story."

"Am I just a story to you?"

She chuckled. De Ja Vu. "You know what you are to me." She kissed him again.

"How much did you hear tonight?"

"All of it. I'm sorry I doubted you. I actually thought you might have killed your father for a while! I'm so sorry. Baby, I hope you forgive me."

He chuckled. "You jumped into a black and swollen river to save my life! How can I not forgive you? Honey, I love you. There's nothing to forgive because you shouldn't say sorry."

"So now what?"

"Well, for starters, if we get back home safe, I want to marry you."

She laughed. "Nope. You can't even walk, and I'm walking down the aisle, honey! My parents will kill me if I don't give them a good old fashioned Catholic wedding!"

"Your parents will kill me if they find out about this."

"They won't. How are we going to get out of this one?"

Zack exhaled. "We have to wait til dawn. Then we figure out how to get out of here before the owners of this boat call the cops on us."

"Do you think Warren killed your father?"

"I'm not sure. Everything we found suggests it. But why wouldn't he cop to it?"

"Nice pun, haha," she said.

"He definitely was in on it, but he makes it sound like my mother was, too."

"And your sister."

"Which one though?"

"Becky. The oldest," Julie said with confidence. "Maybe he's protecting her."

"He's protecting someone. Or he did it. I'm not sure."

"Get some sleep, hon; I'll wake you in a few hours."

"It will be light in about an hour. You sleep. I need to think."

* * * * * * * *

When daylight appeared on the horizon, Zack grasped the situation to the fullest: there was no way out. Cops were everywhere. He could see the flashing beacons atop the patrol cars; he could hear the buzz of the ambulances and first responders at the zoo still looking for injured, dead and probably their beloved chief. Zack saw state police cars speeding over the Franklin Street Bridge heading towards the zoo and knew up the river or back into town was not going to work.

His leg ached, but she had stopped the bleeding for him. His chest and shoulder were sore and stiff and bruised. The scratches and scrapes and cuts from the fight and the rose bush burned. The boat was their only haven, and he knew that was only temporary.

He looked at the shore between the boat, the dock and the condos lining them. Small areas of grass, concrete patios, outdoor furniture, an occasional canopy and other water equipment littered the area. He saw jet-skis in docks ready to be launched and several sets of kayaks. Lifestyles of the rich and boring, he thought.

Then he watched a pair of Chicago-style yuppies exit their condo, walk down the stairwell to their patio, grab a pair of kayaks and head to the river. The river and harbor were calm despite the previous night's storms. He shook his head and realized that was their only way out of the river and away from the city.

"Hey hon, remember when you asked me to go kayaking a couple of months ago, and I said no?"

"I forgot about that! Yes!" She got to her knees beside Zack and looked where he was looking. "Why?"

"Well, I'm sore, so you're going to have to do all the work."

"Ok, and then what?"

"We call Andre."

She snorted. "I hate to tell you this, love of my life, but we don't have a cell phone. So how do we call him?"

"I don't know. Maybe we'll find a park ranger."

"Yeah right. A ranger sees you, and he'll call for back up after he shoots you!"

Zack smiled. "Wanna bet he'll let a beautiful woman borrow his phone for one call?"

She shook her head. "Ok, we better hurry. Yuppies don't sleep in."

* * * * * * *

The sunrise was beautiful that morning. The air wasn't ripe with humidity like it had been. That morning it smelled fresh. It was much cooler. Darnell watched it come up from the beginning: saw the many shades of purples, oranges, reds, and yellows before the globe chased off the night and revealed another day.

Darnell realized that for the first time in a long time he was not hungry. He looked for Andre and saw him outside, perched on the hood of the rental car.

They were parked somewhere at a park along the lakeshore. No one would care they were there because the parking lot had several vehicles in it already. People fishing, several walking their dog, two guys were trying to surf the small waves the previous night's storm had created; it was a safe place to hide.

Darnell exited the car and moved beside Andre.

"What time is it?"

"Quarter after six."

"Where are we?"

"Michigan."

"What do we do now?" Darnell stretched. Two hours of sleep felt good.

"I don't know."

They sat there in silence. "We can't stay here." Darnell decided.

"You are more than welcome to come up with a plan. If you have any ideas, please share them with me." Andre examined his fingernails.

"Is it safe here? Two black guys sitting on a car in some park is bound to attract attention."

Andre laughed. "Not everyone is as afraid of blacks as you think. Look around, man. There are two black dudes fishing down there. No one cares. We're fine."

"What about Zack and Julie?"

"We wait." Andre decided. "All we can do."

"But what about Zack?" Darnell persisted.

"He'll reach me as soon as he can."

"And until then? We can't wait here forever."

Andre looked around. "The good thing about this area is that it is all tourists," he said. "Let's go find a place to stay for the night. Or two."

Darnell shook his head. "I would feel better safe inside rather than exposed outside."

Andre got into the car as Darnell got in the other side. "If you exposed yourself anywhere around me, dude, I'm gonna bust you up even more!"

* * * * * * * *

Andre removed the cases from the trunk of the rental car and carried them inside the lakeshore resort condo. The briefcase Darnell threw into the car was still there. He grabbed that one, too. He decided to rent a villa along the lake while they hid. Four people, he, his brother, his friend, and his wife were in town for the weekend. Do some Salmon fishing.

He slid the trunks and the briefcase under the bed, checked his buzzing cell phone and went to the kitchen. He didn't recognize the number. It was an area code he knew was from the area. 219. He took a deep breath. "Hello?"

Five minutes later, Darnell came out of the bathroom clean with the contusions and bruises evident on his face. Andre said he looked like crap. Like he'd been through a fifteen-round cage match and lost. Darnell said he felt like the same thing.

"What do we do now?" Darnell asked as he sat on the couch.

Andre grabbed three cans of soda out of the refrigerator. "We'll figure that out when I go get Zack and Jules."

"What? You're going to get them?"

"You have to stay here. You will be recognized. No one has seen me."

"Zack's sister has."

Andre paused. Always a fly in the ointment. "Well, I'm hopeful she'll keep her promise and not tell anyone about me."

"And if she does?"

Andre shrugged. "Then we're all screwed. I'll be back."

"You know where he is?"

"Basically.   You're staying here.   Don't leave and don't let yourself get seen. You got it?"

Darnell nodded and sunk back into the couch. "I ain't moving for a while."

Andy Gruse
STACKED CASE

CHAPTER 49

The Indiana Dunes National Lakeshore officially started on the west side of Michigan City at a place called Mount Baldy. On weekends, the place was so crowded with tourists and natives alike that you couldn't park in the lot or even see the giant dune. To keep it alive and slow down the deterioration of it, access to the side of the steep dune had been shut off. Climbing up the dune had been a challenge but yet something everyone wanted to do. Unfortunately, the people only helped move the sand and the hill deteriorated. Keeping the last great dune alive was a constant battle. Thus, it was closed, but the battle continued.

Andre stared at what he could see through the oak trees early that morning and knew it would fill up, even though it was a weekday. But it had cooled off considerably so that might keep people away from the beach that day. A large woodpecker flew overhead, called and disappeared into the trees.

The sound of the birds singing filled the air. Andre saw the signs that lead the beach-goers around Mount Baldy, through the forest, and up a wooden walkway to the top of the dunes and to the other side of mountainous sand that blocked them from the lake.

He put on his sunglasses and followed the signs. He walked up the path, climbed the long stairs and finally exited the forest atop the dunes. The swaying grasses blown by the light wind looked majestic to

347

Andre, but he was only there for one reason and didn't care much for the scenery.

He followed the path towards the beach and came to the edge of the dunes where the descent to the beach was inspiring and deep. He saw an orange double person kayak on the shore, looked around but saw nothing.

A pair of Caspian Terns flew along the lakefront. The sun ducked behind a wispy cirrus cloud but showed itself again. Andre turned his back to the lake and walked back. The path dropped between two dunes covered in the sharp reed grasses. A perfect place for an ambush, he thought.

"Hey, up here."

Andre saw Julie kneeling on the edge at the top. He smiled. "Hey, pretty girl. Where the hell is our boy?"

"Right here."

Zack rolled over the side, fell down the sand and stopped at Andre's feet.

"Quit screwing around. Get up and walk."

"I have a hole in my leg, I'm cramped, and I can barely move. Give me a break."

Andre saw the wound, grabbed his arm and lifted him off the sand. The moaning and groaning by Zack were real. He was in pain. Zack was shirtless, and the bruises on his chest the bullets left were deep red. It looked like a group of cats tore him to shreds.

"Jules, can you move? Can you help me with this slug?"

Julie chuckled and hopped down from the dune. "I can help just fine. And we better hurry. The nude sunbather was a little suspicious of me. Thankfully he covered himself with a towel!"

They got back to the car where Andre laid Zack in the back seat. "Don't be bleeding over the upholstery. I didn't take the extra insurance." Andre started the car and left, headed back to Michigan via the long way around town. He made two stops at two different stores, but Zack had his eyes shut, and Julie kept out of sight. Exhaustion knocked him out, and Julie made sure he was comfortable.

Andre drove along the highway; the radio played softly. He kept his eyes pressed to the mirrors and overpasses and under bridges for cops. There were none. Their exit was in ten miles.

"Is Darnell safe?"

"Yeah, he's safe." Andre saw in his mirror one of Zack's hands move to cover his face.

"How the hell did you find him?"

"Dumb luck, man but I'll tell you, the dude's all right, you know that? He could have bolted, but he saved your ass twice last night."

Zack tried to take a deep breath, but the pain wouldn't let him. "Where's my bike?"

Andre chuckled. "Don't worry; it's safe too. I made sure of that first. And you owe me a lot of money."

"For what?"

Andre laughed. "You just do! You may be my boy, but I risked my ass last night, and that's gotta be worth something."

* * * * * * * *

Michelle Borman sipped her Hawaiian born coffee and savored every flavor, every aroma, every last sip. The office was quiet for three days. She worried about Zack and Andre. She tried sorting mail hoping to get payment for services, so she could make a deposit and pay some bills. No dice. It seemed the clients only paid when Zack and Andre made appearances requesting final payment for what they did.

The phone rang. She didn't feel like answering it and lying to another bill collector. Why was the electric company so fussy about a late bill? The machine picked up on the tenth ring.

"Hello, you've reached the Dre-Zack Detective Agency. Please leave a message, and we will get back to you as soon as we are able." The beep followed.

"Michelle, pick up the goddamn phone!"

She spat out the sip of coffee and scrambled for the phone, knocking it off the receiver. "Oh my God! Zack? Is that you?"

"What did I say about coffee in the office?"

"You said, I'm not, how did you, wait? That's why you're calling?"

"I need you to do your thing, honey. Call your FBI boyfriend,"

"He's NOT my boyfriend!"

"Call him and tell him we need to know everything that is going on in this town, OK? Somehow, he needs to get involved and find out everything. If we have any chance, we need to know what they think they know."

"Zack, what is going on? Are you all right? You sound like you're hurt. Are you hurt? Did you get shot? Did you see the news?

350

Were you involved in that gunfight last night? Zack, talk to me! Why aren't you talking to me?"

Zack handed the phone to the front seat to Andre and covered his face with his hands again. Andre talked to her for a few minutes, hung up, and Zack felt the car stop.

"We're here. Let me get a blanket from the room to cover you two. If someone sees you guys, especially you Zack, they might ask questions."

"Yeah, I know. Then we wait."

Andy Gruse
STACKED CASE

CHAPTER 50

"Read that. Almost brings tears to my eyes."

Zack saw the headline. Nothing creative about it but mentioned that several police officers were wounded, several in intensive care and five were killed. But his fascination was with the Chief of Police Warren Sapagio.

"Only five? The rest were lucky."

Andre scoffed. "Two don't have heads left. They're just quiet now. Damage control. They don't know what they got yet."

The report said that during the melee, Warren jumped over the fence to avoid getting shot. He fell twenty feet and broke an arm, wrist, and collarbone. Uniformed police had to shoot and kill a tiger to prevent it from mauling Warren, though the tiger was still safely behind a fence and Warren landed in the moat between the fences. He had already been released from the hospital.

The report only speculated that it was a gang-related drug bust and the cops found themselves overmatched.

Zack put down the paper. "That's it? That's all they have on this thing?"

"We got enough to bury the sonofabitch. Let's do it." Darnell jumped to his feet.

Julie read the article. "They interviewed several of the undercover cops that were there. The same ones that are dirty. They don't even mention us!"

"Because they know they can't. They are hoping right now that we don't talk. If we do, it's over for all of them." Zack tried to stretch his leg and cringed.

"So, we're safe from the rest of the cops, but what about the dirty ones?"

"Well, Darnell, my guess is that they think we bolted town. Hell, they might even think I drowned last night in the river. But they did make a point to steer clear of any mentioning of us, didn't they? Even you."

"That doesn't mean I'm off the hook."

"No, it doesn't," Julie offered. "So, what do we do? Tell them to drop it, or we drop them? I mean, after all, your stepdad is still in charge, and they are going to want justice. The good cops don't know about the bad cops. All they know is that five of their own were killed. Zack, they don't like that."

"Semper fi, cop style, right Zack?" Andre asked.

"Do we leave right now? Get away from this place?" Zack asked.

Julie looked at her boyfriend and then at Andre. "Dre, what about Zack? The chief kept calling him Davey. They're gonna know that Davey is alive."

"Worse than that, Jules. They know where you and Zack live. They know about our agency. And if his sister talks, they'll know I was here and likely the sniper we had protecting them," Andre added.

They were all silent and stared at Zack and waited.

"Zack, babe, what about that?" Julie finally broke the long silence.

Zack closed his eyes. "I have no freaking idea."

* * * * * * * *

Zack and Julie were left alone in the lower level of the villa. Darnell, upon Andre's insistence, went to the upper level and watched a baseball game on a big screen television. Andre had left to meet Michelle's FBI friend.

The two had been silent. Zack slept a lot during the day, but as the sun sank on the horizon, he awoke with his mind loaded with confusion and unanswered questions.

Julie moved next to him, checked the wrapping on his leg and sat beside him. "Looks like you could use a drink. What do you want?"

"Scotch, whiskey, vodka, all of them, whatever works."

She walked to the well-stocked wet bar and poured two drinks. She handed Zack his and nudged alongside him.

"So now what? What's going to happen now?"

Zack exhaled. "I don't know. We don't know how deep this goes. We know he has people at the state level, attorneys, probably even more. We may have enough for someone to investigate if there is anyone left not in on it."

"State's attorney? State police?"

"Maybe. Probably. But if they investigate, and they investigate me," he paused, she saw his eyes get glossy and she put her fingers to his lips.

"Shhhh, baby, shhhh." She stared back at him and handed him his drink. "What about Darnell?"

"Well, if he wants to pursue it, I expect that a civil liberties lawyer, the NAACP or someone somewhere is going to find him. His case would be worth a lot of money in a lawsuit."

Julie was aware of the ramifications. She also knew he hated repeating himself. She wanted to ask again. She wanted to try to understand. "I have so many questions. I don't know where to begin, and if you're not even going to answer me, I don't know if I should bother."

He chugged from his drink, finished it and handed her the glass. "I'll make you a deal: you fill this up, and I'll tell you everything you want to know."

"No bullshit? No lies? No hem-hawing around?"

"Nope. Nothing but the truth."

"Why now?"

He looked at her, his face sunken and hollowed despite the bruises and cuts. "I expect you to leave me, Jules. And I want you to know the truth about everything when you do. I owe you that."

"You sure as hell do." She tried a smile and gently touched the side of his face.

"Drink first though."

"You have a deal."

She returned with the drinks, gave him one and then kissed him deeply.

"What was that for?"

"To remind you every time you feel like clamming up or not telling me the truth that you'll never get that again if I find out you're lying." She smiled.

He showed a smile for the first time since he saw her in the room earlier that day. "Then where do you want me to begin?"

"The beginning: the day your dad was murdered."

Andy Gruse
STACKED CASE

CHAPTER 51

"**I came home early that day**, forgot my practice jersey for basketball, and if I didn't have it, I would have had to run sprints until I puked. So, I drove home quick and ran inside. Detective Sapagio was standing in the living room with my mother. For some odd reason, he seemed to be around a lot. My mom worked as a waitress in a diner, and whenever I'd stop in to get food for my brothers and sisters, he was always there talking to her. At first, I liked him. Figured it was good to be friends with a cop. But something seemed off about him. Anyway, they looked shocked when I came inside. I said I forgot my practice stuff and was going to grab a snack, even though we never had snacks in the house. I figured a saltine would hold me over through practice. So, I ran upstairs, but my jersey was still in the dirty clothes, so I ran downstairs again and headed for the basement. I never paid attention to the detective or my mom."

"Why not?"

"I don't know. I guess I should have seen that she was upset. They were serious. And I never questioned why he was there. I mean, what the hell was another man doing with my mother in the middle of the afternoon?"

"Tell me what you know, Zack. Don't torture yourself with what you think you should have noticed."

He let out a deep breath. "I ran downstairs, flicked on the light, my jersey was on the floor in front of me along with another pile of dirty clothes, but all I saw was my father." He swallowed hard. "On his back, in a pool of blood." He struggled to keep from crying, but Julie saw it and heard it. "He was dead."

"You found your father?"

He nodded. "I ran upstairs to tell the policeman. I was in a panic. They grabbed me and calmed me. Convinced me it was suicide. That I should just go to practice, not say anything and they'll handle everything."

"They told you it was suicide?"

"Yes. My mother was shaking me like I was a rag doll telling me to calm down and stay cool. Then the detective said he'd investigate, but it was imperative that I said nothing, or it could compromise the investigation." Zack shook his head. "So, I went to practice."

"You still went to practice? What happened? How could you practice?"

Zack chuckled. "I forgot my jersey anyway, and coach made me ran stairs for a half hour, then I practiced with the team then I ran sprints. I didn't puke. Should have passed out. Don't know what kept me going."

Julie rubbed his back. "I do." He went silent. "Tell me why you left town. Because Darnell was arrested and convicted?"

"After the trial, which was quick, and the jury deliberated for about two hours, long enough to get some food I guess, they convicted Darnell. The judge sentenced him not long after that. I went home upset and told my mother that I knew it wasn't Darnell and I was going to the police chief and the D.A and tell them it was suicide."

"She argued that it wasn't suicide. They only told me that, so I wouldn't be afraid of living in the house is what she said." Zack shook his head. "She made a case to convince me it was murder. Reiterated all the lies I heard in the courtroom."

Julie squeezed his arm. "Then what?"

"I believed her. But I told my mother Darnell couldn't have done it. It was someone else. She yelled, I yelled, she yelled louder. 'We are poor; we need the money! How can I raise you kids, how can I raise your sisters and brothers now that your father is gone?' she screamed at me as if it were my fault. 'I need that money to put your sisters and brothers through college! You will not say anything. This case is solved.' Her mind was made up, too, just like the all-white jury."

"Are you sure it wasn't suicide? You knew it was a gunshot wound? How do you know?" She got him another drink. She realized he was talking freer and hoped she wouldn't have to get him drunk to get him to open up to her all the time.

"I was there. I remember the splatter. And I've seen enough gunshot wounds since then to know what I saw and thought was accurate. He was shot point blank in the forehead. A man killing himself would swallow the bullet or blast himself from the side. He wouldn't stare at the gun and then fire. I panicked and freaked out, but I do know that there was no gun there and that he was shot. There was no gun. My father never owned a gun, never shot one as far as I know, and the back door was not open, and nothing was scattered about as if it was ransacked. I remember that much which means it was not the break-in and robbery like they said it was."

"Are you sure?"

"Yes."

"Maybe that's just what you want to remember."

He scoffed. "That's what my mother and her boyfriend kept telling me."

"You knew Warren was seeing your mom?"

Zack looked at her. "No, I didn't. I told you I was naïve."

"So, you left because of that?"

"No. I left because I saw my friend Darnell handcuffed, in an orange jumpsuit heading to prison for a crime he didn't commit. I told my mother I was going to the DA; then we argued. She kept going on about the insurance money. It was the only way, she said. How would Becky and Lindsay and Adam and Jennifer and Christopher get through college? It was my responsibility to honor my father and protect my family, she said. And I HAD to take the interests over that of some Negro, as she called Darnell."

Julie silenced as Zack opened up about the day. She understood why he was so closed but knew they were growing closer. And the best part was that the man she loved did not kill his own father. Nor did he, as she had begun to think days earlier and learned the night before, have anything to do with it.

"So, you didn't want to cross your mother and you left?"

Zack looked at her. His eyes narrowed. She knew he was thinking something. "I'm missing something, I know it."

"Just tell me what you know."

"I got on my motorcycle and left. I was going to tell someone what I knew."

"What happened?" She ran her hand over his ear and through his short hair.

"I wasn't sure what I was going to say. I was really nervous. I stopped at a pizza place to get a sub, sit down inside where it was fairly dark and think it out. After I finished, I felt better, realized that I was doing the right thing and knew that I'd have to somehow support my family. I knew my mom would get some insurance but obviously had no idea of the two-million- dollar policy she and Warren had. In fact, I didn't even know about the five-hundred grand one. I just assumed. Seventeen and naïve, remember?"

"You're being too hard on yourself, Zachary. So, you talked to the DA? Or went to the police?"

"Neither." He looked at Julie.

She saw the moisture from his eyes disappear and turn into anger.

"I parked my bike in the back. I walked back to get it, but before I reached it, someone grabbed me and threw me into the fence."

She put a hand again on his arm, he tensed.

"Detective Sapagio had me against the fence, me on my butt. He tells me the case is closed and it's over. There was nothing I could do about it. I tried to be tough. I told him that it wasn't and that I knew Darnell didn't do it. I told him he was going to have to give back all the awards he got because he arrested the wrong man."

Julie leaned forward to see Zack's eyes, which retreated from her gaze and stared at the ground in front of him.

"There wasn't much after that. He pulled me off the ground and punched me in the gut. I thought my ribs had broken and my lungs had collapsed. He told me in no uncertain terms that I was going to keep my

363

mouth," he paused, "I believe he said, 'you will keep your mouth shut if you know what's good for you.'" Zack exhaled. "He's a monosyllabic moron. I eyed him, still thinking I was tough."

"Then what?"

"He didn't make his full point. He picked me back up and beat me a few more times. Then, for good measure, as I was leaning against the fence on my ass, barely able to breathe, he shoved the barrel of his .38 against my forehead and told me that I was going to leave town right then and never come back. If I didn't, I was going to end up like my father only no one would ever find my body."

Julie didn't know what to say. Her mind circled back to Sara Eckhart and her sixteen-year-old son who could not have looked any more like Zack.

"He threw a wad of cash on my lap, told me to get my savings out of the bank and get out of town before dark. He said the cops would be looking for me and my bike after dark and if they found me, I would have to deal with Warren again."

"Jesus, Zack, I'm sorry," Julie said. "You never told me. Is that the truth?"

Zack chuckled. "No, I made up the part where I got the shit beat out of me and almost pissed my pants because a loaded and cocked gun was pressed against my head. That's a story to tell at parties, isn't it?" He took a deep breath. "I did what he said. By six o'clock that night, I had everything worth anything to me in my backpack and was on my motorcycle heading east. And I never looked back."

She digested what he said. "Was that everything? There wasn't any other reason?"

"What other reason would I need?"

Ok, let's push this. "Didn't you have a girlfriend or something? What about her?"

"At the time, yes I did. But not getting my brains splattered all over a nameless alley seemed to be more important to me."

"Did you say anything to her?"

"No, of course not."

"Were you close to her?"

"Yes. We were boyfriend-girlfriend. Dated throughout high school. But Warren's threat was real to me." Zack exhaled. "I let Darnell down, I didn't come through for him when I could have saved him all those years in the clink." He looked at her. "That's why I came back. Not to save my name or hide any evidence. It was to make up for Darnell what I was too weak to do back then."

She ran her hand through his hair again and smiled.

"So, this girlfriend, did you sleep with her?"

Zack looked at her. "Julie, for Christ's sake, if you're going to question me about every girl I've ever seen, then one of us has boundary issues."

She stared at him.

"Fine. Sara Eckhart was her name. She was the only girl I dated in high school. If you must know, I lost my virginity to her and her to me and like every other teenage romance we were sure it was true love and would last forever. Only I left town and never talked to her again."

He didn't know! "Zack, it's not that, I'm not jealous."

"Sure as hell sounds like you are. Then there was Michelle if you must know, but we haven't dated or done anything in years, long before you and I became a couple and other than one one-night stand while stationed in Germany, you are the only other woman I've slept with. Happy now?"

She was surprised. *Only three other women? Wow.* "I just didn't know if you were running from her for some reason, that's all."

"Why would I? I never did anything to hurt her, other than to just up and leave one day and never talk to her again." He shrugged. "Certainly not chivalrous, but under the circumstances, I thought my actions were justified."

No, he didn't know. And I'm not going to tell him. "So now what?"

"Have I told you everything you want to know?"

She smiled, happy with the results. Her arms went around his neck. "Yes."

They kissed. She poured him another drink. The effects of the alcohol started to make her feel light-headed, but she figured they both deserved it. He sipped his glass and put it down for the first time since he started.

"Tell me about your family. Your brothers and sisters."

"Why? You still have the fairy tale dream of me taking you to the house one day to introduce you to them?"

She giggled. "Well, I don't see it happening. But it's nice to know you came from somewhere. Start with the oldest and work your way back."

"Becky?" He scoffed. "Kidnapped her the other night." He sipped the drink but held it. "We were close. At least I thought we were. Lindsay and Jennifer were a few years younger, and into the doll thing and Adam and Christopher were too young to play ball with. So, Rebecca and I were close. Friends." He chuckled. "But it's funny because after a while in high school she started spending a lot of time with mom. In fact," he sipped again and smiled, "they were always trying to talk me into going out with this girl or that girl or do this or do that. They must have thought Sara and I were too serious or something." He laughed. "It was funny. Heck, at times it felt like they were conspiring about my life," and he realized what he was missing. He stared at her computing his thoughts and then said: "I have to call Barnes."

Andy Gruse
STACKED CASE

CHAPTER 52

The morning came too quickly for Zack. He stayed up way too late talking with Julie who kept feeding him drinks. He understood why after his eyes cleared when he remembered what they did: talk. He looked for her but couldn't find her.

He tried to get off the couch but was stiff from head to toe. After struggling for awhile, he got to his foot and hopped into the kitchen where he leaned on the fridge, opened it, found a can of Pepsi and drank it.

He heard heavy footsteps come down the stairs after he leaned for he didn't know how long against the refrigerator.

"Where the hell is everyone?" Darnell's voice sounded like he had a few drinks too.

"I'm not enough for you?"

Darnell moved Zack off the fridge, found some juice and drank straight from the container. "No, man. You're not. Where's everyone else?"

"How do I know? I've been asleep. What time is it?"

Darnell saw the digital clock on the stove. "Says eleven thirty."

"So now what do we do?"

Zack couldn't help but laugh a little. "Well, as long as it doesn't involve violence or quick movements, I don't care."

"Go take a shower man; you stink like stale blood and bad booze."

Zack laughed again. "You don't smell too good either."

Four hours later, both men cleaned and dressed in whatever they could find, Andre and Julie entered the villa. Julie carried a laptop case; her hand fixed to the strap over her shoulder. She saw Zack and smiled. Andre walked to Darnell, shook his hand and did the same to Zack.

"How are you boys feeling?"

"I'm hungry," they said simultaneously.

Julie laughed. "I heard there's a good burger joint nearby. We'll grab something there after we take care of this."

"Take care of what?"

Julie sat down next to Zack and kissed the side of his face that wasn't swollen and bruised. Andre sat next to Darnell and jokingly tried to kiss him, but Darnell pushed him away.

"I never get any loving," Andre joked. "Well, man, thought you'd like to know that you're a few hours away from at least having your latest arrest and the parole violations expunged."

"What about the murder wrap?"

"One thing at a time, Darnell. But we think at least that charge will be dropped. From what we could ascertain, Warren is talking with IA. Apparently, he was keeping a file. Now granted, it will be days, weeks, maybe months before any of this is released. Who the hell knows, it may never be released, and the public may never know about any of this. Well," Andre took a deep breath, "at least the version that Warren is orchestrating and looks like IA and everyone else is eating it up."

Zack leaned forward. "Eating what up?"

"Eating up the fake bullshit Warren so readily gave up on the five dead cops. He had a file, Zack. And I think it was all set up so all he had to do was insert names and he had his guinea pigs to take the fall. "

"Are you kidding me? Nothing came of this? Nothing?"

Julie grabbed Zack's arm and understood his incredulity. "No one was investigating Warren, Zack. There was no reason to. He blamed everything on the dead cops trying to do a deal with Diablo's gang. Said they were dirty. The church, Darnell's uncle, the shootout, everything, all blamed on five dead cops being dirty."

Zack leaned back and covered his face. "All in what? Two days?" He shook his head. "He was prepared."

"So, what do I do now?" Darnell asked. "I mean, so what about the drug charge being dropped? I got nothing. My uncle is dead. The church my family built decades ago is gone. I got nothing. No one left in this town and I don't even want to be here. So where does that leave me?"

"The briefcase under the bed is full of money, Darnell," Zack said. "Take it. It's yours."

"I don't want that money. It's dirty."

"It's a fresh start. Rebuild the church, start a life for yourself. Make some good come from all this."

"Screw that, Zack. There's no one left here. Every time I would look at that church or whatever I did with the money I'd be reminded that it was money spent to kill me. And you and Julie. I don't want it. And not only that, you know damn well I can't live here! Your stepdad will find me and have me disappear! You know it. I can't stay here, and if I leave I violate my parole and end up in prison again and probably dead there, too!"

Zack nodded. "We're both kind of screwed."

"So, what do we now then, man?"

Zack stared at Darnell and then looked at Andre and Julie. "Well, what do you two suggest?"

"We should probably eat," Andre said and looked at Julie for support. She looked at Zack. "Baby, we should just get lunch and then go home."

CHAPTER **53**

Zack covered his face with his hands as he listened to the recent developments. The spin on the truth as it was created over the years. He leaned back and let out a deep sigh. "It's not over yet."

"It's over, Zack." Andre stood and patted Zack's shoulder. "It's over."

"If you were Warren, would you let it drop?"

"He's got too much to lose to continue."

Zack shook his head. "He's got too much to lose to let it go."

"Well that's exactly what we have to do, baby," Julie leaned to him and put her hands on his knees. "We have to let it go and get out of here."

"And do what? And go where?"

"We have to get back. We have to organize everything we have, and if we can build a case, then that's what we do. But we can't do it here," Andre said.

Zack leaned back and motioned to the waitress. She hurried over with a smile and asked what he needed. "Can you bring me the largest mug of beer you have?" She asked a flavor, listed off about 20 and he settled on a Sam Adams Seasonal. Julie looked at him, but he waved off her look. "Ok, so let's sum up. In two days since the meeting, he has ratted out the five dead cops as dirty drug-dealing cops who turned on their police-mates but were overmatched and killed. He also tied them with Diablo and his gang and pinned the burning of the Church and murder of Darnell's uncle on Diablo's gang. Am I correct so far?"

Julie and Andre nodded as the waitress brought back the beer and Zack took a long pull off of it. Darnell watched and ordered the same.

"And now you're telling me that the city council, based on Warren's recommendation and the recent violence that he started but is blaming everyone else has condemned the Triangle and approved the redevelopment of it. Meanwhile, the city cops have mobilized and moved into the area to run Diablo and his gang out, but they have moved on, so there is no one to run out of that area. But, the people, quote-unquote, are demanding justice for the zoo incident and Warren has sworn they will bring anyone else involved to previously demanded justice. Am I still correct so far?"

Julie took his mug and drank from it as the waitress brought Darnell's and motioned to bring another for her which she fully intended to share with Zack. She put her hand on the back of his head and gently massaged it.

Andre looked at his watch. "Yes, you are. But Zack, you had to know we weren't going to stop the development of the Triangle. It was too far along when we learned about it, and nothing Michelle uncovered would have stopped it at this point unless we rat you out and I for one am against that."

Darnell shook his head. "Nothing about it is legal! We tied that piece of shit to everything illegal going on in the Triangle! We saw it! We know it! How the hell can he get away with any of it?"

Julie sipped her beer when it arrived and put it down. "The city needs jobs. It needs revenue. It needs to clean up that part of town to get the tourist dollars because that is the only thing it has to offer. Warren knew this and orchestrated it all. And now he is going to profit from it. And we, my dear," she picked up her mug and lightly tapped his mug with hers, "have nicely packaged and accelerated the whole deal for him."

"Ok, ok, wait." Darnell shook his head. "So, your stepdad is going to get richer, big deal. We can't stop it, and we can't prove anything about the death of your old man. I get that. I don't want to sound like a selfish asshole here, but you guys are talking about leaving and I can't. So, sorry to interrupt, but what the hell do I do now?"

Zack finished his beer at the burger joint near the lakeshore in Michigan that Zack remembered everyone raved about when he lived there. It was like a Mecca. When it opened in the spring, his schoolmates would flock there and brag about being the first and talk about how great the burger and fries were. World-renowned was what some called it. Zack had the double. Hated onions so none of that vile weed, as he called them, were allowed near but plenty of pickles and ketchup. Basic, he knew it. He didn't care. It was still supposed to be the best burger he ever had.

He enjoyed it, but even after swallowing Lake Michigan water, he still didn't think it was that great. Never was to him. The beer was better than the burger, in his mind. To Zack, if he could only pick one burger joint to go to as his last meal, he would go to a place called The Nook in St. Paul, Minnesota. Best he ever tasted, and he had tasted a lot of burgers. But, some traditions never died, and since this was likely the last time he'd ever be at this shack of a burger joint, he accepted it for what it was: a decent burger at a unique place.

He took a deep breath and focused on the conversation. "Well, Darnell, we have a private detective agency back in Baltimore. It's a small operation. Just Andre, me and a secretary named Michelle. You heard her chew me out when I called, remember? Occasionally a sassy investigative reporter will help me or use me to get a story, and I have a good friend who's a cop. Right now, we are broke because I used all our money to bail someone out of jail, but I'm looking to hire someone who is smart, can read people, who I can trust and who I think would be a great asset to the firm. What do you say?"

"Why would I want to do that?"

"Because you can't stay here, man." Andre sipped his iced tea. "You said it yourself. No way."

Darnell chuckled. "Man, I'd be freaking crazy to work for you!" He sucked down part of his beer. "But it's the best offer I got."

"It's the only offer you got!"

"I'd be stupid to say no. I'd be breaking the law though."

"Let me talk to Barnes about that. Maybe he can help," Zack said.

"Worth asking," Andre decided.

"Why would you do that? Aiding and abetting?"

Zack drank from Julie's beer as she intended. "Because you're my friend and you're innocent. And maybe, in time, we can prove it. You just come with us, you stay the hell off the grid and don't cause any trouble. We go to Barnes immediately, and hopefully, we can make this work for a while."

"I'm cool with that. Baltimore, you say? I like seafood. When do we go? And more importantly, how about this Michelle? Is she hot? I could use a woman."

Zack shook his head. "Out of the question." He looked at Andre. "Dre, what do you think?"

"I still think that this is over. I think Warren can't mention us because of what we know. He is hoping we won't mention what we know because he knows David Staechel is alive. And we all know what happens if that becomes public knowledge."

Zack shook his head. "No, it isn't over. But, right now we have to focus on our next move."

"Our next move is to get the hell out of here," Julie said.

Zack was about to argue when Andre's cell phone rang. As his usual, he left the area to talk.

After two quick minutes, he returned and sat down. "Lieutenant Barnes wants to apologize for almost knocking your teeth out and to congratulate you for almost succeeding in your quest."

"That's why he called?"

"Well, he's pissed you and Jules aren't answering your phones."

"I imagine he would be. But we don't have phones any longer. What else?"

"Well, he said we need to get back there immediately."

Within the hour they were on the road headed back east. Julie drove the rental car, Zack and Darnell were passengers and Andre followed on the motorcycle. They stayed off the interstate as much as they could. Zack guessed it might be ok to just hop on the tollway and cruise, but he wanted nothing to do with police for a while. Not even back home. He wanted peace and to be left alone, but that wasn't going to happen because Lieutenant Ted Barnes was waiting for them when they got to Baltimore.

CHAPTER 54

The greeting by Lieutenant Barnes was not as warm as Zack expected when he arrived in Baltimore. Julie tucked herself under his arm to help him walk. No handshake, no smile, not even a head nod. They met at Julie's apartment per Barnes' instructions. He handed Zack a manila envelope and sat on her couch.

"You wanted this case. You got it."

"I want a vacation," Zack answered as Julie helped him sit on a loveseat across from Ted.

"Well," he looked at Darnell who sat at a table near the kitchen just behind Zack. "Who's he? A charity case?"

Zack knew that Barnes knew exactly who Darnell was and all about him already. "He's an asset, Ted."

Barnes opened his mouth but said nothing, closed it and shook his head. "Ok, what do you need from me?"

"I need him safe and off the grid."

Barnes looked at him, waiting for more.

"And I need your blessing."

Barnes shook his head and rolled his eyes. "I used to have such a promising career." He rubbed his brow with his fingers as if trying to rub away the stress. "And then I met you." He exhaled. "Michelle I'm sure can fix the grid problem. Hell, she did it once already. At least this time I'll know about it."

"Ted, I said I was sorry. I explained everything. I," Zack hesitated.

"I get it. I got it. I understand why you did it. Hell, I would have done the same damn thing," Barnes said. "I forgave you. But this isn't going away, and you and I are going to discuss this further, but not now because we have bigger problems. I got a few phone calls and requests in the last couple of days."

"Requests for what?" Julie asked as she sat down beside Zack and handed him some pills and a glass of water. "Ibuprofen. Drink up," she ordered him.

Barnes leaned back in his chair. "It seems a certain police chief from a quiet little Northwest Indiana city has an interest in the Dre-Zack Detective Agency and a certain freelance reporter. It seems there might be a connection between you guys and the, as he put it 'attack on several of his officers' as they tried to make an undercover bust on a gang at a zoo."

"And how in the hell did he make that connection?"

"Your business card was found at the scene. He said they were ambushed and witnesses say they saw a white man and white woman along with a black man running from the area and they might have been armed."

"Well we were running from the area, but in that rain and darkness and that area, no one saw us. There was no one around! And no way anyone could have seen if we were armed!" Darnell said.

"The business card is what concerns me." Zack looked at Julie.

"Shit, he took it from my purse when they kidnapped me!"

"Well," Barnes said, "they know where you live anyway and there isn't much I can do. I didn't give them much. Certainly, he does not know about our relationship, but I don't have a good feeling about this."

"So now what?" Zack asked. "Hide?"

Barnes nodded. "Yep. Until I can cool things off. Hence the manila folder I gave you." Zack opened it, but Ted talked as Zack read it. "Well, I followed your lead, your middle of the night call and I have a friend at Interpol. My funds are limited but he can help, and I think it is your best interest to take an extended vacation out of the country."

"In Amsterdam?"

"You're the one so certain that is where Granders is. So, you're going to find him and his wife. I'm sure Michelle's FBI friend can do whatever the hell they do and make sure no one is tracking your passports."

"That was plural."

"Yep," Barnes stood and pointed at Julie. "She's going to and so is Andre. We don't know what kind of enemies you made in Indiana and what they are willing to do but if anything you have shared with me is true, then you three need to worry. And I have enough problems already in this town, so I'm getting you guys the hell out of here."

"For how long?"

He smiled. "What's the rush? Consider part of the trip a wedding present. Keep in touch, answer your damn cell phones," he said with enough emphasis, "and I'll let you know when you can come back."

Zack looked at Darnell. "What about Darnell? And Michelle?"

"Oh well, I'll keep him occupied, and Michelle will get him off the grid. I'll have your office under surveillance and Michelle will work from home. Your office is going to be closed."

"What about money?"

Barnes walked to the door. "Seriously? Do you really want to talk about money? You have a freaking suitcase full of it!" He looked at his watch. "I want you on a plane headed to Europe by nightfall. Understood?"

* * * * * * * *

Zack fastened the safety belt on the airliner next to Julie who settled into the first-class seat and sipped champagne.

"I don't know how you can drink champagne at a time like this!"

Andre placed his bag in the overhead and sat on the other side of Julie. Zack hated the lack of legroom but still insisted on the window seat saying he preferred to see when they were about to crash.

"Relax. Nothing is gonna happen." Andre sat and buckled in. "Why are you drinking champagne anyway?"

Julie smiled and flashed her wedding ring finger. A huge diamond ring adorned it.

Andre did a double-take then smiled. "Did my boy finally mature and ask you to marry him?"

Julie laughed. "Not sure about the mature part, but yes to the second question."

Andre waved to the flight attendant. "It seems we're celebrating an engagement, so we're gonna need more champagne!"

Zack shook his head. "You two do understand how much I despise flying, right?"

Julie squeezed his hand. "Baby, you're going to be fine!"

He didn't say anything.

"Lighten up, Zack. We can celebrate a little." Andre laughed as he got his glass.

"Since it may be the last time we're alive together, fine."

Andre sipped his champagne. "Did you buy that ring with the money paid to have you killed?"

Zack chuckled. "No, I'm classier than that. I had some saved up for the ring. The hit money is paying our bills, for this trip and Michelle. I just hope we have a business to salvage when we get back."

"We will," Andre said and sipped more champagne.

Zack rubbed his head. "I think I had a concussion or something. My head still hurts."

"You must have a concussion, or you wouldn't have proposed!"

"Funny, Dre." Zack settled back in his seat. "I made some investments for us, too. Someday maybe we'll be able to retire from this and not care about high maintenance broads and the men who screw them."

Andre laughed. "Then what will we do?"

"I have no idea, but I'm looking forward to finding out."

* * * * * * *

Passing through customs wasn't as much an ordeal as Barnes suspected it would be. The three breezed through and carried their bags, one each except for Julie who had three, through the airport towards a car rental agency.

"Suit, two o'clock."

Andre glanced at a dark-suited white man who stared at them. "What do you think?"

"Cop."

"Here he comes."

"Excuse me, gentlemen, and ma'am. I don't mean to alarm you," the man greeted and pulled out a badge. "My name is Eric Peters."

Andre looked at Zack. "Does that qualify as two last names?"

"It may, but because the Peters has an S, it may nullify that rule."

"Excuse me, what?" The suit looked confused.

Zack leaned closer to the badge. "Oooh, Interpol. Nice. We've finally reached the stratosphere of International Law Enforcement."

Andre looked again. "Looks fake." He looked at Eric Peters. "How do we know that isn't fake and this isn't a hustle?"

Peters smiled. "Barnes said you two would give me a hard time." He motioned his head for the two to follow him. "Come on; you want to find this Granders guy, right?"

"No, we're looking for his wife."

Eric Peters stopped. "Really?"

"She owes us money."

"Well, let's see what we can do about that. Come on; I have a car waiting for us."

* * * * * * * *

Lieutenant Barnes stopped his car in front of Darnell's new apartment, exactly three doors down from Zack's and turned off the car.

"That's the five-cent tour of the area. Any questions about the setup or the routine until Stack gets back?"

Darnell stared straight ahead.

"What is it, Whittaker?"

"You think I'm just another hood, don't you?"

Barnes shook his head. "I've seen enough to know the difference and if I thought that we'd be having a different conversation. Stack says you're good; then I'm good with that."

Darnell nodded. "Why you like that cracker so much?"

Barnes smiled. "You can drop the street slang. What's important is that I do."

"That's why you're helping me out?"

"That's exactly why I'm helping you out."

"So, what's the deal with that Michelle chick?"

Barnes laughed. "Don't stick your pen in the company ink, Whittaker. Especially that ink. Zack won't like that."

"He's with Julie."

"Yep, he is." Barnes looked at him. "Take my advice: don't go after her. Any other questions?"

"So, you'll be training me while Zack is gone?"

"You need to know some basic things, and I want you properly trained. I'm sure you're capable of defending yourself, but we can teach you some things that will help. And you need to pass a test to get your license to be a private detective. If you want to do this, then you're going to do it my way until Zack gets back."

"This shit ain't over, is it?"

Barnes sighed and stared straight. "I hope to God it is." He exhaled again. "I really sincerely hope to God it is." But he knew it wasn't.

CHAPTER 55

Zack looked at his watch late that afternoon. He sat in a car with the Interpol agent and added the days he had been in Amsterdam so far. He counted fifteen, and though it was nice, so far, he barely had any alone time with Julie. His mind constantly went back to the situation he left back home. But the silence was uncomfortable.

"So how do you know Ted?" Zack finally asked, breaking the hour-long silence inside the car with the agent.

"Teddy? Theodore and I went to the U together. Met in ROTC. Did the whole term together. After we got out, he went to Baltimore, and I went across the Pond and joined Interpol. We've been friends for years."

"I didn't know he was ROTC."

"He doesn't talk much about this past. But get a few drinks in him and watch out!" Eric Peters laughed. "Man, that guy can party. Used to anyway. Married life and kids were good for him."

Zack and Peters sat in the car across the street from a café in Amsterdam and watched the people pass. Andre sat on the inside, read a paper and nursed a coffee.

"You must know him pretty well."

Zack shrugged. "It took a while until I think we considered each other friends, but since that point, we've gotten to know each other well."

"I bet. I was surprised to hear from him and then when we got a lead on this Granders fellow, for him to ask for a favor for you. Well, it's unusual."

"You're welcome, by the way." Zack smiled. Why he wanted Peters to know where the lead came from, he didn't know. Acceptance?

"Regardless. It's still unusual."

"Because we aren't law enforcement?"

"Bingo."

"Perhaps extradition isn't so easy from Holland."

Peters laughed. "Well, Ted's a good man. He's looking out for you. I know him well enough to know you don't want to screw that up."

Zack knew he heard something in that sentence. He nodded. "I don't intend to."

They were silent for some time. Zack looked at his watch. He thought of Julie. Convincing her to stay at their hotel was difficult, but after he promised her the exclusive she relented.

"Well, our surveillance saw him coming in this café about the same time every day. He always disappears though. We think he's meeting someone. It could be Kate, though we've yet to see a brunette that fits her description here. Why did you think she's here in Amsterdam?"

"Only after I realized something was missing the other day in an unrelated case I realized that she was setting me up all along. She wasn't acting like a typical heart-broken wife who found out her husband was cheating on her. It was a con. I wasn't supposed to see the airline tickets. I don't think they planned on me showing up at all."

Eric listened.

"The dead body planted with evidence making it look like I was guilty was because they suspected I'd figure it out. I remember seeing a bag of weed in her house during an interview. She said it was for her grandmother's glaucoma. Made sense at the time until Michelle discovered her grandmother, who did have glaucoma, has been dead for six years. So, Amsterdam makes sense."

"A bag of weed automatically makes you think of Amsterdam?"

"No, the fact that her maiden name is Van der Hollen made me think that."

Eric nodded. "And you had Barnes call me looking for leads on Doug Granders, Allison Greene and Kate Granders here based on a maiden name and a bag of marijuana in a house in Baltimore?"

"Yep. Well that, the airline tickets on the suitcases and the set that Kate tried to hide when I stopped at her house to tell her Doug was bumping uglies with the other chick and the fact that Dougie was using one of his offshore accounts under a different name sending money to a privately owned company here in Amsterdam made me tell Barnes that. The offshore account was pure luck. She got sloppy and left a receipt from a bank out. I barely caught a name but didn't think anything of it. Til later. And now here we are."

"Well, if you get lucky and they appear, what's your plan?"

"I'd like to shoot them all, but I don't have a gun. So, probably just beat them senseless, tie them up and ship them in a cargo box back to the states where I can collect my gun and shoot them."

Eric laughed. "Teddy told me I'd like the way you think after I got past the oddity of how and when your thoughts come together."

"This is where you've been spotting him?"

"Mostly, but not every day. I don't think he's going to show. How many days do you plan to stay here and look? It's already been fifteen."

"As many as it takes or until Teddy tells me to come back home." Zack watched a tall blonde walk past and enter the café. "Man, there are a lot of good-looking blondes here in Holland!"

"I know. I love it here."

"I haven't seen many brunettes."

"They're here, but blondes are everywhere."

Zack nodded and watched one walk past.

"Wow! See the ass on her?"

"You aren't married, are you, Eric?"

Eric laughed. "Hell no. That institution is not for me."

Zack was curious to hear Eric Peters' reasons now that he was freshly engaged to Julie. "Why not? It certainly has its perks."

Eric laughed. "In your America don't at least half of all marriages end in divorce?" He shook his head. "Seems like playing roulette has better odds."

Zack knew otherwise. Roulette odds were far worse than that.

"I don't need the shackles. I like my freedom. And what if you end up in a relationship you can't get out of and fall in love with someone else? What do you then? You can't kill your spouse these days."

Zack looked at Eric. "What do you mean these days?"

"Oh, maybe 15-20 years ago you could have gotten away with it, but now with the forensics we have today."

That was too close to home. "Wouldn't divorce just be easier?"

"Sure, if you don't mind being broke the rest of your life. So, your only hopes are that your ex gets married right away so you don't have to pay alimony and heaven forbid you have children, and you have to pay child support. And if that doesn't work, back to killing."

Zack knew Eric was being facetious, but it made him think. "You really think people would kill their husband or wife just to get out of a marriage?"

"Yep."

"And then frame someone else for doing it?"

"Well, you'd have to or else you'd be the first and only suspect. Even a bumbling idiot of a cop could probably get a collar in that situation."

Zack nodded. "Yeah, even a bumbling idiot of a cop."

Eric Peters looked at his watch. "Well, I've had enough for today. Why don't you go back to your hotel and rest? Go see some sites, travel about. Hell, go see Germany as you mentioned. If anything happens here, I'll call you. You just got engaged so go celebrate with your fiancé."

Only Zack didn't feel much like celebrating.

Andy Gruse
STACKED CASE

CHAPTER 56

Zack stared out the window of the train as it traveled through Germany. Julie was by his side. Andre and his girlfriend went to France instead. Andre argued that France was way more romantic than Germany and that Zack was ruining a perfect opportunity to relax, unwind and clear his head. Zack just smiled and said when France has beer halls like Germany, he'll travel there instead.

He had seen a doctor in Amsterdam, and that lead to two more visits. But he was healing and not limping and felt pretty good. It bothered him though, leaving Amsterdam. He hated losing, and that's what it felt like...again.

Julie knew something was bothering him. He had been silent, more silent than usual. Despite three weeks already alone together in Europe and every night together, they really hadn't talked. She was afraid to because of what she knew. And what he might think when he found out. Still, she wasn't going to let him pull away.

"Babe, talk to me. What is going on inside that pretty head of yours," she asked playfully with a nudge of her shoulder.

"Something isn't right. I missed something back in Indiana. And I missed something back in Amsterdam." He looked at her finally, into her eyes. "I hate losing."

"You haven't lost anything. Darnell is free and alive. We're alive. We're in Europe for Pete's sake! You are looking at things wrong."

"No, the Granders' are still out there, and I know they are in Amsterdam. And Warren is still out there, and we're afraid to go back to our regular lives. I haven't gotten any closer to finding out who killed my dad other than convincing enough people it wasn't Darnell or me!"

"Honey, please, you're torturing yourself."

"Plus, I was set up from the beginning. With Kate Granders. Why did they pick me? It doesn't make sense."

"You need to forget about it," Julie reiterated.

"No, I can't. You heard Warren. He said my mom was going to stay with Frank. Give him another chance to prove himself. He had the idea, remember?"

She did remember. "What idea?"

Zack shook his head. "I don't know. He kept all his stuff locked in a footlocker his father brought back from the war. We weren't allowed even to touch it. Warren said my mom still has it."

Julie thought that was odd to think. "Why would she keep it?"

Zack shrugged. "Suppose she wasn't the one who pulled the trigger and secretly did want to stay with Frank, or at least see if Frank would finally succeed at something. Maybe she kept that locker as a reminder. Who knows? People do strange things."

Julie shook her head. "I'm shocked if that footlocker wasn't in a landfill for the last seventeen years."

Zack knew that. "I know." He fell back to silence, and Julie knew she had to cooperate.

"So maybe they hatched the scheme to kill your dad to get the life insurance? Or maybe Warren paid one of his dirty cops off to do it, and Louise had no knowledge of it?"

He shook his head and thought. "I really don't think Louise did it. All the evidence we could gather suggests Warren did it. But I couldn't get him to admit it. So maybe he didn't pull the trigger either. But they know who did it." He stared into her eyes and only momentarily saw the blue that he loved so much. "And they're protecting that person."

"Baby," she whispered to his ear, "you have got to get past that. We're getting married. You have a business to run. You have Darnell and Andre counting on you. And you have me! Isn't that enough?"

"Yes, of course it is! You're enough for me; you know that. But Warren isn't going to let us ride off into the sunset."

She kissed him and suspected he was right.

He didn't notice her expression. "So, I have to go back. Maybe I can talk to Becky. Maybe she'll know something."

"You aren't going back. I won't let you, Andre won't let you, Darnell won't let you and you know damn well that Barnes won't let you so get that foolish thought out of your head!"

"I never saw Becky at school that day. Usually, I'd pass her in the hallway heading to my independent study class right after lunch."

"Zack, drop it. Ok? I've had enough of it!"

He looked at her and knew she was upset. He frowned. "Shit, I'm sorry. You're right. I've been obsessed with this and have completely neglected you. I'm sorry, Jules. I'll clear my head, and you have all of me again."

Her conscience finally got the best of her though. She let out a deep exhale. "Well, first, we have to talk."

That woke him up. "Uh-oh. Those are the four words no man in a relationship ever wants to hear. What did I do?"

She let out a deep breath. "Ok, there's no real way to say this. I met your high school girlfriend."

"Sara Eckhart?"

"Yeah. I was trying to find out what happened. Darnell gave me her name after he kidnapped Becky. It was worth a shot."

"You talked to her?"

"Yes, Zack. I did. And I have to tell you she's gorgeous."

"Well, I don't pick ugly women!" He tried to joke, but the humor was lost on her.

"She has a kid."

"Really? Good for her. I knew she'd find a man and settle down."

"She never found another man."

She took a deep breath. He wasn't getting it, and she hoped he would.

"Look, honey, I wasn't going to tell you, but after I thought about it when we were in Amsterdam, I knew I had to. You promised me no secrets, and I promised the same."

"Being engaged I would think that would be something you wouldn't have to debate!'"

"Oh, Zack, shut up and listen to me!"

"I'm listening," he snapped. "But unless you're going to tell me that my high school girlfriend's child has something to do with the murder of my dad, I really don't care about her or the kid!"

"He does, Zack." She took a deep breath. "That child is yours."

He stopped everything, and his face went white. "What? That's impossible."

"Is it?"

He thought about it. "Well, I guess not impossible but...wait. Her son is mine? You're saying that I have a son with Sara Eckhart?"

She nodded. "I saw him. He looks like you."

"And you weren't going to tell me?"

"No! I mean yes! I mean, well, not at first but then I realized I had to. I am telling you because I know if you ever found out that I didn't tell you that you'd never forgive me! Zack, you have to understand. Everything we did there was to protect you! This is no different."

He tried to think and process but couldn't. In a million years he wasn't expecting that. "She said she was on the pill."

"Zack, no birth control is full proof."

"Are using that same pill?"

She blushed and shook her head. "Zack, do you understand what I said?"

"Duh, of course. But Jesus Christ."

"Zachariah, my mother will slap your face if you ever say that in front of her!"

"Freak an aye, then! What do I do now?"

She moved to him. "Zack, you can't....do.... anything." She watched his mind struggle. "Baby, no one loves you or understands you more than I do. And I know that what's best here is that you do one thing: let......this......go!'"

At least thirty questions entered his mind as he processed what she told him and what she felt was the net result. Let this go, she said to him, and he thought maybe she was right. But there was no way he could. How could he? He nodded and returned to the intent stare out the window. *How the hell could she ask me to let it go minutes after telling me I have a sixteen-year-old son?*

CHAPTER 57

The French Riviera seemed a nice place to conclude the second month of their extended stay in Europe. The beaches were beautiful, the weather was beautiful, and if they paid attention, the group would catch a sighting of some celebrity and their families. The day before it was Bono of U2. Zack even talked to him. Not the typical big-fan-get me an autograph stuff that stars went to the Riviera to avoid, but it was a conversation.

Zack had to apologize for spilling a drink on Bono's beach towel as he and Julie walked past. That lead to a nice conversation and then to a dinner invitation later that night.

Bono even said if he ever needed a private investigator or extra security at a gig, he'd call Zack and Andre. When the Edge showed up that night it turned into quite a night: A lot of drinks, a lot of laughs, some music, some karaoke, one of the most fun nights of the trip. Zack even told Jules the next afternoon on the beach he forgot about everything and had fun.

Julie and Andre's girlfriend disappeared on the beach that day and left their boyfriends alone on a beach crawling with skimpy and gorgeous two-piece bikini wearing women. Neither worried. Julie commented that the two men wouldn't know what to do with one of the models walking around. Zack thought to himself that he knew exactly what to do but wasn't going to try to find out. He had who he loved. So, the girls left the two alone. It was the first time Andre and Zack were completely alone since Indiana.

"You cool, man?"

Zack nodded. "About as cool as I can be all things considered."

"I thought you'd freak about your kid. When Jules told me, I freaked."

Zack shook his head. "Deep down I'm still freaking, but more importantly I hope no one else knows about him."

"The mother certainly knows. Let's hope Warren or anyone else doesn't try to connect the dots to draw you back there."

Zack wondered about the 'anyone else' part of that sentence. "You know it's inevitable, Dre. You know it."

"Maybe not. You still ain't going back there anytime soon. That would be suicide."

"Or murder."

They looked at each other. "Yeah, Zack, that's been bothering me. Granders had you and us investigated by someone. Meaning someone else might know about this whole messed up ordeal."

Zack nodded. "That crossed my mind."

"So, we have yet another problem," Andre acknowledged. "I always suspected your real identity might come back to haunt us. I just never thought it would be so soon. I figured it would be like one of those Nazis that escaped to Brazil and wouldn't get caught until you're like in your seventies!"

Zack opened another drink from the cooler beside them. "Yeah, I know."

"So, what are we going to do about it?"

"About which problem are we talking? My stepfather possibly hunting us and plotting to have us eliminated, so he is never exposed? The murderer of my father knowing I'm alive possibly and wanting to eliminate me, so he or she is never exposed? Or, the fact that we were sent to Amsterdam to find Kate and Doug Granders but they have seemingly disappeared because they don't want to be exposed, and the probable private investigator who found us and my relationship with Barnes and could use that to expose us? Am I missing any?"

Andre chuckled. "You forgot how we are still in debt after you mortgaged our business to get Darnell out of jail and how now there is another liability in the equation: your son and her mother. Your mom and Becky know about her."

"They may know about the son being mine."

"Maybe."

"Jules said she's an optometrist. Has a giant house and looks like money? You said we're broke; maybe I should go back there?"

Andre cut him off laughing. "I don't think so, Don Juan! Julie will have your junk in her purse anyway, so you are off the market." He drank a beer. "But white women seem to like me so maybe I could go after her," he laughed.

Zack smiled. "Maybe." He drank again and thought about everything else. "We can always get money."

Zack smiled. "You're on a roll. No, stick with me. Brunettes. So, if you are a brunette with a nice body on the run from the law and us, what would you do?" "Well, we have to get some results first."

"We can always get results, brother. That is what we do."

Andre smiled, looked at Zack and the two clinked their beers. "So, what now, Zack?"

There was a long pause before Zack looked at Andre. "You know what there are a lot of in Amsterdam?"

"Places to buy pot?"

"Yes, but even better: blonde females with nice bodies. You know what there aren't a lot of?"

"Fat chicks?"

Andre smiled. "If I'm moving to Amsterdam, I'm either getting fat or becoming a blonde. What are you thinking?"

"I'm thinking we have a list of problems."

"Yeah," Andre said, "I guess you could say we have a stacked case load."

"Funny, partner. Here's what I'm thinking: let's start at the top and hope for a snowball effect with solving them. I'm getting kind of tired of this beach flavored paradise. Let's go back to Amsterdam."

"I'm in. But let's enjoy the rest of today first."

Zack nodded and smiled as he saw Julie and Andre's girlfriend walking back. He focused on Julie's amazing orange two-piece bikini and how sexy it looked on her golden tan skin and amazing curves.

"Yeah, that's a good idea. And tonight, too."

The End

Andy Gruse
STACKED CASE

Andy Gruse
STACKED CASE

Author's Note

Arriving to this point has not come easily or lightly. I always tell my sons to never stop dreaming and to never stop chasing those dreams. After all, a dream worth having is a dream worth striving for, in my opinion. I haven't achieved it yet, but I am working toward one of several.

To that end, I would be remiss and seem ungrateful if I don't thank a few people. First and foremost is my mother. Now, I understand many are eye-rolling right now as thanking your mom is about as cliché as cliché can get. However, bear with me and you'll understand why this is not just because she brought me into this world.

When I was about 12 years old one summer, may have been younger, while growing up in Michigan City, Indiana, it was one of those hot and humid days of what seemed like a long summer at that age. (Now they are not nearly long enough!) My older brothers, Rich, Bob, and Joe, were off and not around for me to bug and my little brother, Jon, well, I don't know where he was, but I know I was home alone with my mom. She was doing housework like you'd expect there was a lot of that to do since she had five sons and at least one dog. Basically, I had nothing to do.

And then I made a mistake I have never made again, and my sons will attest that they have heard me repeat what my mother said to me that fateful day.

I found her in the house and said "Mom, I'm bored."

Without a second's hesitation, she said to me "Boredom is a sign of stupidity," with a hint of either disgust or impatience in her voice.

405

(Later, at a book signing while telling this story to my uncle Tom (brother of my mom), he told me their mother (my grandmother if you are keeping score) said that to them when they were young! As much as I am not a stick-to-traditions type of guy, I am glad this one continued!)

Well at about 12 the last thing I would think any child would want to hear from his/her mother is that you show signs of stupidity! I don't recall if I had a reply, I'm guessing I didn't and I'm not sure what else was said but I do know that moments later she handed me two or three books and said, "Read these."

My parents were voracious readers. My father had a new novel by his lunch box I think every week when he worked at the steel mill in Gary. And my mother, when she wasn't cleaning up after us or feeding us and trying to stay sane being the only female in the house, read as much as the free time she could find would allow. But until that day it never occurred to me that another world existed: the world of fiction novels.

I did start reading immediately. The two I read first are still two of my favorites: P.S. Wilkinson and Fruit of the Poppies. P.S. Wilkinson, I have read at least five times and at one point my mother donated a few boxes of books to our school library. I was pulling the books out of the box, saw my favorite and said, "No way! This stays with me." I still have that book in my closet and both of my sons have read it. (Interestingly to me, Fruit of the Poppies is incredibly like a Denzel Washington movie made many years later.)

That summer of experiencing more books, I fell in love with fiction and my imagination took over. My first short story was called Raise Your Hand, about our sixth-grade science teacher we all liked, and

406

how he disliked blurting out answers in class. He eventually snapped and started hacking the kids that blurted out answers with an axe. Looking back, the premise is probably better than a lot of horror movies I've seen…but the point is I've been writing ever since.

So, long story short: Thank you, Mom! I may be called stupid occasionally, but I can guarantee you that it is not because of boredom!

I must thank my dad as well, for being my dad. My mother says I have his sense of humor, which is why throughout high school, he'd wait for me to come home from school before he had to leave to tell me a joke he heard the night before. He and I would laugh while my mom groaned and rolled her eyes. I still love a good pun!

I must thank my brother Bob, too. He has read all my stuff and was the one to push me to make it better. He's still pushing me and I'm still working at making it better. Of course, how can I not thank Rich, Joe, and Jon also? Terrific brothers and influences, still learning from all of them and Goddamn, I wish the five of us could get together more often than once every decade!

And of course, most importantly, thank you, the reader. It is because of you that books continue to be written and published, new worlds explored, and dreams are pursued. I hope you enjoyed this fiction story and if so, please tell your friends about it! Zack, Andre and the gang will be back soon! See you then.

-Andrew Thomas Gruse

Andy Gruse
STACKED CASE

_____

www.ingramcontent.com/pod-product-compliance
Lightning Source LLC
Chambersburg PA
CBHW060341260626
47160CB00006B/2172